The lockers on either side of the corridor were hanging open, supplies scattered in the aftermath of the search. Something off to the right went thump and crack, and Felix turned to look.

A woman in black mercenary armor stepped out of the largest storage locker, the one where the spare environment suits should have been. She pointed her sidearm at him, and for a moment they regarded one another silently.

There was someone else in the locker, slumped over to one side, unmoving: a man with thinning gray hair, a string of drool hanging from his thin lips, eyes closed.

Felix inclined his head toward the man, without taking his eyes from the gun. "Mister Thales, I presume?"

TWILIGHT IMPERIUM™

The
FRACTURED
VOID

TIM PRATT

ACONYTE

First published by Aconyte Books in 2020

ISBN 978 1 83908 046 3

Ebook ISBN 978 1 83908 047 0

Cover art by Scott Schomburg

Distributed in North America by Simon & Schuster Inc, New York, USA

Printed in the United States of America

9 8 7 6 5 4 3 2 1

ACONYTE BOOKS

An imprint of Asmodee Entertainment Ltd

Mercury House, Shipstones Business Centre

North Gate, Nottingham NG7 7FN, UK

aconytebooks.com // twitter.com/aconytebooks

For Effie, a player of games.

CHAPTER 1

Felix waited in the darkness on the lower deck of the *Temerarious*. The only illumination came from faint guide lights running along the floor, pulsing in the direction of designated exits. Carefully, silently, he began to move, confident that he wasn't being watched, at least for the moment. He crept along a corridor and moved past unoccupied crew cabins, converted to storage for emergency relief supplies. He moved slowly, looking into each crowded room for a moment before moving on, listening for the faintest whisper of sound, and feeling for minute disturbances in the stale air.

Felix was *hunting*.

He considered taunting his prey, trying to provoke an error he could exploit, but it was a risky move, and better tried when he was in a more defensible position. He paused at the end of the corridor, with open doors on his left and his right. In a more demanding posting, the cabins on either side would provide housing for two crew members;

instead, the cabin on the left held pallets of potable water, while the one on the right, for some reason, held crate after crate of signal flares. The mysteries of military procurement were doubtless baffling in all societies, but in the Mentak Coalition they were even stranger – the various supplies the raider fleets pillaged had to end up somewhere, and an overstocked quartermaster had taken the opportunity to cram the *Temerarious*, with its whole deck of unused space, full of odds and ends of no great use to anyone.

He ducked into a side room and crouched behind a pallet of shrink-wrapped air purifiers, listening hard, but the only sound was his own breath. He jostled the pallet and gasped, short and swiftly cut off, as if he'd injured himself and made an involuntary sound. He immediately, silently, moved to the far side of the room, waiting to see if his bait would be taken. There was no movement, no sound, nothing. He might have been alone down here, in the dark, but he knew better.

Felix crept back out into the corridor, carefully scanning for the most minute shift in the shadows, the slightest disturbance in the air. Nothing. His quarry was elsewhere. He considered the T-intersection before him: if he went left, he'd reach the deserted lower galley, and if he went right, he'd reach a workout room full of unused training machinery. There were more hiding places in the galley, but–

Something clattered in the cabin on his left. It sounded like a water bottle jostled by mistake, bouncing off the frame of a bunk, and skittering across the floor. Felix immediately spun and faced right instead. There was no way his subtle and deadly prey would make a sound like that by accident.

The little monster was trying to distract him, which meant the ambush would be coming from the *other* side –

In fact, the attack came from above: a weight crashed down on Felix's neck and shoulders, driving him to his knees, and a slick smooth limb he couldn't see snaked around his throat. Felix was bigger and heavier than his opponent, though, and he threw his weight back, hoping to crush the attacker between his own body and the wall, or, failing that, at least dislodge her. Instead, she slithered around his body, shifting from his back to his front, so all he did was rattle his *own* spine on impact.

"Die, scum!" a voice hissed, hot breath on his face, but there was no *face* there, just a sort of shimmer that made his eyes water if he focused too hard, and strong thin fingers wrapped around his throat–

The overhead lights came on brightly, and the voice of the ship's security officer, Calred, purred laconically from hidden speakers all over the deck: "Captain, if you and Tib are finished playing hide-and-seek, we have an urgent message from one of the colonies."

The shimmer stopped shimmering and resolved into the round green face of Captain Felix Duval's first officer Tib Pelta, her yellow lamp-like eyes shining as she smiled, showing all her teeth. The rest of her body, dressed in the uniform of the Mentak Coalition navy, came into focus a moment later. The Yssaril ability to hide from sight – "fading" – wasn't technically invisibility, but functionally there wasn't a big difference. As an infiltration specialist, her uniforms and spacesuits were woven with rare fabrics that could bend light and augmented with devices that stymied detection of heat signatures and other life signs.

Tib let go of her captain's throat, straightened his collar, and patted him gently on the cheek, before hopping off him and heading for the elevator.

"Acknowledged, on our way up," Felix said. Then: "We weren't playing hide-and-seek. We were conducting tactical training exercises to keep ourselves sharp. That's really something you should be organizing, as security officer."

"My job is to keep you from getting killed, and to prevent this moderately valuable ship from getting blown up," Calred said. "Not to keep you entertained."

"I won," Tib said as Felix fell into step beside her, though she had to take two steps for every one of his. "Current score is seven hundred and five to me, one hundred and twelve to you."

"It's one-thirteen to me, Tib," Felix said. "You always leave out that time when I was fourteen, and I tracked you through the ventilation system to the station administrator's secret wine store–"

"That doesn't count, and it will never count. I wasn't trying to hide from you, so the fact that you found me is not a win – it's just you being nosy."

"You were going there in secret, hoping to sell the wine for yourself, so you were hiding from everyone, and by extension, therefore, you were hiding from me."

They continued the old argument – which was less a real disagreement after all these years, and more a pleasant exercise in call-and-response – as they took the lift up to the command deck. Not that it was much of a command, Felix thought; he was in charge of himself, Tib Pelta, Calred, and a bunch of drones. The drones obeyed instantly without arguing, which was nice, but they were otherwise terrible company. It was hard to radiate the effortless aura of mastery Felix wanted to project when your crew consisted of your best friend since childhood and an unflappably competent and unimpressed Hacan soldier. The ship was nice enough, if nothing special: the *Temerarious* was a Freebooter-class cruiser, a lightly armed ship built for speed, meant to strike fast and disappear – the sort of vessel that played a crucial support role in the Mentak Coalition's military fleet, and made up the bulk of its unofficial raider forces.

Of course, in this remote posting, there was little need for speed or armaments, light or otherwise. The *Temerarious* was stationed here to "defend and lend material support" to the three coalition colony worlds (two planets, and one moon orbiting a gas giant) in this system. Felix and Tib had grown up on a shipyard space station near the core of the Coalition, and being way out here on the fringes was teeth-grindingly dull. This posting was both a punishment *and* a promotion. Felix had been first officer on a ship in the raider fleet, and had acted with great daring and courage in a raid, winning glory (and also riches) for the Coalition... but he'd also ignored orders from his captain in order to commit said daring act. The fleet commander had been impressed and pleased with the results, but Felix's captain had been understandably furious about the method, and after some consultation a compromise was reached: in recognition of his service, Felix would be promoted to captain of his own ship and as punishment for his insubordination, he would be assigned to the backwater Lycian system, home to a scant million inhabitants scattered over three worlds, who produced a minimal quantity of resources that nobody back home much wanted anyway.

The unstated but clear message for Felix was: show that you can obey orders by being a good boy out on the edge of everything for a few years, and you'll be welcomed back to do something that matters. The arrangement had seemed reasonable to Felix at first, but after eight months of making a slow and pointless circuit of three colony worlds, he was bored. The colonies were small, scattered, and rural, and none of them had much of a nightlife, so even R and R was in short supply – though there was a cute medic with great legs on one of the planets, and an enjoyably burly gas-extraction engineer on the moon, so Felix wasn't entirely without entertainment, even discounting the running game of hide-and-seek – no, damn it, *tactical exercises* – with Tib.

Mostly Felix fantasized about something *happening*, some occasion he could rise to, some world-shaking challenge he could overcome or disaster he could avert, thus shortening his penance and returning to the fast track. He wanted to sit at the Table of Captains one day, and help guide his polity to ever more greatness. The beautiful thing about the Coalition, this pan-species nation founded by prisoners of the old Lazax Empire's most brutal penal colony, was that *anyone* could rise to the greatest heights, no matter how humble their origins, if they demonstrated the wit, the speed, the daring, the ingenuity – all qualities that Felix, unburdened by false modesty, knew himself to possess in ample supply.

There were no opportunities to demonstrate those qualities, though, because nothing ever happened out here. Sometimes there was a storm or a flood, and in those cases Felix delivered food and blankets. He was also responsible for picking up and delivering cargo from the colony worlds to supply ships, and bringing back medical supplies and trade goods. Not exactly the intended use for a fast warship, but the Coalition had lots of cruisers, and this one had plenty of empty room for crates.

Felix and Tib stepped from the lift onto the bridge, a semicircular room dominated by a large viewscreen that currently showed nothing but the empty star field before them, the brighter glow of Alope standing out in the lower left. Alope was the next planet on their circuit, a world rich in timber, ore, mildew, mutton, and bristly predators called wolferines, who were still delighted by the sheep and goats the colonists had introduced to the ecosystem decades earlier.

Tib went to the comms and navigation station, not that there was much navigating to do, since they more or less just went around in circles. Felix dropped into his command chair: best seat in the house, even if the house wasn't all he might wish. "What's the problem? Did a sheep wander off? Are we urgently needed to help with a barn-raising?"

Calred, an immense Hacan with braids in his mane, shook his leonine head. He stood at the tactical board, which was even less use here than the navigation controls. "Something stranger than that, and my requests for clarification have gone unanswered."

"Show me."

"The message is audio-only." Calred manipulated the board, and a crackling voice blared out from the blank viewscreen:

– unknown – landed outside settlement – jammed – boosting as best we can – immediate assistance – armed

The message ended abruptly. "Where's it from?" Felix said. There were scores of communities on Alope, from small timber camps and mining towns to the relatively booming trading city and sole spaceport Solymi, home to a whole fifty thousand souls (and that cute medic Felix liked to visit).

"A small farming settlement on the northern continent," Calred said. "Doesn't even have a name on the surveys, though I gather the locals call it Cobbler's Knob."

"Do they really?"

"So I'm told," Calred said. "The message came from their emergency distress system, which is probably the only communications apparatus within a hundred kilometers powerful enough to get a message this far."

Could this be it? Felix thought. Could something finally be *happening*? Probably not. It was probably a prank. Felix thought about how bored he was, and extrapolated out to how bored a teenager living in a place called Cobbler's Knob must be. But then, if it were a hoax, you'd think they'd say something more dramatic: "We're being attacked by alien invaders," maybe, or at least, "Help, a wolferine ate my mother."

"Let's get down there," Felix said. "It's probably nothing, but it's not like we were doing anything else."

Calred nodded. "With my amazing tactical prescience,

I anticipated your order. We're already heading there at speed. Does that count as insubordination? I hope not. I'd hate to be assigned to some remote posting as punishment."

"We'll call it the sort of initiative that befits an officer of your stature." Felix had no idea why Calred had ended up on this ship, but he must have annoyed *someone*. The Hacan would only say, "I go where I'm assigned." He was competent, gave the impression of being effortlessly deadly, and was completely unflappable, not that they encountered many things worthy of getting into a flap about out here. In a storm last year, though, Felix had seen Calred wade into a surging river that had burst its banks, rescuing a young boy who would have been swept away, and returning him to his tearful family. Calred had done it as matterof-factly as Felix might take a bottle down from a shelf. He hadn't known Calred anywhere near as long as Tib, but he'd already come to depend on him.

The planet grew, a greenish disc in the corner of the screen. "Something's moving," Calred said. "Looks like a shuttle, coming from the vicinity of Cobbler's Knob, heading into orbit."

"That doesn't make any sense," Felix said. "Where's it *going*?" A shuttle didn't have the range to make it to one of the other colony worlds, and there was no space station. "Is there anything in orbit for the shuttle to rendezvous with?"

"There isn't," Calred said. "Maybe they're just sightseeing."

"Or," Tib said.

"Or what?" Felix said.

"Or there is something in orbit, and we just can't see it. Let me see." She bowed her head to the terminal, and the screen shifted through various false color arrays, visualizing discrete pulses of sensor data. "*There* it is," Tib said, voice a throaty murmur. "A ship, orbiting Alope."

Felix leaned forward. The screen was back to true color, and there was no orbiting ship to be seen, though the shuttle was highlighted, a silver lozenge rising from the planet's surface. "Show me."

"I can't show you. The ship is using some sort of stealth technology – I think it's a variant of light-wave deflection."

"Then how do you know it's even there?"

Tib rolled her eyes, and given the size of her eyes, that was very dramatic. "Felix. I have a particular interest in stealth, and no system is perfect. It can hide from sensors, and even bend light to avoid visual detection, and against a big expanse of empty black, that's almost always enough. Against the backdrop of a planet, though, there are visual distortions, little shimmers and glimmers, and you can see them if you know where to look, kind of like we detect black holes by seeing the light from stars bend around them."

Felix took her word for it. Yssaril were famed throughout the galaxy for their skill as spies – they'd taken their natural ability to fade, augmented it with technology and training, and spent centuries building their networks. The Tribes of Yssaril sold their skills throughout the galaxy, and doubtless used what they learned to pursue their own interests and imperial ambitions. Tib had never been within a billion kilometers of the Yssaril homeworld, but she had all the natural abilities of her species combined with the legacy of the Mentak Coalition, the descendants of thieves, renegades, smugglers, and *survivors*. The Yssaril members of the Coalition were the backbone of their clandestine forces, and Tib had vanished for a year once for "special training" that Felix assumed included plenty of spooky spy techniques. She'd certainly gotten even better at playing hide-and-seek afterward. "Who could it be?" he asked. "Why would anyone come out here in the first place, let alone in a stealth ship?"

"It's not a dreadnought or something," Tib said. "Not that those are really built for stealth anyway. The distortions indicate something cruiser-sized."

"Don't give them any indication that we've seen them," Felix said. What *was* this unfamiliar feeling, like his blood was fizzing? Oh, yes: excitement. The thrill of the hunt. He'd missed it. Stalking Tib in the basement was a poor substitute for the real thing.

"My communications array just lit up." Tib put the incoming message up on half the screen, the other half still tracking the slow ascent of the shuttle as it inexorably approached the big red question mark Tib had generated to indicate the location of the stealthed ship.

A dirty-faced woman hunched over a console in a small dark room appeared, her eyes wide and wild. "They took Mr Thales!"

"This is Captain Duval of the *Temerarious*." Felix leaned forward. "Who took who?"

She ran a hand through her messy hair. "These soldiers, five or six of them, they wore armor and had these guns, they broke into his house and dragged him out! They took him and a bunch of his stuff – we asked what was happening, who they were, and they told us to shut up or they'd *shoot* us!

I tried to call before but they did something, they jammed the signal or something."

"I guess now we know who's on the shuttle," Tib said. "I've pinged the vessel, but there's no transponder, and they don't reply. No indication where it's from or where it's going."

"Should I blow up the shuttle?" Calred said.

"There's probably a kidnapped civilian on board, so no," Felix said. "Can we move to intercept the shuttle, disable it, scoop it up?"

"Sure. Assuming we're faster than the invisible ship, which we might be. Also assuming the invisible ship isn't better armed than we are, which is more doubtful."

"Start moving that way. Weapons hot. Hail the shuttle again, Tib. Tell them if they don't respond we'll be forced to disable them." Felix returned his attention to the woman on the screen. As far as he knew there was nobody worth abducting in this system, at least not for conventional reasons like ransom. Felix had been furnished with a list of notable citizens when he came here, mayors and heads of local business concerns, and none of them seemed like targets for a heavily armed strike team with stealth tech and jamming equipment. Thales hadn't been on it anyway. "Why did they come for this Thales? Who is he?"

"I don't know," the woman said. "He moved here not quite a year ago. He mostly keeps to himself, and when he doesn't, you wish he had." She paused. "I mean, everyone here hates him – he's terrible, really – but I don't know why anyone would bother to *kidnap* him."

"Huh. Thanks for notifying us. We'll take care of things from here." He ended the call and watched the shuttle get bigger in the viewscreen as their courses converged.

"The shuttle just answered us," Tib said.

"What did they say?"

"'Stand down, or die.'"

"Oh," Felix said. "I don't much like either of those options. Cal, you know that ship we can't see?"

"I am familiar with it."

"The shuttle is still pretty far away from said invisible ship, right?"

"It's outside the maximum blast radius, if that's what you're asking."

"That is what I'm asking. There you go, showing initiative again." Goodbye boredom, Felix thought. "Let's turn that invisible ship into a cloud of radioactive dust, shall we?"

CHAPTER 2

The missiles Calred launched did not, in fact, turn the invisible ship into radioactive dust. Felix hadn't really expected them to. He had, however, hoped the mysterious ship would be forced to drop out of stealth in order to deploy countermeasures, and that's what happened: the empty space on the screen was suddenly full of spaceship, its countermeasures dazzling the incoming missiles with guidance-disrupting lasers, sending them spinning off on harmless courses to burn up in the atmosphere of the planet below.

"Looks like the Federation," Calred said. "A cruiser, built for speed, not violence."

The Federation of Sol, Felix thought with reflexive irritation. Sure, he was human himself, but he was from the Coalition, and he knew being human didn't make him particularly special – something his ambitious, expansionist cousins-by-ancestry didn't seem to grasp. The Coalition had decent relations with the Federation, insofar as their interests ever overlapped, so what were they doing sneaking around and kidnapping people out here? This Thales must be pretty important to risk an act of war over. Unless… "Are we sure it's from the Federation?"

"Not necessarily," Calred said. "We've even got a few Federation ships in our raider fleet, and they sell their old military cruisers sometimes."

"There's no transponder indicating that they're an accredited diplomatic or trading vessel," Tib said. "They're running dark. It could be anybody. Anybody with the resources to field a snatch team and operate cutting-edge stealth tech, anyway."

"Target lock the shuttle, and tell the big ship to stand down," Felix said. "If we can see them, I assume we can yell at them."

"Are we going to actually shoot down the shuttle?" Tib asked. "That would prevent them from abducting one of our colonists, the same way cutting off my head would stop me from sneezing."

"I'm still thinking about it," Felix said. "How long do I have to think about it, Cal?"

"In about five minutes, the shuttle will be close enough to the ship that firing on one will mean firing on the other."

Felix considered. "If the shooting starts, would we win?"

Cal shrugged. "They might die of heatstroke before we die of thirst."

Felix had served with Calred long enough to know that was a Hacan phrase that either meant it was a no-win situation or, more generously, that the fight could go either way. He almost asked for clarification, but both interpretations were bad, so he didn't bother.

"There's an incoming transmission from the ship of mystery," Tib said.

Half the screen filled with a visibly irritated human woman's head and shoulders. She wasn't wearing a uniform, but she was wearing the sort of armor favored by the better class of mercenaries – and she wasn't even part of the ground force that did the snatch, so who knew how they were outfitted? What Felix could glimpse of the enemy bridge (they had an enemy now – how exciting) was bare of insignia, flags, or other identifiers. She glared, but didn't say anything.

"Hello," Felix said. "Return the person you abducted, and we won't kill you."

"We're capturing an escaped prisoner," the woman said. "He's not a citizen of the Coalition. He's a fugitive from justice."

"Assuming that's true, we have diplomatic relations with the Federation, and there are channels for this sort of thing. You're not allowed to drop in and kidnap people without turning in the appropriate paperwork first."

"We never said we were from the Federation."

Felix smiled. "I apologize for the assumption. Maybe you're from Jol-Nar? Or are you from a faction we don't have diplomatic relations with? In that case, I'm pretty sure this is definitely an act of war, instead of just probably. Do you want to reconsider this…" he waved his hand in the air. "… whole thing?"

She gritted her teeth. "We are independent bounty hunters."

"Interesting. What crimes did Thales commit, and in what jurisdiction?"

She winced. She was clearly unhappy that Felix knew that name. Felix was just sad he couldn't play cards with someone who wore her emotions so clearly on her face. He quite liked taking money from strangers. "Phillip Thales is guilty of theft, murder, and destruction of property."

"Where did he do this thieving, murder, and vandalism?"

"That's classified."

Calred laughed out loud. "By whom? Let me guess. Also classified?"

Felix cupped his chin in his hand and looked at her. "Thales must have stolen something pretty big if you mentioned the theft part before the murder part. Cobbler's Knob is an unusual choice for spending ill-gotten gains, but to each their own, I suppose. I'm sure we can clear all this up. If you're bounty hunters, just send the credentials proving you're authorized to operate in Coalition space."

She worked her mouth like she'd taken a bite of something sour and couldn't decide whether to swallow it or spit it out. "Perhaps we could come to some other arrangement."

"Are you offering me a bribe?" Felix said.

She shrugged. "Where I'm from, we have a saying: every Coalition ship is a pirate ship. The man we took is not one of your citizens, and none of your citizens were harmed in the course of taking him. We'd be happy to send you a substantial quantity of Federation credits if you'd agree to let us leave in peace, and refrain from filing any sort of official report. Everyone goes away happy."

"How substantial?" She named a sum. Felix went hmm. "What's the exchange rate right now, Tib?"

"One-point-five Federation credits to one Coalition credit."

So, not that substantial, but still. "Sure. Tib, send them the account info."

The woman blinked at him. "Really?"

Felix shrugged. "Why not? I like money." He almost said, "I'm Coalition. What do you expect? I'd sell my mother's teeth if I could get a credit for them, right?" but decided that might tip his hand.

After a few moments, Tib said, "Transmission complete. From an untraceable account – very slick."

"Thank you for your generous contribution to the Bereaved and Orphaned Benevolent Fund," Felix said. "The Coalition will be eternally grateful. Now, release your prisoner, or we will fire on your ship."

"We had a deal!" she shouted.

Now Felix shrugged. "I gather my people are famously untrustworthy. Shall I count to, let's see, five? One, two–"

He didn't get to finish, because the other ship fired on them, and the *Temerarious* had to deploy their own countermeasures. Felix was surprised. The *Temerarious* had the shuttle target locked, and surely the enemy ship knew they were well matched tactically, but they still chose to fight? Bounty hunters were all about balancing risk against reward: these weren't bounty hunters. (Well, obviously. The amount they'd paid Felix was more than any bounty he'd ever heard of.)

"Do we return fire?" Cal said. The shuttle was so close

to the ship now, it would inevitably be destroyed if the *Temerarious* fired back.

Damn it. Maybe Thales was a citizen – Felix wasn't about to take the word of the people shooting at him on that – but even if he wasn't, someone was willing to go to a lot of trouble and expense to abduct him, and that meant he was valuable. The Coalition really liked taking valuable things, and didn't like having them taken away. "No, pull back. Can we keep up with that ship when they run?"

"Unless their stealth technology is better than anything I've ever heard of before, yes," Cal said.

"Good. Then let them go, follow at a safe distance, extrapolate their likely course, and see if any of the raider fleets are in a position to intercept." There was no regular military way out here, but they weren't far from a shipping route, and there were often a few of the Coalition's irregular troops lurking in the dark between the stars, keeping an eye out for easy targets.

The *Temerarious* withdrew as the shuttle disappeared into the belly of the enemy cruiser, which rose out of orbit and accelerated away.

"They must know we're going to call for help," Felix said. "What's their plan?"

"I think their plan was 'don't get caught,'" Tib said. "It's a reasonable plan, way out here, where we're the only possible threat in the system. It's just their bad luck we happened to be passing this way. Otherwise, they would have been long gone by the time we heard about the abduction. Their new plan is probably 'run fast and hope for the best.'"

Felix nodded. That wasn't a good plan, but he didn't

judge the humans too harshly: after all, they didn't have any other plans available. "See what we can find out about this Thales, would you, Cal?"

"I'm already compiling a dossier. It's going to be short, though, I can tell."

"Good news," Tib said. "I've got Commander Meehves and a small fleet that should be able to intercept our new friends in half a day or so."

"Good old Meehves," Felix said.

"Oh, we can catch them." Meehves slouched in a chair in her quarters, a drink in her hand, her grayish skin and blank eyes revealing her Letnev ancestry. Those eyes made her damnably hard to gamble against, as Felix had learned during officer training. Meehves taught tactics occasionally, with a special emphasis on surprise and misdirection, and had cheerfully explained that taking money from her students constituted teaching them a valuable lesson in her areas of expertise. "Do you want to lead the boarding party?"

"It would make a nice change from flying around in circles, if you don't mind."

Meehves waved her free hand lazily. "We've just been lurking out here waiting for a fat, lonely cargo ship to drift by. Thanks for bringing us something to do. I'm a bit baffled by the whole thing, though. Who is this Thales, anyway? Why would the Federation, or someone hiring a bunch of mercenaries, go to so much trouble to kidnap him?"

"We don't know much." Felix flicked his fingertip and scrolled through the information Calred had scrounged up in the past several hours. "We don't have any record of him on Alope until about ten standard months ago, when he showed up in Cobbler's Knob–"

"*Whose* knob?" Meehves said.

"I had the same question. It's just what the locals call their little patch of grazing land, a river, some fields, and a few housing modules. Maybe it was founded by someone named Cobbler, or there's a mountain nearby that looks like a shoe or something. Anyway, this Thales immigrated, perfectly legally. Claimed he was from the Federation of Sol and, I regret to say, the security officials didn't poke too hard at his identity, or they would have realized all his documentation was fake."

"Doing deep background checks on colonists to remote worlds isn't a good use of resources," she said. "It's not like Alope is a prime target for terrorism. Most of the people who immigrate to places like this have shady backgrounds and no other options."

"Fair enough," Felix said. "He showed up in Cobbler's Knob looking for a place to live, and for some reason the good country people didn't just steal his money and throw his body down a well. Instead they fixed up an abandoned cottage for him, one with a big root cellar, which he was particularly pleased about – he said he could use the space for his work, without saying what that work was. He shut himself away and only came out to buy supplies, and to complain about the food, the weather, the hygiene of his fellow colonists, and every other subject imaginable. No one had any idea what he was doing there, and he didn't volunteer information. The locals thought he might be an artist or a writer, a reclusive genius devoting himself to his work, or else that he was hiding out from the law. There was some disagreement on that score, but everyone *does* agree that he's rude, unpleasant, and a total bastard."

Meehves sipped her drink, a perfectly clear liquid that Felix suspected was highly flammable. "People don't usually send stealth ships full of mercenaries to kidnap artists, and whoever came for him wasn't the law."

"The locals took the opportunity to snoop around his house after he was taken, and there's no sign of any artwork anyway. They're not exactly trained investigators down there, but they say it looks like the kidnappers took everything but the furniture with them. No documents, no personal effects, nothing."

Meehves swirled her drink. "Maybe he was a fugitive, but if so, why not reach out to us through normal channels? Why risk a fight with the Coalition?"

"I was thinking about that. Maybe he's a special kind of fugitive – the kind with a head full of state secrets the Federation, or whoever, is afraid he'll give away. Or maybe he stole something they were really keen to recover?"

"Why not just kill him, then?" Meehves said. "They had the firepower. Honestly, they could have paid someone in Cobbler's Knob two sheep to kill him, the way it sounds."

"They need him alive, then, for whatever reason," Felix said. "Maybe it's not something he has, but something he knows."

Meehves nodded. "So he's not a brilliant artist, but he could be some other kind of brilliant – some useful variety. You hear about people kidnapping Hylar scientists sometimes, trying to get a jump on weapons research."

"Or he could be a spy with intel that's not recorded anywhere, or he was witness to something and they need his testimony, or, or, or. Suddenly I can come up with all sorts of scenarios."

Meehves shrugged. "We'll find out soon enough. Unless they kill him when we try to board their ship, in the spirit of, 'if we can't have him, no one can'. Unless they all choose death before dishonor, though, one of them will tell us what's going on, anyway. We just have to ask them the right way."

"Mercenaries don't tend to sacrifice their lives for honor."

"They do not," Meehves agreed. "So let's hope they're mercenaries, and not some flavor of true believer. We should intercept their vessel soon." She pushed herself out of the chair. "I'm going to make sure the guns are loaded and the boarding pods are prepped. Or, rather, tell other people to make sure of those things – the burden of command, you know." She leaned down and looked into her screen, and through it, into Felix's mind. "The money you scammed out of them for the Benevolent Fund. How much did you skim?"

"Only two per cent," Felix said. "I'll split it with my crew, of course." No one expected an officer of the Mentak Coalition to be scrupulously honest – it would have been suspicious if they had been – but you didn't want a reputation for being too greedy, either, or you'd lose out on crucial opportunities to profit in the future.

"Fair enough. Not many opportunities for plunder out in the territories, are there?"

"There's plenty to steal, as long as you want to steal dirt or sheep," Felix said. "Unfortunately, it all belongs to people I'm supposed to protect instead of profit from. I call first pick on any personal weapons we recover on the enemy ship. Carrying a regulation sidearm is so basic."

"Spoils of war, eh?" Meehves switched off.

CHAPTER 3

The kidnappers had the good sense to stop running when a destroyer and its attendant fighters appeared before them (and beside, above, and below them). The *Temerarious*, which had lagged behind at a distance where they could counteract any attacks lobbed at them, rapidly closed the gap to cut off the last avenue of retreat.

"They're trying to send out some kind of encrypted communication," Calred said over Felix's helmet radio. "It's adorable, really."

Felix grinned. Meehves had jammed outgoing signals, of course. He clambered into the *Temerarious*'s shuttle and let the computer chart the course. The little hemispherical boarding pods were already spinning off from Meehves's ship, *The Bad Cat*, and would soon attach to the hull of the enemy vessel like leeches on a swimmer. They weren't quite sure what they'd find inside – the enemy ship was shielded against deep sensor scans, like most vessels with military specs, so they had to guess at the interior layout and the crew complement. The boarding pods were full of electronic countermeasures and security circumvention tools meant to convince ships to pop open their airlocks, and, if those failed, they also had lasers, cutting blades, and acid nozzles to make their own openings through the hull.

Usually, the pods weren't necessary. The unofficial raider fleet of the Coalition wasn't in the murder business, nor did they wish to discourage interstellar trade; they were basically just a toll you had to pay if you strayed too close to Coalition space without making proper prior arrangements. The merchant vessels knew to bring along a little extra so they could satisfy the raider captains and still make an appropriate profit, and worked that expense into their projections of the cost of doing business. Every once in a while, you encountered a ship with a crew that didn't understand the rules and needed them explained, in person, at the end of a gun. Even then, there was usually no reason to kill anyone. After all, if you murder someone, you only get to steal from them once.

This ship wasn't like the others, though, and would not be extended such courtesies. Once you fire on a Coalition vessel, especially an official one like the *Temerarious*, negotiations are pretty much over. By the time Felix's shuttle was close enough to dock, the boarding pods had taken control of the aft airlock, and Meehves's first officer, an Xxcha named Qqmel, was on board waiting for Felix. Being confronted by hulking reptilian bipeds was inherently disconcerting for humans who hadn't grown up around Xxcha, so who better to lead the party?

Qqmel was patient and thoughtful, but those qualities tended to come across to strangers as emotionless menace, an impression compounded by the elaborate shouldermounted cannon he wore. The cannon moved independently, with audible whirs and clicks, to remain pointed steadfastly at the face (or equivalent) of anyone he target-locked. "How would you like to handle this?" Qqmel said.

"Oh, right. I'm the ranking officer here." Felix straightened his shoulders.

Qqmel made the weird little cough that Xxcha used for laughing. "I'm in charge of the boarding party, reporting to Commander Meehves. You're tagging along. But Meehves said I should ask you how you'd go about it, to see if you learned anything in tactic class."

Felix slumped, but he thought about it. "They'll have Thales in some remote part of the ship, where he's safe, with a guard or two, while the bulk of their forces try to keep us from reaching him. Except they must know we have overwhelming force, so they'll also have some plan to escape this ship, maybe an escape pod they'll try to slip away in unnoticed with Thales, to reach some predetermined rendezvous point. So, why don't you and your large violent comrades do the big noisy seizing-the-bridge thing, and I'll creep along the service corridors and see if I can find the actual prisoner? They'll either be hiding in the tunnels, or using them to reach their means of escape, I bet."

"Acceptable," Qqmel said. "If you lose Thales, though, you'll be the one who gets the blame, not me or the commander."

"Yes, I realize that. Good tactics on your part."

"Want to take a marine with you?"

Felix shook his head. He had a secret weapon, and didn't need a big obvious one too. "I'll be faster and quieter on my own. I'd better go silent, too, so don't contact me; I'll contact you. I'd welcome any schematics we have for the ship, though."

After briefly scanning the layout in his heads-up display (the diagrams were for the generic model of this ship, so any modifications would be an unwelcome surprise, but it was the best they could do), he moved left down a passageway to a service access hatch.

Felix had grown up on a shipyard space station near the center of Coalition space, and was comfortable clambering through the innards of vessels, though he'd moved a lot more easily as a ten year-old than he did nearly twenty years later. He moved quietly, ducking under bundles of cable, turning sideways to slip past pipes, occasionally consulting his display to make sure he hadn't become lost. The only light came from thin strips along the floor, turning the tunnels into a shadowland, but Felix had no trouble negotiating such environments. He had all that practice hunting Tib, and being hunted. This was the same thing, except at the end of this exercise, his prey might really try to kill him.

He heard occasional booms, shouts, and thumps that told him battle had been joined elsewhere on board. The raider fleet was expert at boarding hostile craft, and came armed for that specific purpose with anti-personnel weapons, lethal and non-, so he didn't worry much about whether his people were winning. He *was* beginning to feel silly, though, because he'd gone through a whole lot of tunnels without seeing anyone. Maybe he was giving his opponents too much credit, and they weren't that clever after all – what if Qqmel was waiting impatiently with Thales already in custody up on the bridge? Felix considered risking the use of his comms to ask –

Ah ha, what's this? He reached a narrow, downward-slanting passageway that wasn't marked on his schematics, which meant it was an after-market alteration to the ship's design, which meant it was potentially interesting. He started to make his way down, toward the belly of the ship – home to the shuttle, and cargo, and maybe other things too. A secret hidey-hole, maybe, for a small escape pod.

He slithered down a vertical shaft barely large enough to accommodate him. That gave him more doubts: it would be hard to manhandle a prisoner through a space that cramped, though he supposed if someone pointed a gun at him and told him to start crawling, he would. No way to tell where he was going until he got there, so on he went. *If I end up in a trash compactor or something, Tib will never let me live it down…*

Felix crawled through a duct on his hands and knees, toward a vent, the grille that should have been covering the opening dangling askew. So, either this ship was maintained in a slovenly fashion, or someone had come this way before him. He eased forward on his belly and peered through the opening.

The vent led to a small cylindrical room, about the size of an airlock, with no visible points of entry. An escape pod shaped like the closed bud of a flower filled most of the space, leaving a thin strip to walk on all the way around. A woman in black mercenary armor – but no helmet; that was lucky – crouched by the pod's entry hatch, tapping away on a handheld terminal. There was no sign of Thales, but he might be inside the pod already.

Felix unclipped a noisemaker, set it for a five-second delay, then slung it toward the woman. The small object bounced off her head, making her curse and lift her eyes to him. She was the one he'd talked to earlier, the one who couldn't hide her emotions and who'd tried to bribe him. How nice to see her again.

Noisemakers were little blue spheres, sized to fit comfortably in the hand, and when you set them off they released sonic waves of such intensity that they obliterated thought and left their victims dazed, blinking, and bleeding from the ears and nose. Felix, of course, had his noise-cancelling earpieces in, so the onslaught was just an unpleasant whine for him, and a rumble that made his skeleton tingle. He scrambled out of the vent, dropped to the floor, and dashed to the woman. She was on her back, staring up blankly – but, wait, her ears weren't bleeding, and neither was her nose, so –

Felix flung himself to one side just as she raised her sidearm and fired. The energy blast melted a section of the wall behind him. Damn. She must have protective gear on too. He scrambled toward her, getting too close for her to shoot easily, and tried to pin her gun arm down. Even using both hands, he could barely manage – her armor was powered, making her easily twice as strong as he was. His own suit was made for infiltration rather than brute force, which had seemed like a good idea at the time.

She started punching him in the side with her free hand,

and if he didn't make her stop soon he was going to end up with broken ribs, as his armor was not as comprehensive as hers. She snarled and yelled things, calling him a traitor to humanity and so on, but he ignored that, flicking his eyes across his helmet display, selecting the countermeasure he really should have queued up earlier, and blinking to activate it.

His suit used most of its remaining battery life to discharge an electromagnetic pulse, and her eyes bulged as her armor locked in place. Felix's suit systems went down too, of course – EMPs didn't discriminate – but *he* had a secondary, shielded, temporary power source that kicked on immediately to compensate. He took her gun away and threw it aside, then peeked into the escape pod.

It was empty.

He sighed and looked down at her. She still had one arm raised, armor locked in position, fingers twisted into a claw. "Where's Thales?"

"Gone." She grinned savagely. "Long gone. You're too late. My team leader escaped with him."

"You mean you aren't the team leader? Wait, never mind – of course not. They left you on the ship, after all, while the competent people went down to do the actual job. Oh well. At least tell me why you wanted him. What's so special about Thales, anyway?"

"I'll never tell you anything, pirate scum."

"That's hurtful." He leaned against the rounded side of the escape pod, crossed his arms, and gazed down at her. "I don't have much experience with Coalition interrogation methods – that was never my area of training – but I gather they're quite effective. We'll find out what you know eventually, so you might as well spare yourself some trouble and tell me now."

"Never." She clenched her jaw, grinding her teeth, then spasmed, foamed spit through her lips, and went limp.

"Great Edwin's ghost," Felix murmured. He hadn't expected *that*. Had she bitten down on a suicide pill or something? He hadn't realized people actually did that, outside spy adventure serials. He prodded her with his foot, in case she was faking, then checked for a pulse in her neck. Apparently, people did.

Felix considered himself a patriot, but really, there were limits. Did this mean Thales was so important it was better to die than to risk the Coalition even finding out why?

He activated his comms. "Qqmel, I found one crew member trying to escape, but no sign of Thales. She killed herself before I could ask too many questions. Tell me you had better luck?"

"We took some very nice guns off some corpses. The armor is mostly ruined though. No survivors among the enemy up here – they fought to the last. We offered nicely to take them prisoner, but they preferred certain death. Where's the percentage in that? Your cousins are strange, Felix."

"Tell me you just forgot to mention recovering their hostage."

"Sorry, Felix. No sign of the mysterious Thales. We're still searching, so don't give up hope yet. We found a bunch of documents and equipment, the former encrypted, the latter mysterious. My techs are digging through the ship's computers, but there's nothing yet to indicate who hired these people or the purpose of their mission. If I had to guess, I'd say it's a classic black ops setup, verbal orders only, highly compartmentalized, all need-to-know. Clearly no one thinks *we* need to know."

"Did you lose anyone?" Felix asked.

"No, we came in heavy, since your reports indicated they were pretty geared up. We sacrificed mobility for armor. Lieutenant Roarge will be out of commission for a while – they got lucky and shot his arm off at the elbow, so the medics will need to grow him a new one – but otherwise it's just bruises and dents."

"Glad to hear it. I'll come up and help with the search." He looked around, but there really weren't any doors, so it was back through the ventilation hatch again. That was an unnecessary addition of insult to injury.

Hours later, Felix sat slumped in the captain's chair on the enemy ship, where the woman he'd watched die had snarled at him not long ago. "Where did they *go*?" he said, not for the first time.

"I don't know, but *I'm* going back to my ship." Qqmel's shoulder-mounted cannon drooped like a wilted flower, pointing at the floor. "We've searched every inch of this vessel, found two more of those hidden escape pod bays – both with their pods still in place. Maybe they jumped out an airlock with a personal propulsion device, something too small to show up on our sensors, and met up with another stealth ship. Wherever they went, they're gone." Qqmel patted Felix on the shoulder. "This was some kind of well-funded clandestine operation, so take heart – you didn't accidentally declare war against anyone, since the assets were obviously deniable. The raider fleet gained a nice new cruiser and a bunch of guns, and you'll get a share of plunder deposited in your account, which you official military types don't usually get to enjoy. The analysts back home will keep researching this Thales, and maybe we'll figure out who wanted him, and what for."

"Maybe." Felix wasn't cheered up. He'd really believed this was it: his ticket out of backwater patrol and back to the fast track, where he belonged. He'd spent enough time gambling over the years to know this feeling well: seeing the big score vanish from sight with one bad turn of the cards or roll of the dice. "Guess I'll head back to the *Temerarious*. Give Meehves my best."

"She said to tell you she'll send you a bottle of something nice. Said you'd have sorrows that need drowning?"

"She knows me better than she has any right to," Felix grumbled.

Felix returned to the airlock where his shuttle was docked. The lockers on either side of the corridor were hanging open, environment suits and supplies scattered on the floor in the aftermath of the search. At least cleaning up the mess was someone else's job. He punched the button to open the inner doors, entered the airlock, waited for it to seal shut, then unlocked the doors leading to the shuttle. He ducked as he stepped into the long, low-ceilinged space. The shuttle was simple, a box of air attached to engines and a guidance system, the interior just a row of seats and walls made up entirely of storage compartments, without so much as a window.

Once on board, he strapped into one of the front seats and ordered the computer to begin the detachment sequence and return to the *Temerarious*. The shuttle's mechanical voice droned a countdown, and when it reached zero the shuttle kicked away from the captured vessel and began its journey back home.

Something off to the right went *thump* and *crack*, and Felix turned to look. A woman in black mercenary armor stepped out of the largest storage locker, the one where the spare environment suits should have been. She pointed her sidearm at him, and for a moment they regarded one another silently. He'd never seen her before, and he would have remembered: she had a face made of diamond-sharp edges, with dark and merry eyes, topped by a crown of spikily short dark hair. Her grin was as self-satisfied as any Felix had ever seen in the mirror.

There was someone else in the locker, slumped over to one side, unmoving: a man with thinning gray hair, a string of drool hanging from his thin lips, eyes closed.

Felix inclined his head toward the man, without taking his eyes from the gun. "Mister Thales, I presume?"

"Doctor, actually," she said.

That was interesting. "What kind of doctor?"

"Based on our brief interactions," she said, "he's a doctor of being a huge asshole."

CHAPTER 4

"So, not the medical kind," Felix said.

"Nope," she replied. "He won't be any help at all after I shoot you in the knee."

"Ah. Could I persuade you *not* to shoot me in the knee?"

"The knee is already my compromise. My first impulse was to shoot you in the face."

"But I'm too pretty?"

"Not from where I'm looking, no," she said. "You are a giant pain in the ass, captain Duval. You very nearly ruined everything, but fortunately I'm a professional, so it can still be salvaged. You took my ship, so I'm going to take yours. I won't need it for long, and then you can have it back. You can captain with one knee, I'm sure."

"I'm grateful, understand, but why did you decide on maiming me rather than killing me?"

"After your people killed all of mine, you mean?"

"That is the question that arose in my mind," Felix admitted.

"My people were all willing to die for this mission. So am I, technically, but I'd rather keep it a hypothetical willingness. They were doing their job, and you were doing yours. Even if I didn't need you alive to give your crew orders, I don't operate based on revenge." She rolled her head around on her shoulders. Probably had a cramp from being jammed in a locker that, while big enough for spacesuits, was not really made to hold spacesuits with the people still inside them. "If I did, I'd be more likely to go after the analyst who told us your patrol ship would be on the other side of the system yesterday."

"Ah, that. We had to leave the system to pick up an emergency delivery of antivirals for one of the mining outposts a few days ago – they picked up some nasty bug in a mineshaft, makes the eyes swell shut and get all crusty, disgusting business. That altered the patrol schedule a bit, but it didn't matter, because nothing ever happens out here."

"I guess I'll spare the analyst's life after all then. Sorry to shatter your bucolic peace."

"Oh, no, it's been a welcome distraction. Until this part, anyway. You mentioned orders. What orders am I meant to be giving? Where are we taking the old man?"

"I'll tell you when you need to know–"

The woman's jaws snapped together, she twitched and spasmed, and then fell over.

"You took your time about it," Felix said mildly.

Tib Pelta shimmered into view, putting her stun gun back in its holster. "I wanted to see if she'd say anything useful, but you are very bad at interrogating people."

"I'm excellent at flirting, though."

"You think so? She certainly wasn't flirting back."

"I was still getting warmed up." He sighed. "You could have *told* us they'd stowed away on the shuttle, Tib, and saved us all a lot of time." He untethered himself and tried to figure out how to remove the enemy's armor.

"Don't be stupid. She would have heard me if I called you on the comms. It's not like there's a quiet corner in this shuttle where I could go to make a call, and opening the doors to go out would have drawn attention. I'm sneaky – I don't teleport."

"You're extremely insubordinate today."

"Ah. I meant to say, 'Don't be stupid, captain'. Better?"

"Much. Forgive me. I'm just annoyed." He thumped the armor. "How are we supposed to crack this shell?"

Tib crouched beside him, pressed a spot on the armor that looked like any other spot, and the plates separated with a hiss of escaping air. The enemy was wearing a plain white jumpsuit underneath. Still no identifying marks, not even a ship name. They wrestled her out of the armor and propped her in a corner. Felix put her weapons in a locked compartment while Tib opened a supply panel and brought out a roll of gray industrial tape. Perfect for binding wrists and ankles. "How'd all this happen, anyway?" he said. "I wondered where you'd gotten off to. I almost called you."

"Don't worry. I turned off my comms in case you tried." She bound the prisoner's wrists while Felix did the ankles. "I was creeping around the ship, being as invisible as possible, like you ordered." She paused in her work long enough to give a little salute. "I followed along behind the boarding party, to see if anyone tried to slip away behind them. No luck. I did the same thing during the search, in case someone was moving around to hide in places they'd already checked, but still nothing. So I wandered back here. Just luck that I happened to be faded out, still. I was planning on jumping out at you later and making you wet yourself."

"I would not have wet myself."

"No? You know you're supposed to stay hydrated, captain. Instead, I found her, tossing our spare environment suits into the corridor with the rest of the search detritus, and hiding in the locker. I spent a long time staring at the closed door, wondering if I could wrench it open and knock her out before she killed me, but I could just picture her, holding her gun in front of her, ready to fire at the slightest movement of the door."

Felix could picture it too. "So you figured you'd wait for her to come out."

"I knew she would eventually. A suit locker isn't much of a long-term residence. If she'd stayed sealed in until we got back to the ship, I could have slipped out after you and then we could have cut the oxygen to the shuttle and knocked her out or something."

Felix nodded. "You did well, Tib. On balance. With extra points for style."

"Feel free to reward me with bonus money in addition to praise." She inclined her head toward the woman. "What do we do with her? And with *him*?"

"Ask them various pointed questions, I would imagine."

"Sounds important," Tib said. "Very much captain-level work. You can do that part."

The prisoner stalked back and forth in the brig – which was

halfway filled with cases of emergency rations, of course, so at least she wouldn't go hungry – while Felix watched her on the screen from the bridge. Half the screen, anyway: the other half was filled with the dossier Calred had compiled on their prisoner, based on DNA and facial recognition results.

"Amina Azad," Cal rumbled. "Citizen of the Federation of Sol. Ten years in their navy, the last three as a training officer specializing in close combat and incursion tactics. Most of her service record is redacted, even in the Federation databases our analysts aren't supposed to be able to access. She was discharged two years ago, and set up shop as a freelance security consultant, with a confidential client list. So confidential I'd be willing to bet none of the clients actually exist."

"You think she's still working for the Federation of Sol as a deniable asset?" Felix was neither shocked nor appalled by the possibility. The Coalition had its share of unofficial state actors, after all – a whole raider fleet of them.

"Seems likely. The Federation doesn't like to let valuable people go any more than we do."

"She's some kind of black ops super soldier, and we were still able to find out more about her than we were about Doctor Thales?"

"I know," Cal said. "Makes you curious about what *he* does for a living, doesn't it?"

"Is he awake yet?" Felix asked.

"In and out," Tib said over the comms. She was in their infirmary, watching over Thales. His status was a bit fuzzy: he wasn't a Coalition citizen, as far as they knew, but the Coalition was certainly interested in him, so he was somewhere between a guest and a prisoner. "Azad hit him with a massive dose of sedatives, and the safest approach is just to let them work their way out of his system. I could counteract the effects with *more* drugs, but he's on the far side of middle age, has high blood pressure and some arterial clogging, and I don't want to shock his system."

"Let me know when he's lucid. I suppose I'll go chat with Azad in the meantime."

"Captain. Neat trick back on the shuttle. Our analysts said you had an Yssaril on your crew, but I didn't realize she came to my ship with you. You fooled me once, which is one more than most people get."

Felix sat outside the brig, on a crate full of cloned eel-meat canned in red jelly – the drones had moved several crates into the corridor to make room for Azad. He thumped the side of the box. "Cloned eels. Ever had them? I guess I'd eat them, if it was the aftermath of a disaster and the choice was cloned eels or nothing at all."

"They're better in yellow jelly," Azad said. "Why are we talking about eels?"

"I'm attempting to establish a conversational rapport with my prisoner for purposes of interrogation."

"Try harder," she said. "How's *my* prisoner?"

"You mean Thales? He's not yours any more. He'll be all right, though no thanks to you. That level of sedation? Pretty dangerous for someone his age."

"One of my people is an expert at judging that sort of thing. Or was, before you killed him. I guess Thales hasn't started talking yet, or you'd see why I wanted him unconscious and quiet." She leaned against the bars, gazing at Felix with disconcerting directness. "What are you going to do with me?"

"Hand you over to the Table of Captains. Or, rather, their general staff. They'll ask you various difficult questions, and then decide if keeping you alive has any strategic value. Or you could cooperate with me, tell me everything right now, and I'll use my influence with the Table to intercede on your behalf."

She snorted. "Ha. I'll pass. My analyst said you're competent, but reckless even by Coalition standards, which is why you're stuck running a glorified transport ship in one of the most remote systems in Coalition space. Thales came way out here precisely because it's the middle of nowhere. Scratch that – the deep dusty back corner of nowhere. I think I can live without your influence."

"You can live for a little while, anyway, though it might not be very pleasant."

"Going to make me walk the space-plank?" she said. "Keelhaul me?"

"Nobody ever really walked planks, and keelhauling someone on a spaceship isn't very effective. It's just not the same unless you're being dragged underwater across a hull covered with barnacles."

"There's a sad shortage of barnacles in space, I've noticed. Just the usual interrogation techniques and methods of execution, then? That's too bad. I was hoping for exposure to the local culture."

"I'm sure you'll find our little customs fascinating. We're

meeting up with Commander Meehves in a few hours and transferring you to her custody."

"Is this commander taking custody of Thales too?" She tried to make the question sound casual, and didn't do a very good job.

"I'm afraid not. The general consensus is that you and Thales shouldn't be on the same ship, if that can be avoided, in case you're tempted to do something reckless."

"Aren't you afraid I'll do something reckless *here*?" She smiled. With a smile like that, she would have made a pretty good pirate.

"Desperately." Felix took out his hand terminal, pushed an icon on the screen, and a clear sheet of unbreakable plexi slid out of the ceiling to cover the bars of the brig. "That's what this gas is for."

"You absolute piece of–" Azad crumpled to the floor before Felix could learn any new Federation of Sol insults.

Qqmel came over to escort Azad back to *The Bad Cat*. She was unconscious and restrained on a floating stretcher. "Be careful with her," Felix said. "Nobody's that arrogant without at least a little to back it up."

"Oh, I don't know about that," Qqmel said, eyeing him with reptilian amusement, but his cannon clicked and whirred and shifted to fix on her face.

"When do I get rid of Thales?" Felix said.

They strolled from the brig toward the airlock, with one of Qqmel's marines pushing the stretcher along. "Ah, the good doctor of nobody knows what. The commander says you should return to your usual patrol route and babysit him for the time being. You'll receive further orders after a while."

Felix frowned. "I'm not sensing a lot of urgency."

"The Table hasn't decided what to do with the man yet, Felix. We could return him to Cobbler's Knob, deport him to wherever he's originally from, make him disappear – all options are on the table, because we don't know why he was abducted. We're not sure any of this is Coalition business, honestly."

"None of our business!" Felix pointed at Azad.

"Obviously, Azad fired on you, so *she's* our business. She may have some useful intelligence from her time in the service, so we'll get what we can from her before we lock her up, or shove her out an airlock, or someone in the clandestine branch tries to turn her. Thales, though, isn't nearly as interesting to our superiors. We don't know why she came for him. Maybe he's just a wealthy recluse Azad wanted to ransom. Who knows? He's the victim here, anyway."

"Come on. He must be important. If the Federation sent a black ops team–"

"That's just Calred's theory," Qqmel interrupted. "He's a security officer, which means he's professionally paranoid. We checked out the dead, and they're all freelancers, just like Azad. Our working theory is that they were hired to do a snatch-and-grab that went disastrously wrong, and the Federation doesn't have anything to do with this mess at all."

Of course. "The Table doesn't *want* to believe the Federation was involved," he said. "Or at least they don't want to admit to the possibility officially. Because that would mean the Federation of Sol sent an armed vessel secretly into Mentak Coalition space, which then proceeded to fire on one of our ships. That's the kind of thing that endangers diplomatic relations and trade deals and all sorts of other things."

"That kind of speculation is for higher ranks than me," Qqmel said cheerfully. "I just break open ships and steal stuff. But I may have overheard the commander musing along similar lines. She always said you were smarter than you look. Look, we're going to interrogate Azad, but she's going to be tough. Why don't you see if you can get Thales to talk, and if he says something interesting, pass it on? You can handle one old guy, right, Felix?"

"Right." Felix saw his hope of glory receding. Even if he found out Thales had some big secret, and he told the Table, they might choose not to hear him, because of politics. He watched Qqmel load Azad onto his shuttle, and once they were away from his ship, took a nice deep breath. At least that woman was someone else's problem now. Maybe he had time to grab a bite or a nap or both before –

"Captain." Tib spoke in his comms, voice sharp. "Thales is awake. You'd better get down here."

"I'm on my way." Someone shouted in the background. "Are you all right? What's going on down there?"

"He's throwing things at me and calling me names," Tib said. "I've heard worse, but I'd rather have you here than me."

"Get that slimy sneaking frog away from me," Thales snarled, crouching behind the exam table in the infirmary. His gray hair stuck up in wild whorls, and he held his fists up like he was about to get into a brawl.

"OK, monkey." Tib glanced at Felix. "May I be excused?"

"I think I can take it from here," Felix said. "Doctor Thales, I'm Captain Felix Duval, of the *Temerarious*. I'd appreciate it if you'd stop hurling abuse at my first officer."

"You know what those creatures are like," Thales said. "They're spies, you know, all of them, they sneak and steal and sell your secrets. I can't believe you have one on your ship! Are you some uncommon variety of idiot?"

Tib shook her head and left, the door sliding shut behind her. Felix perched on the edge of a counter. "She's a valuable member of the crew and my oldest friend, so I'm not the right audience for this little show. Let's move on. How are you feeling? Do you have everything you need?"

"I don't have *anything* I need. Where are my files? My equipment?"

"Everything we recovered is here in storage." Meehves didn't want Azad and the files on the same ship either, just to be safe, so Felix was babysitting those, too. "Could you answer a few questions for me, Doctor Thales?"

He scoffed, but lowered his fists and stood up. "Why should I?"

"Courtesy, since you're a guest on my ship? No? Gratitude, because we saved you from a team of mercenaries who attempted to abduct you? No, not that, either? How about pragmatism, because I can make your life easy, or I can make your life difficult?"

"Hmph." He sat on the exam table. "Go ahead. Ask. I can't promise you'll understand any of the answers."

"Where are you from?"

"Oh, all over." He waved his hand vaguely.

Right. "Why did you choose to settle on Cobbler's Knob?"

"I like peace and quiet and privacy. It's good for my work. People are always trying to steal my work."

"What is your work, exactly?"

Thales blinked. "You mean you don't *know*? Ha. I'm a scientist, boy. My research is going to transform the galaxy."

"Oh, is that all. What kind of research?"

Thales stuck his little finger in his ear, wiggled it around, looked at the tip for a moment, then wiped whatever he'd found off on the edge of the table. "The kind that's going to make me very rich." He looked down at the floor and spoke more quietly, as if to himself. "There's no going back to Alope – they found me once, and they will again. I used the last of my funds getting settled out here, establishing a fresh identity, covering my tracks… I can't afford to do all that over again. Hrmph. I need resources." He looked up and met Felix's eyes with his own bloodshot ones. "I suppose the Coalition is as good a partner as any. All right. If your government will help me complete my work, I'll give them the privilege of buying the results." He waved his hand. "Convey my offer to your superiors at the Table."

"I'm going to need a lot more information before I bother the captains."

He glared. "It's not enough for you to know the Federation of Sol wants me? I thought you people were *pirates*."

Felix pinched the bridge of his nose. "Just tell me why the Federation wanted you."

"Because whoever controls my invention will rule the galaxy."

Felix waited for a moment. Nothing more seemed to be forthcoming. "That was a good line, really, and well delivered, but, again, I'm going to need more context."

Thales sniffed. "I'm not sure your clearances are high enough to hear this."

"You're not going to talk to anyone higher ranking anytime soon, Thales, and you don't *work* for us, so nothing you have to say is classified in the Coalition."

"Fine. What do you know about wormholes?"

Felix frowned. "As much as anyone does."

"And what's *that*? I may travel in more informed circles than you do, and I don't want to leave out any *context* you might need to understand."

Felix was beginning to see Azad's point about keeping the man sedated. "Wormholes are naturally occurring portals, scattered randomly throughout the galaxy. They link distant points in space, so they're one of the main reasons interstellar nations and trade are even possible. They're vitally important strategically – control a wormhole, and you control vast swathes of space. A trade dispute over the Quann wormhole a few thousand years ago turned into a shooting war that brought down the old Lazax Empire."

"Solid grade-school-level overview," Thales said. "Except for the bit about them being naturally occurring. Some of them might be, but they can also be *made*. The Creuss do it."

Felix shuddered. The Ghosts of Creuss. He didn't know much about the aliens – nobody did – but they were bogeymen, beings composed of energy instead of matter, difficult or impossible to kill or even fight, with a mastery of technology beyond anything the other races of the galaxy possessed. If Thales said the Creuss could make wormholes, he believed him. "If you say so."

"My personal area of expertise is wormhole physics," Thales said. "When we found out the Creuss could create wormholes, replicating their technology became my personal mission. Creating wormholes isn't easy for them, apparently – they do so rarely, at great cost, and mostly use FTL ships like everyone else. Still, if the Creuss can do it, that means it's possible, and I refuse to believe there's anything they can do that I can't, given sufficient time and resources. I turned my mind toward the problem, and quickly began to make progress. Just knowing it *could* be done removed the greatest psychological block." He leaned forward. "Tell your superiors I've found a way to open wormholes anywhere I want, anytime I want. Tell them, if they can afford me, I'll give them the keys to the galaxy."

CHAPTER 5

"You're saying you can make wormholes. You can actually, really, physically make wormholes." Felix was staggered by the implications. Thales might as well have said he could eat a planet.

Thales showed all his teeth in what must have been intended as a smile. "Imagine what a bunch of pirates like the Coalition could do with my technology. You could open a wormhole, without warning, anywhere you wanted. You could drop a fleet into orbit around any planet or station in the galaxy, strike your target, and then vanish. I can *close* my wormholes, too, so no one will be able to follow you back. Ha. What do you think of that?"

I think it sounds too good to be true. "I think extraordinary claims require extraordinary evidence."

"I always knew I'd have to give a demonstration to potential buyers. I'm prepared to do that, if the Coalition will help me complete my prototype. The theoretical basis is essentially complete – at this point, I just have to solve a few small engineering problems."

"What exactly are you asking for?" Felix asked.

"I'll require the Coalition's full support in gathering the resources and materials I need, and protection from the forces arrayed against me. I was hoping that security through obscurity would prove sufficient, but the Federation found me, so I'll concede that security through being surrounded by armed people with guns also has its advantages." He waved his hand. "Go on and tell the people who pull your strings my terms."

Ordered around by a civilian on my own ship. Felix snapped off a salute so formal and stiff it could only be read as mockery, turned smartly on his heel, and marched out of the infirmary. Then he initiated quarantine procedures so nothing short of a catastrophic hull breach would allow the door to open. At least he could keep Thales from wandering loose on his ship.

Felix didn't get to talk to a representative of the Table of Captains, of course. They were far too busy and important. He invoked the name of the well-respected Commander Meehves, opening contact with a higher echelon of officials, and after a circuitous route of transfers, his screen connected to the office of the assistant undersecretary of special projects, a Hylar named Fololire Jhuri. Jhuri was a member of a sub-species that didn't require any special breathing apparatus to live out of the water, and he spoke through an artificial voicebox in tones clearly based on the human star of a popular adventure romance serial– a mellow, deep voice Felix found a bit incongruous coming from a bulbous green head trailing fronds of tentacles, with a face glistening with cybernetic implants.

"It all sounds a bit implausible," Jhuri said. "We've heard stories of what the Creuss can do to space-time, but there are so many outrageous tales about them it's hard to know what's true and what's nonsense. Wormhole physics isn't my area, but I reached out to a few of the local experts, and they haven't heard of anyone making the kind of progress Thales claims. Since he refuses to give his real name, I can't vet his qualifications, but on the whole, I'm inclined to think he's overstating the level of his research at best, and outright lying at worst."

Felix felt a little disappointment, but it was mingled with relief. An exciting mission would have been nice, but having Thales on board the *Temerarious* was like having a splinter under a fingernail. "So, should I drop him back at Cobbler's Knob?"

The Hylar's tentacles undulated. "I didn't say that. Commander Meehves assures me that significant resources were expended trying to capture Thales, so we can't discount his story utterly – someone wants the man for *something*. Once we properly interrogate the mercenary you captured, we may find out more. In the meantime, we are willing to provide Thales with limited support, at least until it becomes evident that he's a fraud. It's a gamble, but we're the Coalition. We try things. Honestly, I don't believe his claims, but if he *can* do what he says it's worth exploring just on the off-chance. We don't want to be the fools who threw away a winning lottery ticket."

"What are you giving him?"

"I'm authorizing the reassignment of some Coalition

personnel to provide protection for Thales, and to assist him with logistics, and the acquisition of any necessary materiel."

At least Thales wouldn't be Felix's problem any more, though his sympathies went out to whatever crew had to deal with the man. "Understood. Where am I taking him?"

"Anywhere he wants to go, I suppose," the Hylar said.

"Wait," Felix said. "What? Oh."

"Quite. You, your ship, and your crew have been seconded to my office, temporarily reassigned from your patrol duties. Officially, you and your crew are not operating as military assets, but as contractors and consultants hired out to a civilian scientist." The Coalition sometimes rented out personnel for money, so the explanation wasn't implausible. "In reality, you're working for Operation Chicane, and reporting to me."

Felix had various questions, but for some reason the one that popped out was, "Why is it called Operation Chicane?"

"We have a long list of code names generated by computer. That was the next one."

How unsatisfying. "What about my, ah, regular duties?"

"Patrolling the Lycian system? Your work helping the colonists is vital, of course, in its way, but we can move things around to cover your territory. It's one of the quietest systems we control, after all."

"Historically," Felix said. "I'd like to point out that there was an armed attack on this system by violent outsiders rather recently."

"The first such incident since that system was settled, in fact. You dealt with the attack well, which is why you're being given a better assignment. I'm surprised you aren't more enthusiastic – Meehves told me you were eager to serve the Coalition in a more active capacity. Was I misinformed?"

Felix scrubbed a hand through his hair and let himself look as sheepish as he suddenly felt. "No, of course not, I am eager, it's just… Thales. He's awful. I don't like the idea of working for him."

"Then console yourself with the fact that you're actually working for *me*. Get Thales whatever he needs. Prevent anyone else from abducting him. See if he can build the thing he claims he can build."

"When you say get him whatever he needs…"

"Within reason. He doesn't need a platinum statue of himself, or his own personal warship – but if he asks for something that seems plausibly necessary for his research, accommodate him. Don't start any wars. If you break any laws outside Coalition territory, try not to get caught. Otherwise… use your judgment. If your judgment proves inadequate, well, you're a deniable asset now, captain. If you get into serious trouble, we'll just say you went rogue and cut all ties with you."

"Oh good," Felix said. "That's comforting."

"Come now, captain. Don't be worried. If you do well, you'll be rewarded. Even if Thales doesn't accomplish anything, I'll remember your service, and if he *does* produce a miracle… you'll play an instrumental role in helping the Coalition rule the galaxy. Look at the potential advantages. Anyway, I'm sure it won't be too strenuous an assignment. The man is a researcher. I can't imagine he'll require anything too difficult from you."

•••

"What, all I get is *you*?" Thales said. "Ugh."

Thales was wearing his own clothes again, and sitting in Felix's office, leaning back in a chair and scowling. Felix sat behind his desk, partly to lend himself an air of authority, and partly because it put Thales farther away from him. The authority part wasn't really working; Thales didn't seem impressed by any authority outside himself. "I'm happy to tell undersecretary Jhuri that you don't require our services, if you're unhappy."

"Jhuri, eh? Sounds like a Hylar name. My life is infested with those creatures." He sighed. "Don't be stupid. You're better than nothing, if only barely. Once I give that wriggling squid you report to a demonstration of my technology, he'll start treating me with the proper respect. My whole life, I've had to prove myself to my inferiors. I'm used to it by now. In the meantime… well, you're enough to be getting on with."

"I'm so delighted we meet your immediate needs. We can set you up with lab space on the lower decks. I'll have the files and equipment we recovered from the mercenary ship taken down. We're going to take the *Temerarious* out of this system, since people might come looking for you here, though we're still deciding where to go. It depends on the supplies you need, but we can find a place near a trading route, with a raider fleet nearby in case we need backup. Just give me a list of materials and–"

"All that's fine," Thales interrupted, "but the *first* thing I need, the very first thing, before we do anything else, is Shelma."

"What's Shelma?" It sounded like some kind of chemical reagent, or, possibly, a drug.

"Not what. *Who*. Meletl Shelma. My research partner. I've reached a point in my work where I require her expertise – she's the best engineer I've ever known, and she's absolutely crucial to transition from theoretical underpinnings to practical applications."

Felix sighed. He was going to be a taxi service, then. "All right. Where is she?"

"The last I heard," Thales said, "she was in a prison camp in the Barony of Letnev."

"But you specifically said, don't start any wars," Felix said.

Jhuri was unmoved. "You won't start a war, because you aren't a military operative right now. You're a civilian contractor, and we don't have any treaties or diplomatic ties with the Barony. If Thales really needs this engineer, see if you can get her. At least look over the situation and decide if a breakout is feasible. Try not to get captured yourself – we won't be able to do much for you if the Barony locks you up."

"I thought Azad was contemptible for doing basically what you're asking me to do," Felix said.

"Perspective is so important," Jhuri said. "Anyway, there's a difference between abducting someone from a planet where he's chosen to settle, and rescuing someone from a Barony prison. Their habit of jailing political dissidents is shameful. Tell yourself you're striking a blow for freedom if it helps."

Felix thought about it. Plotting a prison break was, in the abstract, an appealing idea – his whole nation was founded on a prison uprising, after all, and the work certainly wouldn't be boring. "I may need extra resources. Mercenaries of my own, or equipment, or money bribes."

"I realize. I'm providing you with access to one of my department's discretionary funds. There's not enough to retire in luxury – I'd hate to tempt you so – but you should be able to fund a small operation like this. It's amazing the sort of things you can classify as 'research and development' in a budget report. Technically true in this case, even."

Resources, and a mission – this was exactly what Felix had been hoping for. Of course, he was stuck working with Thales, but no situation was perfect. "I assume you'll want regular mission updates?"

"Is that what you assume?" Jhuri said. "The whole deniability thing works better when we don't talk constantly, you know. You needn't tell me about every little prison break. The less I know about what you're doing the better, in some ways. I am interested in results. When Thales has a working prototype, get in touch. Or when it becomes clear he's a complete fraud. Or, I suppose, if you run out of money – though that won't make me happy. Otherwise, do your best to muddle along, and if I want updates, I'll reach out to you." The connection went dark.

"I suppose I've got my orders, then," Felix said aloud. He checked the ship's operating account – the funds held in common to buy supplies and repairs if needed – and saw it was much healthier than it had been a few minutes ago. Time to have a family meeting, then.

Tib was present in the galley, but not visible, since she wasn't in the mood to have abuse hurled at her. Cal sat across the table from Thales, looking at him with those large predator's eyes, taking him in calmly. Thales was smiling at the Hacan in a way that made Felix queasy. He sat at the head of the table, slouching in what he hoped looked like easy and effortless command, not that anyone was admiring the pose. "So," he began, but Thales interrupted him.

"What did your ancestors do to get exiled to the penal colony?" Thales asked Calred. "Currency manipulation, was it? Loan sharking? You Hacan do love your money, don't you?"

"Family tradition holds that my many-times-great grandmother had a disagreement with a representative of the Lazax emperor who behaved rudely in her presence," Calred rumbled. "She ate him." Cal showed all his teeth, which usually tended to render people speechless.

"Devoured a tax collector, eh? Sounds like Hacan."

"Can you *please* be less racist toward my crew?" Felix said. "We have to work together, you know."

"This again." Thales shook his head. "I'm not racist. I hold all the species of the galaxy in equal contempt."

"I don't doubt it, but you're expressing your contempt through horrible stereotypes and–"

"Humans are also garbage," Thales interrupted. He interrupted a lot. "For one thing, they talk endlessly and never get to the *point*. Are we going to break Shelma out of the prison camp or not?"

Felix took a deep breath. "I have been authorized to assist you in creating a prototype of your wormhole device, whatever it takes. I have been given complete discretion and autonomy–"

"You're not a total waste of my time, then. Good. First–"

Felix leaned across the table and flicked Thales on the tip of the nose, hard, making the scientist rear back and blink furiously. "What? How dare you–"

"The Table of Captains think you're full of shit." Felix spoke quietly, so Thales would have to stop sputtering to hear him. "If they believed you, they would have assigned more than three people and one ship to this operation, don't you think? Since there's a small chance you're telling the truth, though, they're willing to waste my time and a small quantity of money to hedge their bets. They see it as a small risk with a potentially large reward." He leaned over the table. "But here's the thing, Thales. You don't have any direct line of communication to my superiors. Everything goes through me. If I tell them you're a con artist trying to bilk the Coalition for money, they'll believe me."

"*You* people are the thieves and swindlers and pirates!" Thales cried.

"True enough," Felix said. "We take pride in being clever and sneaky and getting the upper hand by any means necessary. Which is why we don't trust people who tell us they just need a *little* help to make all our dreams come true. You seem to be under the impression that I have to keep you happy, Thales. I don't. You have to keep *me* happy, because as soon as you annoy me too much, I make a call, declare this mission a waste, and drop you off on the nearest rock to starve to death. Do you understand your situation?"

Thales glared at Felix furiously for a moment, then leaned back, and then began to chuckle. The chuckle built into a belly-rumbling laugh as the scientist smacked the table.

"You showed a little backbone there, captain! I can't work with someone I can't respect, as much as I can respect anyone. I thought you were a pudding-hearted sort of man. Of course, if I *could* push you around, I would, but if you say you have limits, I can accept that. I'll keep my opinions to myself unless they're relevant to the mission at hand, then, all right? The lion and the toad won't hear another harsh word from me."

"He's so much better already," Cal murmured.

"That would be marvelous. I'd like you to apologize to my crew first, though. So we can move forward with a clean slate in a spirit of collaboration." Felix thought that was probably pushing it, but he couldn't help himself.

Thales nodded, and turned to Calred. "I apologize for insulting your ancestors."

Calred inclined his great head graciously.

Thales went on. "If you're lurking around in here, First Officer Pelta, I'm sorry for all the shouting earlier. I had a bad experience with a spy from your tribe, but I'll try to judge you on your personal merits, and leave old associations out of it."

Tib shimmered into visibility. "Fine." She sat next to Felix. "Now that we're all happy and functional, what's the first step toward our glorious shared future?"

Felix said, "Thales tells us everything he knows about his partner Shelma and the place she's being held, and we make a plan to reunite them."

Hours later, Felix lay in his bunk, alone in his cabin, staring up at the ceiling, trying to get some sleep. They were making their way to the nearest Coalition-controlled wormhole gate, which would get them closer to the part of Letnev space where Thales believed his fellow scientist was being held. Life was likely to get very eventful soon, but, for now, things were quiet, and he needed to get some sleep while he could. Of course, his mind was spinning and uncooperative, with better things to do than dream.

His comm channel buzzed, and Felix groaned, rolled over, and squinted at the terminal on his bedside table. Then he sat upright. He had an encrypted message, highest urgency, from a command-level officer. He smoothed his hair down and answered.

Meehves appeared on the screen, face puffy from her own interrupted sleep. "We lost her," Meehves said.

CHAPTER 6

"You lost who?" Felix said, and then realized. "The mercenary, Amina Azad? What do you mean you lost her?"

"I mean the guards in the brig didn't check in as scheduled, so someone went down to see why not, and found both guards dead, and her cell empty. The security footage was erased, which I would have sworn wasn't even possible. Our best guess is, Azad had hidden implants that didn't show up on our scans, super-soldier black-ops enhancements that enabled her to escape and hack into our systems. There was no indication of any ships or pods leaving, no evidence of an airlock opening, so we scoured the ship for her, searching for hours. I finally sent the deck master to do a visual check of the launch bay, and that's when we realized one of our fighters was missing – according to the computers, the fighter is still sitting in its launch tube. She manipulated the security footage, so there's no record of the departure, or which way it went. Those fighters aren't meant for long-range travel, but they're fast, and there are inhabited systems in range on multiple trajectories, so we can't mount a meaningful search."

Felix whistled. "She's just gone, then?"

"We sent out her name and description system-wide, claiming she's wanted for murder, but if she can escape my brig, she can hide. It's a big galaxy."

"She'll go back to her handlers in the Federation of Sol and tell them we have Thales," Felix said.

Meehves shrugged. "If she was working for the Federation at all. We didn't prove that. We didn't prove anything. She just stared at us during our initial interview, didn't say a word, and we were planning a more intense interrogation for tomorrow."

"So, you *don't* think I should worry about the full force and power of the Federation of Sol bearing down on me?"

"The Federation doesn't want a war any more than we do. Even if Azad is an operative, and reports back, she doesn't know where Thales is now. We could have put him in a bunker somewhere. The Federation won't be able to do much about *that*." Meehves sighed. "I'm sorry, Felix. I was hoping to get confirmation that Thales was telling the truth – or that he's full of shit. I hear Jhuri made you his babysitter?"

"I thought that was super secret?"

"This is the best encryption we've got," she said. "Anyway, Jhuri was pretty interested in what Azad might have to say, so we've been liaising. I'm sure now that I'm not helpful any more I'll be left in the dark."

"Do you know the undersecretary well?"

"A little by acquaintance, a lot by reputation."

"Am I in good hands? Or, tentacles?"

"If you prove useful to Jhuri, the undersecretary will take very good care of you. If you prove less than useful, he'll throw you away like a broken tool and reach for a new one."

"I do not find that reassuring, commander."

"Oh, cheer up. For someone in the murky upper echelons of the clandestine services, Jhuri is a pretty straight shooter. Didn't he tell you basically the same thing himself?"

"He said if I succeed, I'll be rewarded, and if I get caught committing crimes outside Coalition space, he'll pretend he never heard of me."

"See? You know exactly where you stand. I'll let you know if we hear anything about our escapee. Good luck with your mission, captain."

"I hate the idea of Azad running around loose out there."

"It's a big galaxy," Meehves repeated. "I doubt you'll ever run into her again."

Amina Azad sat in the deepest darkest corner of a cantina in Misna, the most cosmopolitan city on the planet Ryma, which was primarily a world of temperate oceans inhabited by immense but only marginally intelligent cetaceans. The areas of habitable land included a scattering of archipelagos and one island large enough call a continent, at least by local standards. The city of Misna hugged a bay on the western coast, and most of the nicer restaurants featured views of the water. The place where Azad waited didn't have any windows at all.

She wore a wide-brimmed hat she'd stolen from a booth in the bazaar. Misna was big enough to have cameras capable of facial recognition, and she had to assume she was a wanted fugitive in Coalition space, so it was better to keep her features in shadow. She didn't have any contacts here, but cities were cities, and a couple of discreet inquiries had brought her to this portside bar, and the Xxcha bartender had agreed to make the right introductions. He'd get a finder's fee for his trouble if it worked out, and a knife in the neck from Azad if it didn't. He only knew about the first option.

The woman who slid into the chair across from Azad was Letnev. The wild variety of species present in Coalition space always delighted Azad – back home in the Federation, nonhumans were rare, and most of the times Azad had interacted with other races she'd been shooting at them or getting shot at or both. Having other sorts of interactions was always interesting. A lot of her compatriots in the navy were xenophobic, but Azad had decided early on that she wanted to see the galaxy, and she reveled in the vastness of the universe.

"You have a ship to sell." The stranger was young, wearing dark glasses; the Letnev were sensitive to bright light, but the bar was dim, so Azad figured she was probably just an asshole.

"I don't have the title on me," Azad said. "The ship is salvage. Did you take a look?" She'd passed along the coordinates for the ship to the prospective buyer earlier. That was a risk, but a calculated one. The fighter was locked up tight, the engine wouldn't turn on without her permission, and as a military-grade vessel, it had countermeasures that would make it dangerous for anyone to scrap it for parts.

The fighter was more valuable in one piece, anyway.

"We sent someone to take a look," she said. "We don't see a lot of Coalition fighters for sale, certainly not tucked away in the glass flats outside the city."

"Couldn't dock legally," Azad said. "See above regarding the lack of title. Besides, the fighters are made to evade detection. Why not spare myself the port fees?"

"That's just good financial planning," the woman said. "We're interested. You have the access fob?"

"If you have the money."

The woman slid across a card, and Azad passed her hand over it, the implant in her palm reading the data. More than she'd expected, but less than she'd hoped. Enough to finance the next part of her mission, though. "Acceptable." She slid a teardrop-shaped access fob across the table in return. The woman did her own authentication check, nodded, and left without a look back.

Azad wondered who she'd just sold the fighter to, or who would end up with it in the end. Gangsters, terrorists, revolutionaries? Oh well. It was unlikely to end up shooting at Federation ships, so she didn't really care. Now she had sufficient funds to get off this ball of mud and whales and resume her mission. She paid her tab, left a tip, and went looking for a ship to hire.

As she walked through the narrow, winding streets of Misna, she did her best to focus on the future. Pondering past mistakes could be a valuable exercise, if it prompted you to avoid similar mistakes in the future, but there was no point in dwelling on misfortune. She'd done everything properly, but you couldn't account for bad luck, and Duval and the *Temerarious* being in the wrong place at the wrong time was nothing else.

Azad *could* apportion some blame to her second-in-command for blowing their entire emergency fund on a pointless attempt to bribe Captain Duval, but she'd used her selfdestruct button – as the squad called their poison-filled hollow teeth – to avoid capture, so there was no point. The dead couldn't learn from their mistakes.

Azad had a poison capsule too, but she couldn't imagine using it. There was no scenario where she was more valuable dead than alive, and she preferred redemption over sacrifice. Better to stay alive and look for an opportunity to escape, and the sloppy discipline in the raider fleet and her own hidden enhancements had provided one. Now she could complete her mission: bring home the runaway Thales and put him back to work for the Federation of Sol. Thales wasn't a Federation citizen – he'd grown up among the talking squid on a Hylar world – but he'd made certain commitments and then abandoned them. His only loyalty was to himself. Azad was going to show him the error of his ways.

Azad strolled through the spaceport, a series of landing areas and support buildings arrayed on the edge of the island, not far from the bristling cranes and docks of the deep-water port. If she only looked at the sky and the glittering reflections of sunlight on the sparkling water, or closed her eyes and smelled the salt and exhaust, she could imagine she was back home on Jord, in the fishing village where she'd grown up before joining the navy. The illusion broke when she looked around and saw the Xxcha dockworkers carrying heavy loads alongside humans in exo-suits, the Hacan ship owners supervising, and the occasional head of a Hylar popping out of the water as they went about their business.

Misna was refreshing, and a nice change from cramped ship life, but she'd been here too long already. The pirates would be looking for her. She needed a vessel built for speed, something that could be piloted solo if need be, and, fortunately, the Coalition was full of smuggler's ships.

She settled on a newly arrived light cruiser, low-slung and shaped like a sleek aquatic predator, and approached the obvious captain, a dark-skinned human woman standing on top of a crate and yelling at people while wearing an alluring quantity of leather. (*Stop that*, Azad told herself. She was on a mission. There was time enough for pleasure later, if she lived.)

"I need a ride to Thibah." Thibah was an arid place, almost the opposite of Misna, with small oceans that looked like mud puddles from orbit. Its only virtue was its location, making it an ideal staging point for deep-space exploration – it was the last place to get fuel and supplies before venturing out into contested and unknown lands. It was also the first stop for people returning from those depths with items for sale, usually ore or other plundered resources, but sometimes alien artifacts and stranger things.

Azad didn't have any interest in going there, but it was a plausible destination from here.

The captain looked Azad up and down. "Nice hat. I'm not available for hire. I've got a load of mixed liquor I'm planning to unload on a mining planet."

"Take it to Thibah instead. Explorers like to drink."

"Yes, and I like to fill my cargo hold. I sell liquor, I get ore, I sell ore, I get liquor, and around and around I go. It's a virtuous circle."

Azad leaned back against a crate and gave her a lazy smile. "Sounds boring. You're too young to be that boring. Besides, there are plenty of things to pick up on Thibah. Even if you don't get a decent load there, that's where me paying you comes in handy."

The captain hopped down from the crate. "I'm sure you can find a ship going that way without bothering me."

"I like the look of *your* boat. I want something small, fast, and private. Maybe we could crack open a bottle or two of your supply and enjoy the journey."

She grunted. "What's the offer?"

Amina plucked the card from her pocket and held it up. The captain scanned it, and she *was* young, because she couldn't stop her eyes from widening. "You could almost buy a ship for that much."

"Not one as fast as yours, and anyway, then I wouldn't have any company. What do you say?"

"I say, are you on the run from anybody I should be worried about?"

Azad laughed, deep and throaty. "I never run *from* anything. I run toward things." She held out her hand. "I'm Carmen Goodwin." It wasn't an alias she'd ever used before, and it wasn't the name of her dead aunt or her hometown or any of the other stupid false identity choices amateurs made. She had a list in her head of the names of human women approximately her age who'd emigrated as children to remote parts of the galaxy and never shown up in public records since, and when she needed a new name, she picked one, after a cursory check to make sure they hadn't reentered civilization. As she recalled, Carmen had grown up on a space station until her family went to seek their fortune on a colony world, where they'd probably been eaten by local predators or something. Azad had always possessed a good memory, and the navy had provided technological augmentation to make it even better.

"I'm Zayne ad Itroc," the captain said. "I'll need half up front, half on your safe delivery to Thibah."

"I find your terms acceptable, captain. How soon can we leave?"

"I'm almost done with loading. I'll tell the cargo handlers they aren't needed, and pay the docking fees – no, wait, it's cheaper to bribe the dockmaster here, I forgot – and then we can be on our way. Say two hours?"

"I can't wait."

Azad got something to eat from a kiosk nearby – hot spiced meat wrapped in broad leaves, nowhere near as good as the seafood she could get back home; she had the sinking suspicion it was whale meat – and then hunkered down to wait. She had a tactical engine in her head, and she ran it through various scenarios, but the immediate problems were trivially easy to solve. The bigger issue – tracking down Thales – was harder. They'd planned to put a tracking device on him in case he tried to escape, but with all the chaos and pursuit, they hadn't got round to it. She'd have to find him the old-fashioned way: deduction, investigation, and intelligence gathering. First, she considered what she knew about him: he was a genius, an egomaniac, a bigot, and a holder of grudges. He now probably had the resources of the pirate nation at his disposal. What would he do with those resources? Or rather, what would he do *first*?

Ah. She thought she had an idea. When their mission was being put together, there'd been two potential targets: Thales and the Hylar scientist he'd collaborated with before the whole thing fell apart and they both disappeared into the depths of the galaxy. Her superiors had settled on recovering Thales first because he was the softer target. But Thales would be interested in their other possibility, too – their research showed she was the builder, while he was the theoretician, and he probably needed her to continue his work. Now that he had the resources of the Coalition at his back, Thales might try to get her.

If Azad could get there before he did, and lay in wait, she could recapture Thales. And if she was totally wrong, and he didn't go there, she could break in and take the secondary target for herself. Going back to her superiors empty-handed wasn't an option. If she came back with Thales, all her past transgressions would be wiped away. If she came back with Meletl Shelma, she'd at least get to keep breathing and drawing a paycheck. If she came back with *both* targets… ahh. Her handler would shout at her for excessive improvisation, but, in the end, she'd be covered in glory.

Azad always felt better when her mission parameters were clear. Now she could enjoy the trip with the intriguing captain ad Itroc. At least until the regrettable, inevitable, unenjoyable part.

•••

Once the course was laid in, they settled back in the captain's small lounge with glasses of firewine. Azad made a point of keeping her glass full, trusting that the captain's piratical pride would make her match her, sip for sip. Of course, the captain probably didn't have metabolic enhancements like those Azad used to keep herself from getting tipsy, let alone drunk.

They talked for hours as they drank, swapping life stories – most of Azad's were fictitious, and most of ad Itroc's were hilarious – and flirting. The flirting grew ever more outrageous as ad Itroc got drunker, and soon she was sitting next to Azad on the bunk, nuzzling her neck, one hand sliding from her knee up her thigh.

Azad's control of her own body was greater than normal, but not total, and it was impossible not to react. Her heartbeat sped up, her breath shortened, her face flushed. Azad had been through a long and lonely few months, and the captain was pretty and witty and willing.

Azad took ad Itroc's face in both hands and gazed into her eyes, centimeters away. "You're lovely," she said, and ad Itroc smiled.

Azad twisted the captain's head around savagely, snapping her neck, her augmented muscles turning the head nearly a hundred-and-eighty degrees around. Ad Itroc didn't even have time to be surprised before she died and slithered off the bunk to sprawl on the floor.

Azad knew from past experience that she usually regretted sleeping with someone she'd have to kill later. Looking at someone in the throes of passion and imagining their corpse was a downer. She gazed at the captain's body and sighed. Such a shame – she'd liked the woman – but the mission came first, always.

After Azad used the captain's glazing-over eyes and cooling fingertips to unlock the biometric controls and take over the ship, she kissed ad Itroc on the forehead, then dragged her down to the airlock to jettison her into space. "The Federation of Sol thanks you for your assistance," she said as she watched the body spin away. As good a prayer as any. Most people were no service to anyone but themselves, and even that was hit-or-miss.

Azad went to the cockpit and adjusted the trajectory to take her to Letnev space.

CHAPTER 7

"Have you ever been to the Barony?" Felix asked.

Thales made a face. "I went to one of their colonies, once, for a scientific conference. Beautiful place, full of lush jungles, towering trees, clear skies. Naturally, the Letnev had burrowed their settlements into the planet's crust, living in subterranean tunnels that never saw the sun. They could have grown anything there – it was a classic garden world – but they brought their mushroom farms and cloned meat vats with them."

"Ah, well, everyone enjoys a little taste of home." Felix leaned back in his chair at the galley table. He had to admit, Thales had become less objectionable since they had their little talk. Most of the scientist's conversation still consisted of insulting people (and entire peoples), but he was mostly insulting people Felix didn't like much either, which was more tolerable.

"I don't think the Letnev are allowed to enjoy things. Fascists and bureaucrats. One of them approached me at that conference, offered me a position at one of their scientific academies. From the look on his face, he learned some new Hylar swear words that day, ha."

"Is that why they imprisoned your colleague?"

Thales waved his hand. "No, that was years ago, when I was just a promising young academic at the Universities of Jol-Nar."

"I didn't think there were humans at the Universities," Felix said. Admittedly, most of his knowledge about the Hylar research worlds was based on their appearance in technothriller serials, where they were inevitably home to mad scientists crafting doomsday weapons.

"The Universities accept applications based on merit." Thales grinned. "They mostly see merit in other Hylar, but there are exceptions."

Felix would pass that tidbit of information on to Calred, and see if it helped him discover anything more about Thales. There couldn't be that many humans of his age, description, and purported area of expertise who'd studied or been employed at the Universities, and it might help to figure out his real name and background. Assuming he wasn't lying about any of those details, of course.

"Have you figured out how to break into the prison yet?" Thales asked.

"About that. Calred did some research, and the place you told us about isn't one of the Barony's penal facilities at all. Officially, it's an orbital weather monitoring station above a colony planet. Mentak Coalition intelligence suspects it's a secured research facility."

Thales waved that away. "They can call it whatever they like – it's still a prison. The Barony kidnapped Shelma, just like the Federation tried to kidnap *me*. She's being held there against her will. We have to help her. Especially since I can't easily complete my work without her – or vice versa, so be careful not to let the Barony get their hands on me, or they'll be ruling the galaxy. Besides, this is good news, isn't it? Surely it's easier to break into a research facility than it is to break into a prison."

"You might think so," Felix said. But he did have the inklings of an idea.

"Listen," Thales said. "When you rescue her, don't tell her you're working with me. I want to surprise her when she gets on board. She'll be delighted."

Felix tried to imagine someone being delighted to see Thales, especially when they weren't *expecting* to see him, and he failed, but perhaps he simply lacked sufficient imagination.

"You think all Hacan know one other?" Calred growled. He was lounging in the good chair in Felix's quarters, sipping a glass of clear liquid that could have doubled as engine degreaser and would have probably killed a human. The liquor was distilled from a desert plant native to the Emirates, and Felix kept a bottle on hand for those occasions when he needed a favor from a Hacan. "You're a human – you must know Juan Salvador Tao, right? Are you related?"

Felix sighed. "Don't act so offended. I know your mother did that genealogy project a few years back, and connected up with a bunch of your fifteenth cousins or whatever back in the Emirates. Don't you all share some glorious common ancestor?"

"We're distantly related to the third Quieron, yes. My branch of the family tree is on the disreputable side of the trunk, though. My oldest known direct ancestor once sold a map of the legendary Temple of the Burning Sands to the Mowshir Emirate."

"What's disreputable about that?"

Calred took a sip of his murder fluid. "She also sold it to the Creena clan, and then the governor of Eilaran." Another sip. "Also, the Temple of the Burning Sands doesn't actually exist."

"I begin to see the family resemblance."

Calred snorted. "Yes, fine, it's true. I talk to some of my cousins back in the ancestral homeland occasionally. They like to hear my tales of derring-do."

"No one ever wants to hear the tales of derring-don't," Felix said. "Do you think any of your relatives might have useful contacts for this mission?" The Emirates of Hacan had tentacles – well, claws – in every aspect of galactic trade, including business in the Barony, and Felix was hoping for a crack he could exploit.

Calred stroked his tawny chin. "Hmm. I do have a cousin who works for a consortium in the specialty agricultural sector. She was telling me about something that might prove useful."

"Agriculture? We're trying to break into a space station, not a farm."

"*Specialty* agriculture, I said."

"Ohhhh," Felix said. "You mean drugs."

"In most cases, yes," Calred admitted. "In this case, not quite. Let's just say high-ranking Letnev officials stationed far from the center of the Barony will pay dearly for a taste of home. I'll make some discreet calls, and I should be able to get some information, if you can pay for it."

"Pay? Does family count for nothing?"

"Of course it does," Calred said. "My cousin wouldn't even take *your* call."

Once the *Temerarious* was stripped of its Coalition markings and transponder, and temporarily renamed the *Swift Emergence*, they cruised into Barony space and sent a message to the research station. The response came back immediately: "You're a day early."

"We made up time on Rigel III," Calred said from the captain's chair. Felix was in the first officer's position, Thales was in his new lab, and Tib was… elsewhere. "We won't even charge you extra for expedited delivery."

The Letnev sneer was audible in the reply. "How considerate of you. Approach the cargo bay, and have your manifests ready for examination."

"Don't worry, we know how much you love proper documentation." The channel closed, and Calred raised an eyebrow at Felix. "I'm a natural. I should be captain full-time."

"Good. Then you can deal with Thales."

"I withdraw my request for a promotion."

The cruiser approached the station, an angular collection of dull metal modules connected by gantries and corridors and tethers, which resembled a child's mobile if it were conceived by one of the twisted horrors of the L1Z1X. One of the larger modules was the cargo bay, and Calred guided the ship in to dock.

Once they were settled inside the belly of the station, Cal and Felix trooped down to the cargo bay. They'd rearranged some of the countless crates of supplies that filled the ship for maximum camouflage effect, complete with fake bills of lading and inventory lists. Felix stood beside a stack of crates with a hand terminal and tried to look busy while Calred continued his merchant captain cosplay.

The ship's ramp opened and slid down, revealing the "weather station's" cargo bay. Felix took in the layout in a glance: a cavernous space big enough for five of his ship, with neat stacks of crates and barrels, mostly along the walls. A few robots trundled to and fro, moving cargo around, and there were several cranes, both small mobile ones and larger ones in fixed positions. Stairs on either side of the space led up to a series of catwalks with a guard holding a long rifle stationed where he could see everything below. There were two more guards with sidearms loitering near the doors that led deeper into the station. All three wore shiny black uniforms and full-face masks that resembled stylized skulls with bulging silver eyes. The lower halves of the masks were probably full of filter systems to protect against gas attacks, and those shining eyes would include fancy optics and maybe even automated threat assessment and targeting programs. *That* was a lucky break.

The doors opened, the guards snapped off salutes, and three Barony officials tromped into the bay, one greater bureaucrat and two lesser, all wearing black uniforms with silver accents, all stiff and pale and formal. They mounted the ramp, and the one in the lead looked around at the *Swift Emergence*'s hold and sniffed in disgust, at who knows what;

just general disgust, probably. "Manifest." He snapped his fingers, but, since he was wearing thick dark gloves, they didn't actually make a snapping sound.

Calred tapped his tablet, sending information to the officer's terminal, then turned and gestured to a stack of crates on a pallet. "Here they are. Do you want our help unloading? There's a modest stevedore fee–"

"Wait." The officer frowned, and the two other officers frowned too, though they couldn't possibly know what they were frowning about. "This is wrong."

"Oh?" Calred said.

"It says here you have ten crates of… sunscreen?"

"Yes, that's right."

"Sunscreen," the official repeated.

"Protects you from the sun, as I understand it," Calred said.

"We're Letnev!" The homeworld of the Barony of Letnev, Arc Prime, famously drifted through the void without orbiting a star. It was a lightless place, and the natives lived in vast underground cities oxygenated by fungal growths and heated by the planet's core.

Calred nodded agreeably. "I thought so. The Letnev are a rather pale people. Very prudent to order sunscreen in bulk."

The lead bureaucrat grimaced. "The station is shielded from the light of the local star. We didn't order any sunscreen. We're expecting a shipment of fungal growth matrix." According to Calred's cousin, the botanist for an agricultural cartel, one of the most treasured delicacies in the Barony was a particular mushroom that grew in the caverns of their dank homeworld. Whenever a sufficient number of Letnev congregated in outer space, they brought that delicacy with them, if they could afford it. The mushrooms were difficult to grow, and thus rare and valuable, in their original environment, but when cultivated artificially in hydroponic gardens, using a proprietary growth medium created in the Hacan Emirates, the mushrooms thrived. (Of course, connoisseurs claimed they could smell and taste the difference between *true* cave mushrooms and those grown elsewhere, but that was connoisseurs for you; the results were certainly close enough to satisfy most Letnev, though.) There was indeed a shipment of the matrix headed to the station on the real cargo ship *Swift Emergence*, which would arrive right on schedule sometime tomorrow. The *Temerarious* didn't have any such thing in its stores, so they'd had to improvise.

Calred peered at his tablet, peered at the officer, looked back at his tablet, looked back at the officer, and then brightened. "Perhaps it's both! Sunscreen *and* fungal growth matrix. Think about it: sunscreen protects things from sunlight. Mushrooms hate sunlight. Go on, give it a try. I bet mushrooms grow all over the stuff."

The Letnev took an aggressive step forward, but stopped at that, since he was, after all, being aggressive at a two-and-a-half-meter-tall bipedal lion. "This is unacceptable. We will not pay for this."

"Listen," Calred said. "Your procurement officer checked the box that says if your actual order is out of stock, we should substitute the closest available product. Looks like that's what we did. It's not my fault. If you weren't willing to accept a substitution, you should have said so."

The argument went on, around and around, with various appeals to various authorities. More bureaucrats appeared with more documentation, and Calred remained unfazed, meeting every outrage with a shrug. Eventually, as planned, he agreed to soften the blow of the lost matrix by providing them with a few extra items drawn from their store of emergency supplies, including food and medication; that mollified the outrage somewhat, but not completely, because Letnev were culturally resistant to being mollified. The crowd dwindled once the pallets were offloaded and moved into the Letnev cargo bay, and the officer in charge said, "All right. Be on your way."

Calred put a huge hand to his broad chest. "Regretfully, I cannot leave yet. My trading company has strict regulations regarding rest for the crew, in order to avoid accidents, as stipulated in our contract."

"What crew?" the office sputtered. "It's just you, that useless human loitering by the crates, and a bunch of semi-autonomous machinery!"

"We are the ones who *operate* said machinery, and it's imperative that we get our rest – especially my human. You know how disagreeable they can be when they don't get enough sleep."

"This is preposterous. First you bring us the wrong cargo, and now you want to take up space in our–"

"Peace, peace," Calred said soothingly. "Understand, these regulations are as much for your protection as our own. Last year a cousin of mine – well, a cousin of a nephew, to be precise, for I know how the Letnev value precision – decided to ignore the safety regulations and leave in his ship without first taking his prescribed period of rest. He hoped to earn a bonus for swift delivery of his remaining cargo, you see. Well, he entered the wrong commands in his navigation system, and – because he'd also skimped on proper safety checks – his ship's protective measures failed. His navigation system thought he was departing from orbit, not from within a space station, and do you know what happened?" Calred brought his hands together and said "boom" very softly. "His ship struck the edge of the launch bay while accelerating at unsafe speeds. The containment field on his engine breached, and the resulting explosion took out half the station. The devastation made the station's orbit unstable, and it promptly decayed and began to plummet into the atmosphere. I heard they got almost half the survivors off the station before–"

"Enough." The officer held up a hand, wincing. He had his terminal in his other hand, and scanned through it. "I understand, and yes, there's a provision in the contract that requires us to honor any mandatory rest breaks, on page one-thousand-seventeen, in a footnote."

"You find the most wonderful things in footnotes, don't you?" Calred's good cheer was as relentless as a desert sun. "Might my first mate and I avail ourselves of your shower facilities, perhaps enjoy your doubtless lavish guest quarters–"

"You are confined to your ship," the officer snapped before turning on his polished black heel and storming away. "Your eight hours start *now*!"

Calred crossed his arms and looked benignly on his departure as the ship's cargo ramp slowly closed. Then he turned and grinned at Felix. "Eight hours. That should be plenty of time, even for you."

"Do you think Tib made it out OK?" Felix said.

Calred made a great show of looking around the cargo hold. "I don't see her here anywhere."

"Ha, ha," Felix said.

CHAPTER 8

"My *human* is resting," Calred said, voice relayed to the comm in Felix's ear. "He's the one who needs the sleep. I, however, grow bored. I happen to have a set of void dice here, though, which could help pass the time." Playing void dice was a Letnev national obsession.

"We're supposed to keep an eye on you, not fraternize," a menacing, machine-altered voice said.

"You could keep a closer eye on me if you were sitting in my cargo hold, at this table, playing void dice. I've never played against Letnev, and I'm curious to see how my abilities stand up against those who invented the game."

"Well…" one of the guards said, but the other snapped, "Stop talking to the trader. Mind your duty."

They'd never expected the guards to let their, well, their guard, down far enough to actually play a game, but the back-and-forth distracted them long enough for Felix to slip out undetected through an emergency access hatch. He began to make his way carefully across the cargo bay. They'd deliberately taken the landing spot closest to the interior wall, but Felix still had an intimidatingly large distance of bare floor to cover, especially with the sniper up above. The ship's tactical systems had carefully plotted out a route that should keep Felix hidden from the overwatch guard's view, but the back of Felix's neck itched anyway; he fully expected a blob of molten metal or charged plasma to obliterate the back of his head as he hurried from one pile of crates to another. A normal guard back home, especially this far into a long and boring shift, would have hacked his helmet display to show entertainment vids or scroll the text of a book to pass the time, and could be relied upon to be distracted and inattentive, but the discipline of the Letnev was as legendary as their lack of humor.

The shimmering overlay in Felix's contact lenses showed him the proper route in blue, a narrow path leading from a pile of crates to the shadow of a crane and so on, and would flash red if he so much as stepped one toe off the path. He went carefully, methodically, knowing sudden movement was more visible than slow. Not for the first time, he envied Tib's ability to fade. He supposed humans had their own unique advantages, too, though just at this moment he couldn't remember what any of them were.

To make up for his lack of natural resources, he had a variety of small and useful items in his pockets, the sort of things favored by Coalition raiders, very few of them legal in the galaxy's more civilized jurisdictions.

He finally ducked behind a stack of barrels marked "protein slurry, grade three," slipping into the narrow space between the supplies and the wall. There was a ventilation grille there, and as he crouched toward it, the screen slid aside. Eyes like lanterns shone from within, and Tib's hand emerged and beckoned before vanishing from sight.

Felix had to slither into the duct on his belly. There were maintenance tunnels in the station meant for people his size, but none with access hatches in the cargo bay, and *these* were never meant for anything bigger than a drone repair unit to enter. Tib fit easily, of course, but Felix had to push himself along mostly with his toes, wriggling more than crawling, following Tib's whispered directions in his comms. After a couple of sharply angled turns, and a distressing head-first slide down at about a thirty-degree angle, they finally emerged into a dim room full of thrumming machinery, furnaces, and air filtration systems.

Felix gasped and wiped sweat from his forehead. He wasn't claustrophobic – he'd grown up slithering through tunnels on a shipyard station, though he'd been smaller then – but it was still a relief to stand up and stretch his limbs. A nearly naked Letnev was propped unconscious in the corner, wrists bound to ankles with zip ties. "You've been busy," Felix said.

"I hope the uniform fits."

Felix put on the guard's clothes. The Letnev ran slightly smaller than humans as a species, but Felix was slim. The shirt was tight across the chest, but not enough so that anyone would notice, and the long black gloves would hide the shortness of the sleeves, just as the tall black boots concealed the shortness of the pants. The full-face mask was the best part, though – Felix couldn't pass for Letnev at a glance, but with his face hidden, he could move anonymously through the station.

"What's the lay of the land?" he asked. Tib had spent the past hour doing reconnaissance and acquiring Felix's disguise.

"I think I know where Shelma is being held," Tib said. "Unless there's more than one Hylar on board. She's not in a cell, though – she's in a laboratory or something."

"Or something?"

"All I know is, there are a lot of screens, a lot of terminals, and bits of disassembled machinery all around. She went to get something to eat and she was escorted by a guard, and later she had to return to what I assume are her quarters, and a guard took her there, too."

"She must be a dangerous character."

"She also summoned guards on three occasions to fetch her equipment from other rooms and, once, to remove a spider from a corner of the ceiling. The poor man had to stand on a wobbly table, and she told him not to kill it, just to take it to the gardens, so it could eat pests. She treated the guards more like servants than jailers."

"Maybe she's just valuable rather than dangerous, then," Felix said. "The Letnev must be forcing her to continue the research she did with Thales. Can we get her out?"

"No one seemed to pay attention to her at all, so long as there was a guard walking beside her. You look like a guard. I think we can work out a cunning plan based on those conditions."

"Getting her to the ship and off the station is the tricky part," Felix said. "That's not something a guard would do, and the Letnev ask questions with lethal force. I'd rather get out of here without being murdered. Can we bring her back through the tunnels?"

Tib shook her head. "She's one of the fully aquatic sub-species of Hylar – her tank is set in an exo-suit, and she scurries around on a lot of little legs and manipulator arms. Her rig isn't huge – she can fit through ordinary doors – but she's not crawling through any tunnels."

"Damn," Felix said. "We need to leave here quietly."

"Not a problem for me," Tib said. "I just don't know what to do about you and the squid."

"Maybe," Felix said, "we don't need to be quiet. Maybe we just need to be *less* noisy than something else."

They had to peel open the guard's eyelid and put his head half in the mask to unlock the biometric locks on the operating system, but once they did that Felix had access to a wealth of information about the station. Maps, a navigation system, and even a personnel roster – which notably didn't mention Shelma, but did include a distressing number of guards, a dizzying array of bureaucrats, a few scientists, assistant under-directors, assistant directors, and just the one director. He took particular note of the security provisions, which were extensive, but mainly focused on preventing outside threats – once he was inside, assuming he wasn't challenged, he should be able to move fairly freely.

Tib faded out of sight and went off to handle her part of the operation, while Felix stepped out of the machine room and followed the glowing path to the lab where Shelma was working. He passed a couple of other masked guards, who ignored him completely, and he did the same in return, though he fine-tuned his own stiff walk and ramrod posture to better match theirs. The station was a joyless sort of place, all gray metal and white tile and dim recessed lighting. He turned a corner, entering the corridor that should have led him to the research wing, and almost collided with a dark-haired woman, dressed in the requisite amount of gleaming black, who stood talking to a pair of masked guards. She stopped mid-sentence, looked at him, and frowned.

Felix's heads-up display helpfully identified her: this was Severyne Joelle Dampierre, technically an assistant director, functionally the head of security. Felix automatically noted that she was pretty, in a severe, hair-pulled-back-too-tightly way – not that it mattered. It wouldn't have mattered even if they'd met in some difficult-to-imagine social setting, instead of during a jailbreak. He'd dated Letnev who'd grown up in the Coalition, but the ones from the Barony were by all accounts immune to charm, fun, or entertainment. The old joke was, "Why don't Letnev have sex standing up? Because someone might think they're dancing."

"Where are you going?" she asked, sharp and peremptory.

Well, why not? Unnecessary lies only got you in trouble. "To the Hylar's lab, Director Dampierre."

"That's AD Dampierre," she snapped. "You're on her detail, are you? What does Shelma want *now*?"

"She says one of the tables is wobbly, AD Dampierre. She wants me to level it."

"Someone should level *her*." Dampierre scowled again. "Well? Carry on, don't dawdle in the corridors."

Felix snapped off a salute and went on his way. That had gone better than it could have. As he walked, he scrolled up the available information on AD Dampierre. She'd only served the mandatory minimum of Letnev military service, so she wasn't a professional soldier – maybe her job running station security had been bestowed for political rather than practical reasons, or maybe she was a terrifying clandestine operative whose training was so secret it didn't show up in her public-facing files. Ideally, he'd never have to find out.

Felix's helmet had the necessary authentications to make the next four sealed doors unlock for him, and to open the elevator that led to Shelma's floor. He exited the elevator and approached the blinking icon in his display that marked the door to the lab. A guard stood stiffly before it, arms at his sides. "Is the Hylar in there?" Felix asked, the suit modulating his voice to an amusingly menacing degree.

"Where else would she be during working hours?" the guard replied.

"Good point," Felix said, and punched her in the throat. He had on a pair of rings beneath his gloves that discharged a single-burst electric shock sufficient to paralyze the body and scramble the brain, and the guard slid down the door. Felix's HUD obligingly showed him the location of a storage closet, so he dragged the guard inside, found a roll of tape, and wrapped it around and around the masked head, to serve as a blindfold and to make it hard to remove said mask, which he thought was rather funny. Then he bound the guard's ankles to her wrists and turned to the door.

He stopped, turned back, looked down at the guard, sighed, knelt, and laboriously unpicked and unwound all the tape from the mask. He undid the clasps and removed her mask, then put it on a high shelf, because otherwise when the guard woke up, she would have called for help on the mask's integrated comms. "There's such a thing as being *too* clever, Felix," he muttered.

His display assured him there were no other guards in the immediate vicinity, so he went into the lab, the door sliding silently shut behind him. "Shelma?" he said.

The Hylar was enclosed in a transparent globe full of pale fluid, the sphere set into an exoskeletal body with scores of many-jointed limbs, some for walking, others for manipulating objects, still others for specialized purposes he couldn't imagine. Shelma herself was small, head shaped a bit like a lemon, trailing fronds of tentacles and feelers that wriggled into the controls of the exo-suit. Her large, dark eyes gazed at him. Her skin, a pale green at first, flushed through oranges and reds. Felix knew the Hylar communicated among themselves with color changes, but he didn't understand what these meant.

Apparently, the colors didn't indicate a warm welcome. "What is it? You're interrupting my work." Her voice was querulous and sounded like a human with nasal congestion. Despite her assertion, her manipulator arms continued to solder components into the guts of a torpedo-shaped object resting on the work table.

"I've come to rescue you," he said.

"Oh, by the bubbling crevice," she said, becoming an even deeper red. "Are you from the Federation of Sol? The last time you reached out, I told you, I have no interest in going back. As far as I'm concerned, our relationship ended when our lab was destroyed." She waved a cluster of manipulators at him. "Shoo."

Felix blinked behind his mask. "Ah, no. I'm not from

the Federation. I represent other parties interested in your research. I was under the impression that you were a prisoner here?" A red light began to blink in his peripheral vision.

"Prisoner or employee? I suppose it's a fine distinction." She turned away from him, back to her apparatus. "If I'd refused to help the Barony, they probably would have imprisoned me, and if I said tomorrow that I'd grown weary of my project and wanted to retire to the hot springs of Wun-Escha, I doubt they'd be supportive. But I agreed to work for the Barony, and they have honored the terms of my agreement. Who told you I was a prisoner?"

Don't tell her you're working with me, Thales said. *I want to surprise her,* Thales said.

"Phillip Thales did," Felix said.

She didn't turn around, but the color drained out of her. "He's still alive, then. And still a liar."

"A liar," Felix repeated. "Do you mean he can't do what he claims?" If Thales was lying about his invention, the Table wouldn't mind if Felix stranded him on an asteroid somewhere. It would be the end of glory, but it would also be the end of being sent to infiltrate Barony research stations on false pretenses.

"Did he claim he can share credit, display empathy, or listen to anyone else's ideas without shouting at them? In that case, no, he can't." Sparks cascaded up from the device, but apparently that was supposed to happen, because she kept working. "If he claimed he can create wormholes, though, that part's true. He's the only person in the galaxy who's come close to creating that technology – except for the Creuss, if you believe the rumors, and myself, of course. Thales has a brilliant scientific mind. It's a shame the rest of his mind is a burning pile of garbage."

"Ah. I haven't known him long, but I don't disagree."

"Why did he send you here? Our partnership ended... dramatically."

"He says you're essential to completing his prototype."

"Does he? That's actually flattering. Last time I saw him, he said I wasn't qualified to clean fish tanks. He may have reached the limits of his abilities, though. He was always better at theory than application, and I'm making great progress on a working prototype. It's–" She abruptly went silent. Felix almost felt bad for her. She was a scientist, not a spy, but she was doubtless feeling bad about spilling so much to the representative of some unknown force.

"Is *that* the working prototype?" Felix pointed at the cylinder.

The pause was just a moment too long. "No. No, that's just, ah... an air purifier. The air here, I'm told, is very impure. Smells of mushrooms. I'm helping."

"My ship has a terrible odor. We think something died in the vents. I'd better take the purifier with me." He drew his sidearm, but didn't point it. "You should probably come with me, too, and show me how to work it."

"And see Thales again? I'd really rather not. We didn't part on good terms."

"I'm afraid I must insist."

"Insist all you like. I hit my panic button four minutes ago. Guards should be descending here en masse any moment."

"I noticed. I'm hooked into the station's security system."

He tapped his mask. "'En masse' might be overstating things. There are two guards coming, and they're having some trouble with the elevator. That's fine. We're going out another way anyway. I hope you like service tunnels." Tib couldn't compromise the station security systems from the maintenance area she'd secretly accessed, but she could break a few things, which was why those guards were currently pushing buttons futilely in an elevator stopped between floors.

"I won't go anywhere with you."

Shelma was faced with an armed man, professed agent of an unknown organization sent to rescue – make that "abduct" her – and she was still stubbornly acting like she was in charge. Felix began to see why she and Thales had worked together.

"I'm still insisting. Things are going to get very loud and chaotic on this station, and even though you don't want to be rescued, I've gone too far to stop now." He stepped toward her, and her manipulator arms stretched out defensively. They probably could have soldered, laser-etched, or sliced him up, but they didn't stop him from lobbing one of the objects from his pocket at her – a little thing, the size and shape of a plum – where it struck her glass dome with a splat, sticking to the side.

"That's a very small, inward-pointing explosive, coated in epoxy resin. It's now firmly attached to your helmet. If you attempt to remove the device, it will explode. If I don't disarm it in half an hour, it will explode. The solvent I need to remove it…" He made a show of patting his pockets. "I seem to have left it on my ship. We should go there, don't you think?" He hadn't planned to use the little bomb for *this*, and in fact it wouldn't explode at all unless he triggered it deliberately, but he was a Mentak Coalition officer: they were expected to improvise.

"Severyne won't let you take me," she said. "I'm very valuable."

"Severyne is going to be busy soon," Felix said, and his tactical display lit up with emergency alerts as the first of the bombs Tib had set up in the station went off.

CHAPTER 9

At first, Severyne didn't take Shelma's latest push of the panic button seriously. In the ten months since Severyne had taken over security for this station, she'd learned that the Hylar scientist didn't share the same definition of the word "emergency" the rest of the universe did. The first time the panic button went off, Severyne responded personally, charging into her quarters followed by six elite soldiers. Shelma had looked up from a tablet and said, mildly, "The lights in this room are too dim. Please get me brighter ones."

Severyne had dismissed the soldiers and given Shelma a stern talking-to about the proper channels for maintenance requests. "I tried those channels," Shelma replied. "They said they would add my request to the non-essential queue. That is not acceptable. I thought perhaps this button might bring a more rapid response, and I was correct."

"That button is for moments when your life is in danger, or when you have reason to believe this station is under attack, or that our security has been compromised."

"I believe that's what *you* intended the button for,"

Shelma said. "But I'm an engineer first and foremost. I'm interested in what things actually do, not merely what they were designed for."

After that, the Hylar used the panic button indiscriminately, for the most trivial things, until, in desperation, Severyne finally gave her a dedicated comms channel and a small rotating group of guards who could take care of her endless insignificant needs – the lights too dim, the liquid in her tank an imperfect pH, her tools not calibrated perfectly to her liking, her quarters not the right temperature (even though she could control the temperature of her tank!), and a thousand other trivial details. After that, her use of the panic button trailed off, but didn't stop entirely, especially when she was in a bad mood or frustrated by setbacks in her work. She enjoyed spreading the annoyance around.

So when the panic button went off this time, Severyne sighed and dispatched a pair of guards to look in on the scientist, then went back to working on the duty rosters. Lestrande had shown up for his last shift with a tiny blot of protein slurry on his elbow, and such slovenliness must be punished, so she decided to assign him to be one of Shelma's babysitters for the week, and put a note about conduct unbecoming in his file. He'd probably never be promoted again with a mark like that against him, but he should have thought of that before he ate like a slough-beast.

One of the guards she'd dispatched reached out over comms to say there was a malfunction in the elevator. A tingle of foreboding started up at the back of Severyne's mind. She was a creature of order who loved routine, and disruptions gave her an almost visceral twinge of disgust. The panic button was one disruption, albeit a common one. The elevator breaking down was a second. And there was a third – the merchant ship, the *Swift Emergence*, was still idling in their cargo bay. There'd been some fuss about the manifests, the ship carrying the wrong cargo, that she'd picked up on the assistant director-level comms channel – Melisante Couray, the AD in charge of procurement, had been complaining about the mix-up. *Was* it a mix-up?

Officially, this was just a research facility studying weather patterns, but Severyne knew anyone who looked at them closely would realize there was something more serious going on. Their delivery schedule, for example, would reveal they seemed to be feeding and supplying more staff than such a station would normally require. Had someone gotten curious, and sent spies to see what they were doing here? Or, had someone already *figured out* what they were doing here, and come to stop them, or steal their research – and their star researcher? They were only in this station at all because the Federation of Sol had discovered Shelma's previous lab and sent her a message trying to tempt her back to their service. Had they tracked her down again, and decided to take a more direct approach?

The deck beneath Severyne's feet vibrated. That didn't set off another tingle of foreboding. That set off an *earthquake*. The screens hovering before her eyes, projected from her contact lenses, blared red: there was hull damage in one of the hydroponic gardens, though apparently no injuries. She called the assistant director of resource management and barked "Report!"

"There was an explosion – that's all I know so far. It could have been caused by a build-up of static electricity, discharging and igniting a hydrogen tank–"

Another boom rocked the room, this one much closer, and another section of the station diagram hovering before Severyne's eyes turned red and started flashing. This time, an explosion had torn apart the lab at the top of the station's central hub, where the weathermonitoring equipment was located. There were no injuries there, either, because no one actually *worked* in that section; the lab and all the equipment were purely for show, to make their cover story plausible.

"My new theory is enemy action," the voice on Severyne's comms said. She cut the contact without a word and called the leaders of all her guard divisions, on-duty and otherwise: "Scan the ship for more explosives, and report anything unusual immediately." An array of affirmatives cascaded into her ears. "Second squad, go check on Shelma. I *know* the elevator is out – go through the maintenance tunnels!"

She gritted her teeth as she watched the blinking dots of her guards spread out through the ship diagram. Could this be internal sabotage? The Barony was full of competing political currents, and some factions thought this station – dedicated to the work of a Hylar who was somewhere between a defector and a prisoner – was a misallocation of resources, either because they had a natural distrust of other species, and/or because they thought the idea of generating wormholes on demand was a ridiculous fantasy. Usually attacks from within the Barony were rather more subtle than this. You didn't bomb a station to shut it down; you snarled the station in red tape and did your best to encourage small, deniable problems that added up into cumulative disasters. When the heating or plumbing broke, you made sure the work orders got lost, or that the repair crew showed up with incompatible parts, and contrived to make it look like incompetence on the part of the station head. Or you introduced errors into the supply chain, to deny the crew their necessities and their comforts –

That thought reminded her of the cargo ship – the one that had shown up a day early, and with the wrong supplies. Severyne had ascribed that error to either a genuine mistake, or petty political maneuvering… but what if the ship was more than that? What if the enemy had come from *outside*?

She pulled up her security override panel and began to lock down portions of the station, simultaneously calling her guards in the cargo bay. "Don't let that ship go anywhere–" she began, and then the hangar bay where *her* fighters and support ships were docked exploded.

Felix crouched beside Shelma's exo-suit as boots pounded in the corridor around the corner. The guards were headed to the Hylar's lab, and if they'd been a little faster, they would have run head-on into Felix. Fortunately, he was beyond their entry point, but adding some distance was a good idea.

"Come on," he muttered, adjusting the straps of the duffel over his shoulder. The bag contained various data-sticks, which didn't weigh much, and Shelma's torpedo-shaped device, which weighed so much he assumed it was made of lead-wrapped osmium. He hurried along the narrow tunnel, past bundled cables and humming pipes, with Shelma clattering along ahead of him.

They reached a corridor that led to the cargo bay doors – the ones with guards on the other side – and he paused to call his ship on their private comm channel. "Calred, I'm on my way back with our guest."

"Are we being noisy or quiet?" Calred said.

"I'm hoping for the latter, but let's be prepared for the former." He glanced at Shelma, who waited with poor grace, her many-jointed legs delicately bent. Her skin was bright red; she looked like a walking danger indicator. "Don't say anything during this next part." She glared at him, which he supposed counted as agreement.

The doors to the cargo bay slid open as they approached. He could see his ship, barely fifty meters away, but you could die a lot of times in a lot of ways in the course of fifty meters. The guards on the door turned to face him, guns held up.

Plan A was just to brazen things out. "The bomber took out our hangar!" he said, voice modulated with menace. "AD Dampierre sent me to commandeer that civilian vessel and get the Hylar to safety." Felix thought it was a plausible cover story – he was pretty proud of it – so he was disappointed when they kept pointing their guns at him. He promptly stepped behind the Hylar, hoping they wouldn't risk shooting through her to get to him.

"Drop your weapon!" the first guard said.

"You drop yours!" Felix said.

"Right now!" the second guard shouted.

"Guess we're going loud, then," Felix said.

The guards dropped, with barely a second between the falls. Felix looked past them to Calred, who stood on the ramp of the *Temerarious*, holding his favorite precision plasma rifle. He'd placed second in the all-Coalition long-range target shooting competition the year before, and wore the silver pin he'd earned on the collar of his uniform with pride. Taking out two men from fifty meters was nothing to him; Felix was surprised he hadn't worn a blindfold or something to make it more interesting.

Seeing Calred poised with his weapon reminded Felix of the sniper, up there on overwatch. Calred was shielded from fire by the roof of his own ship, and Felix and Shelma were partially protected because they were still in the corridor, and hadn't yet passed into the cargo bay. A sufficiently eager sniper could hit the legs of her exo-suit. If her suit was disabled, that was it – Felix couldn't manhandle hundreds of kilograms of metal and liquid and Hylar five meters, let alone fifty.

Felix crouched down, imagining the long barrel pointed right at him, attempting to calculate the angles, creeping forward to get a glimpse of the sniper, knowing if he could *see*, he could *be* seen –

The sniper was poised, pointing his gun right at Felix, and he flung himself back, trying to hide behind Shelma again. No shot rang out, no plasma seared the deck plates or sheared off Shelma's legs – nothing happened at all.

Felix edged forward again in time to see the sniper's rifle fall from the catwalk, bounce off the top of the *Temerarious*, and fall onto the deck with a clatter. The sniper appeared to be choking himself, hands clasped to his throat as he stumbled jerkily to and fro, bouncing off the railings of the catwalk. The sniper's mask came loose and went flying and falling to the deck, flung by an unseen hand.

"Let's get on the ship, shall we?" Felix prodded the back of Shelma's tank, making the liquid inside slosh.

"Is that guard having some sort of seizure?" Shelma scuttled toward the ship's ramp. "Did you disperse a nerve agent in here? Their masks can filter most of the common ones." Her voice held nothing but professional interest. Scientists were so strange.

"Oh, no, he's just being strangled by an invisible woman. It's a disconcerting sensation, as I know from experience." The sniper finally stopped struggling and slumped to the catwalk floor, as if gently lowered.

Felix had instructed Tib to set bombs with the aim of crippling pursuit capabilities with minimal casualties, and he'd hoped to get off the station without killing anyone, but that was hopes for you. Sometimes he thought they existed just to be dashed.

Shelma went up the ramp, delicate legs spidering her along, and paused in front of Calred.

"Greetings," Calred said. "Welcome to my humble merchant vessel."

"Get this bomb off me, captain," Shelma demanded.

"Hey, *I'm* the captain," Felix said, turning to look back at the cargo bay doors. Trouble could come bursting through them at any moment.

"He seems much more commanding than you do," Shelma said.

"You are keen and perceptive," Calred said. "Once we're underway, we'll get that bomb off you." He handed Felix the precision rifle, a device of exquisite craftsmanship that was largely wasted on the captain. Felix had placed in the bottom hundred in the long gun competition – he was more adept with sidearms, at least – but even he could hit a personsized target at this distance. Calred escorted Shelma deeper into the ship, while Felix watched the doors and waited for Tib to shimmer into visibility. Once she got on board, they could close the ramp and get out of here –

"You aren't where you're supposed to be," said a voice in his ear. Felix flinched – he'd muted the station's internal comm channels, since all the yelling and blaring of alarms was too distracting – but, of course, certain people would have override codes. "Which means you aren't *who* you're supposed to be – you're an outside agitator in a stolen helmet. Did the Federation send you?"

"Assistant Director Dampierre," Felix said. "I'm sorry for all the fuss we caused." He paused. "The guard I took this helmet from is fine, if you were wondering."

"He won't be once I get my hands on him," she snapped. "Neither will you."

"I'm afraid our meeting will have to wait for another time. We're about to be on our way, and we won't bother you again."

"You won't bother *anyone* ever again."

Felix had a sudden stab of insight, dropped the rifle, and undid the clasps on his helmet. He flung the mask away just as it sparked with electricity and thumped, smoking, on the deck. He picked up the rifle with trembling arms, heart pounding in his chest. Of *course* the Letnev would have corrective and coercive measures built into their standard-issue equipment. He wondered if that electrical discharge would have killed him, or merely incapacitated him. He kicked the helmet as hard as he could, sending it spinning off the ship and into the cargo bay. For all he knew, it was packed with explosives too.

Tib materialized, dancing out of the way before the helmet could hit her. "Good idea. They could track you with that thing."

Among other things. "My thought exactly." The ramp receded as she raced up it. The ship's cargo door started to lower just as a crowd of guards poured through the hangar doors, taking up an attack formation with drilled precision, the ones in front kneeling to clear the field of fire for the back rank. Tib and Felix flung themselves behind piles of crates as blobs of superheated metal and streaks of energy struck around them. When the cargo bay was sealed, Felix shouted, "Calred, get us out of here!"

"I'd be happy to," he drawled. "Once someone opens the door."

"Oh, right," Tib said, and pressed a button on the chunky bracelet on her right wrist.

Tib's bombs blew open the station's closed bay doors with a dull *whump*, and she and Felix were pressed against the stack of crates as the ship accelerated out through the hole she'd made. They rose, shakily, and Felix went around to the other side of their makeshift barricade. The fire from the guards had shattered the crates and their contents, and bits of jellied eel oozed out onto the floor. "It's going to smell like fish in here forever," he lamented.

"Better than smelling like our dead corpses," Tib said.

"Oh, the day is young," Felix said. "What kind of pursuit are we looking at?"

"I blew up their cruisers and shuttles and fighters, but I couldn't shut down their comms," Tib said. "They won't be chasing us from the station, but they'll call people who *can* chase us, soon enough."

"Do we have enough of a head start to lose them?" Felix said.

"I'm good at disappearing," Tib said. "I think we'll be OK, but we probably shouldn't come back this way anytime soon."

Felix grinned. "What a shame. It was such a nice place to visit. You did excellent work back there, Tib."

She grinned back. "This is why I went to raider school. Breaching charges work just as well when planted on the inside of a vessel as they do from the outside. Of course, we used up all our heavy explosives back there, so you'll have to come up with more subtle plans next time."

Felix picked up the duffel and gave it a pat. "I think we're out of the black ops business. We got the expert, and we got her data and her prototype, so Thales should be good to go. Let's organize the happy reunion."

CHAPTER 10

Severyne was having a bad day. Her superiors were not pleased – the station director had shouted at her until she went hoarse, then paused to take a throat lozenge, then screamed some more. "I won't let your disaster bring me down, Dampierre," she concluded. "I can contain this situation, and blame the damage and casualties on accidents and executions for insubordination, but we have to get Shelma *back* before my superiors get suspicious."

"Of course, director." Severyne stood stiffly at attention, as she had been doing for the past hour. Her calves ached, and her feet hurt, but she would never let her discomfort show.

The director was in her chair, perfectly at ease, frowning at something parsecs away. "Do you think the Federation is behind this attack?"

"Perhaps, director." Severyne had reviewed the security footage from Shelma's lab. The kidnapper was masked, of course, and he hadn't confirmed he was from Sol, but he appeared human, and he'd claimed he was working with

Thales. The Federation had attempted to co-opt Shelma before, and it made sense that if they were after her, they'd gone after her old partner, too. The Barony had been interested in Thales too, of course, but they hadn't been able to track down his location. "We aren't sure."

"What *are* we sure of?" The director's voice was soft, and that seemed more dangerous, after all the shouting.

"Their ship, the *Swift Emergence*, was ostensibly a Hacan merchant vessel, but the real *Swift Emergence* is a day away. The attackers spoofed their transponder. The captain of the *real Swift Emergence* insists he has no knowledge of an imposter, and that someone must have stolen their schedule and data, but we can't rule out collaboration–"

"I've already canceled their contracts," the director snapped. "Don't worry about any of that. Worry about finding Shelma and getting her back. What do you know that can help with *that*?"

Precious little, but Severyne wasn't about to admit it. "If they're going to Federation space, they're doubtless on their way to the Kellkillian wormhole. We can send interceptors to–" An alert filled her vision – something serious, if it overrode director-level privacy settings; the boss didn't like being interrupted when she was dressing someone down. Severyne scanned the message and suppressed a gasp. "Forgive me, director, there's a visitor to the station. She claims… director, she says she has information about the people who took Shelma."

"Then go and talk to her," the director said. "Find out what she knows, even if you have to squeeze it out of her with a vise. *Get me my squid back*, Severyne. If I go down for this, you'll go down with me, but it will be *so* much worse for you. I have friends, influence, connections, and all *you'll* have is me for an enemy. I still might end up assistant head of operations on some horrible tropical island somewhere in the sun, but I'll use those same connections to make sure you rot in a Barony cell."

"I understand," Severyne said.

The director flicked her hand. "Dismissed. Don't come back until you have good news."

Severyne turned and walked calmly out of the director's office.

Once the door shut behind her, she broke into a sprint.

"Amina Azad." The Barony head of security was a little younger than Azad, her hair pulled back in a severe bun, her uniform perfect even though portions of her station were still literally on fire. "An unemployed Federation navy veteran. What possible use can you be to me?"

"I was part of a small team sent to capture Phillip Thales," Azad said. "He was hiding out on some backwater in Mentak Coalition space. Unfortunately, we ran afoul of a raider fleet, and now the Coalition has Thales." The Letnev's expression didn't change, and Azad felt a grudging respect for her self-control – the news of Coalition involvement had to be a surprise, but the woman didn't show it. "It occurred to me that the Coalition might want to complete the set and get their hands on Shelma, too. We knew where she was being held – my employers looked at liberating her ourselves, actually, but we decided Thales was a better target."

"Your employers. The Federation of Sol?"

"Sorry, I couldn't say. Confidentiality, you know. Let's just say, interested parties. Tell me about the attack. I might know who your enemies are."

The woman grudgingly gave an account of what she knew. It was a decently slick operation, Amina thought, heavy on the pirate shit, but it wouldn't have worked if *she'd* been running security. "Play me a recording of the guy's voice?" she asked. "Let me confirm a hunch."

The speakers crackled, and a male voice said, "I'm afraid our meeting will have to wait for another time. We're about to be on our way, and we won't bother you again."

Azad nodded. "That's captain Felix Duval, of the Mentak Coalition, though I'm sure they'd claim he's on vacation or he's been discharged or whatever. He's got a pet Yssaril, she's probably the one who snuck around and planted the bombs. Don't feel too bad – she even got the drop on *me*. Natural advantages, sure, but the Coalition must have trained her to be sneaky too, and I bet her suit has countermeasures to make her even harder to detect."

"Never mind the Yssaril," she said. "Duval." The word was a curse in her mouth. "He will pay for what he's done."

"I've got a bill to present to him, too." Azad considered. The Letnev was smart, but she was also desperate, the right lie, deployed at the right moment, could work wonders. "Anyway, I have a tracking device on Thales–"

That got the Letnev's attention. "You can track them?"

The hook was set. "Not with any precision from this distance, but if I can get even a weak ping, that will give us a direction, and once we're in the same system as their ship, I can narrow things down."

The woman frowned, though her default expression was *already* a frown, so really it just deepened. "We had trackers on Shelma, too, in her containment suit, but they were deactivated."

"The tracker I put on Thales is hidden rather deeper. What I'm saying is, we put it in his body. Implanted while he was sedated, so he doesn't know he's on a leash." That had been the plan, anyway. "The device should be undetectable to their bug sweepers, too – it's the latest tech."

The woman looked at Azad for a long moment. "You will give me the device you use to track him." She extended her hand.

"Please. I *am* the tracking device." Azad tapped her temple. "It's integrated technology, connected to all my other tactical systems, left over from my days doing special jobs in the navy. If you try to break open my head to get the tracking system out, all the tech will fuse itself into slag. No good for my brain, but no good for you, either. It's a standard countermeasure, prevents enemies from extracting Federation technology."

"Sol technology?" She turned up her nose. "Your species just crawled out of the gravity well yesterday. You're still basically drawing on cave walls and poking each other with pointy sticks."

Ha, she was livelier than she looked. Azad smiled. "I seem to recall we kicked your pale Barony asses a few times."

The Letnev sniffed. "You had superior numbers, not superior technology. No one denies your people can field a large force. I blame your prolific and unrestrained breeding."

"It's a big galaxy, lady. Somebody's gotta fill it up. Might as well be us. What do you have against unrestrained breeding, anyway? You have to pass the time somehow."

"You sicken me," the woman said. "You humans careen around the galaxy, disrupting the balance of power, causing chaos, and demonstrating a reckless disregard for the traditions and values of the elder species of the galactic community."

"When you put it that way," Azad said, "you make us sound pretty badass."

The woman pressed her fingertips to her temples as if massaging away a headache, and for a moment she looked younger, less severe, and almost vulnerable. Then she looked up, and that glimpse of the woman underneath the uniform was gone – her eyes were once again ice floes adrift in a frozen sea. "I am not opposed to a temporary strategic alliance in order to further our mutual interests."

Azad cackled. "You mean, we can use each other, as long as we both get something out of it?"

"That is *literally* what I said. My name is Severyne Joelle Dampierre. I am the head of security for this facility."

"Were you head of security yesterday, too, or are you replacing the person who oversaw this monumental fuck-up?"

Severyne bared her teeth. "Officially, there hasn't *been* a fuck-up. Not yet. If I can get Shelma back soon, no one ever has to know what happened here."

Azad nodded. "I can do that dance too. I won't be welcome back home if I arrive empty-handed, but if I can recover Thales, all will be forgiven, hearts and flowers, big parade, backslaps all around. Except none of that actually, because officially I don't exist, but there are other rewards, not least of all my continuing status as an alive person. I have a tracking device, and I've studied Thales like you studied for the boot-polishing final, so I can make some educated guesses about where he's headed next. What do *you* have to offer this partnership?"

"The key to this cell, for one thing," Severyne said.

Azad shrugged. "I escaped from a Mentak Coalition pirate flagship. I can usually get out of cells on my own. You haven't impressed me with your ability to stop jailbreaks so far."

"We'd be more careful with you than we were with Shelma. She was more of a highstatus guest, with various privileges. You will be denied those privileges."

"Yes, fine, you showed me the stick, and it's a big scary stick, I'm very impressed. Let's move on to the carrot."

Severyne wrinkled her nose. "I can offer more tangible benefits. Access to a fast gunship, and weapons, and the assistance of my own personal security force."

"The security force likewise hasn't impressed me, but I do like gunships. I came here on a freighter, and it only has enough firepower to nudge the odd asteroid out of the way. So let's say we set out together, and chase down our fugitives, and I get Thales, and you get Shelma, and then we dissolve our partnership?"

"Those terms are acceptable to me," Severyne said.

Azad shook her chains. "Take these off?"

"I have a sidearm," the Letnev said.

"How nice for you. Guns are a great comfort when you're in a room with me, I'm told."

Severyne looked off into space, interacting with some heads-up display Azad couldn't see, and a moment later her shackles unlocked themselves and slithered back into recesses in the table. "There. Partner, not prisoner."

Azad spat into her palm and reached across the table. "Shake on it to seal the deal?"

Severyne stared at her hand with undisguised horror. "Is this some horrible human custom? I will never touch your hand, let alone your hand when it is covered in – in *saliva*."

Azad shrugged, wiping her hand off on the table. "Oh well. I can settle for a verbal agreement." She could tell that needling Severyne was going to be fun. The Letnev was cute when she got horrified. You had to find entertainment where you could.

Severyne cleared her plan with the director, which wasn't very difficult, as the director snapped, "Don't tell me what you're doing, just do it, and you'd better succeed or I'll see you rot forever in your own filth." Severyne tuned her out after that, turning her mind toward logistics. She was good at logistics.

Severyne's own authorizations were sufficient to requisition a gunship, though it took a bit of creative paperwork to account for why she needed to bring a ship from the planet instead of using one from the station hangar, since said hangar was officially still intact. The station director would eventually fake some equipment malfunction, ideally blamed on a mistake by an outside contractor, to account for the damaged and destroyed parts of the station, but, for now, Severyne had to work within the constraints of their cover. You didn't rise this high in the Letnev service without learning how to convince the system to do what needed doing, though, so she got her ship.

Officially, Severyne's mission was to investigate reports of pirate activity in the system, and to neutralize any threat they discovered. Under that aegis, she could stay out for several days, or even a week, without triggering an oversight check from the accountability office. Such flexibility was rare in the Barony, but their station was a high-security covert facility, and their rules were consequently relaxed, at least by Letnev standards.

Her ship arrived: the *Grim Countenance*, a heavily armed cruiser previously assigned to protect the thoroughly unremarkable and unthreatened planet below, and the best ship available in the system. The displaced captain had taken over the next-best ship, and that displaced captain the next after that, and so on; somewhere at the bottom would be a captain left with no ship at all, but that was life in a hierarchy. If you didn't like it at the bottom, you should have worked harder to get to the top.

The *Grim Countenance* had a small crew, now under Severyne's command, consisting of engineering and pilot and navigation personnel, but the rest of the complement that tromped aboard when the ship docked was composed of her personal, hand-picked guards, the best security people on the station, or at least the best ones that weren't dead after Duval's cowardly sneak attack. Casualties has been surprisingly low – that would help with the cover-up – but she had lost her best sniper.

"I'm good with a rifle," Azad said beside her, and Severyne realized, to her horror, that she'd muttered some portion of her thoughts aloud. That was a shocking break in her customary discipline.

She covered it with hauteur. "Good by human standards, or Letnev ones?"

"The Barony was banned from the last round of pan-galactic games on account of being fascists, so it's not like I have a lot of data about your peak marksmanship, but the human who won the bronze in target shooting? I broke her record at the last interservice rifle competition, so it's kinda like I took the silver, at least."

Severyne grunted and refused to be impressed. They walked along the ship's corridors, toward the bridge. "If you're so good with a rifle, why didn't you compete in the games yourself?"

"You've heard of the L1Z1X? Sometimes they take a break from fighting with the Nekro to cause trouble for actual people, so I was busy shooting cyborgs on a colony world way out in the eastern spiral arm. Sadly, there were no impartial judges on hand to score my shooting, and they weren't ideal competition conditions, since some of the targets were shooting back. There were twelve hostiles, though, and I took out eleven with headshots. I think that gives you points for style."

"Eleven of twelve?" Severyne said. "Imperfect. My sniper would have hit the whole dozen." The doors to the bridge slid open before them, and they passed through side-by-side.

"Oh, I hit the last one," Azad said. "I just shot him in

the stomach. He killed one of my squad-mates, so he didn't deserve a clean and easy death. I wasn't even sure if those cybernetic types could feel pain, but then he started hollering and wailing and carrying on when I perforated his guts, so I guess they do."

How distasteful. One's enemies should be crushed, of course, and it was sometimes useful to cause gruesome injuries as an example to others, but as the last killed, that victim had provided no such instructional value. "Do you enjoy inflicting pain?"

"Huh." Azad appeared to take the question seriously. She followed Severyne, standing beside the captain's chair when Severyne seated herself and surveyed the bridge, glaring at the crew going about their preparations. "Nobody's asked me that since my psych evaluation when I first joined the navy. I don't enjoy hurting people on its own merits, no – not like some people do. The thrill of combat, for me, is about pushing yourself to new heights of excellence. Plus, you never feel more alive than you do when death is right there beside you. But, I will admit, I'm sort of a grudge-holder. I find spite and vengeance highly motivating, and yeah, I do like to hurt people who've hurt me. Does that make me a terrible person?"

"I am sure you are a terrible person for many other reasons as well."

Azad grinned. She had a scar on her cheek that made her look quite rakish when she smiled, and it annoyed Severyne, because the mark could have easily been removed with a simple cosmetic surgery, which meant Azad *wanted* to look that way, that she knew it made her look dangerous and,

and a bit *alluring* – She shook herself. Despite superficial physical similarities, the woman wasn't even the same *species* as her.

"What about you?" Azad said. "Do you have a sadistic streak? I'd like to know, since I'm likely to annoy you occasionally, just being who I am."

"Pain is a tool. If it is the proper tool, necessary to achieve the desired outcome, then I wield it as readily as any other."

"We're going to get along really well, Severyne."

"We are not."

"See, you say that, but I sense this spark between us. Talking to you is thrilling the same way being in combat is. We're going to push each other toward new heights of excellence. Is there a shooting range on this ship?"

"That was an abrupt transition," Severyne said. "There is a holographic training simulator, yes."

"Eh, a virtual range can't compete with the feel of real rounds hitting real targets, but it's good enough. I'll teach you to shoot."

"I am fully qualified for my rank," she said frostily.

"Sure, but fundamentally, you're a supervisor, yeah? An *officer*."

"You say that like it's a bad thing."

Azad seesawed her hand in the air. "It's a different thing. I don't deny being an officer requires a certain set of skills. But this Duval is a pirate. Sometimes you have to shoot pirates, and being good enough to get a passing score in officer training might not be good enough for *that*. What do you say? I'm a resource, Severyne. Exploit me."

"We'll see," Severyne conceded. "If we have time.

Speaking of time – I think it's time you told me where we're going, don't you?" She gestured to the crew, all at their stations, awaiting orders.

"How about I just give you a heading first. I'll tell you the destination once we've got some distance between us and my cell. I don't want you tempted to leave without me."

"I'm already tempted to do *that*."

"Maybe I can tempt you to do other things too, Sev."

CHAPTER 11

Felix sat down in the corner of the cabin they'd assigned Shelma. The quarters had been full of pallets of sunscreen earlier; their ruse on the Letnev station had also conveniently cleared out some space for the Hylar to move in. "How are you settling in?"

The front of her exo-suit was turned away from him, and she didn't bother to move so she could look at him when she answered. "I no longer have an explosive connected to my tank, so circumstances are improving."

"I was never going to blow a hole your suit, Doctor Shelma. I just needed to motivate you. I'd like to apologize for the, ah, whole situation. Thales gave us the impression you were a prisoner, and that we were on a rescue mission."

"You must not have known Phillip for very long if you believed something he said."

"Our relationship has been brief, but eventful. If you don't mind, I was hoping you could fill me in a little bit about him. We're usually pretty good at digging up background on people, but we haven't found much about him in our database, even with his genetic profile in hand."

"You're probably looking in the wrong places," Shelma said. "I can't imagine why I'd want to help my kidnappers, though."

Felix nodded, not that she could see it. "The thing is, you're here now. We can't call up the Barony and say, 'Oops, sorry, we thought it was a jailbreak, not an abduction – you can have your scientist back.'"

"I suppose not." The exo-suit turned, and she floated in the tank, gazing at him. "The Letnev are not famously forgiving."

"That's my understanding," Felix said. "I want you to know, my employers are willing to provide you and Thales with whatever resources you need to complete your work." That was close enough to the truth, anyway.

"From the Federation to the Barony to your mysterious employers. I'm quite popular these days. You're with the Mentak Coalition, aren't you? I'm assuming, based on the unusual makeup of your crew."

"I should probably deny it, but I'm sure Thales will tell you soon enough. Yes, we're Coalition. Can I ask how you ended up working for the Letnev?"

"They were the least bad option available to me at the time."

"Who were your *other* options? The doomsday cult on Tendil Two? That swarm of homicidal machines out in Nekro space? Some kind of large, angry, carnivorous monster?"

Her tank bubbled as she moved her tentacles in what Felix interpreted as a shrug. "The Letnev aren't that bad.

They're a bit unimaginative, but they respect science and technology, and they take research and development seriously. The Coalition is prejudiced against the Letnev because the Barony is such a disciplined culture, while your lot enjoys playing the rogue."

"Who's playing?"

The Hylar burbled a laugh. "You really don't know much about Thales at all, do you?"

"Almost nothing. We only want him because the Federation of Sol was willing to send a black ops team to snatch him, so that means he's probably worth having. Do you agree?"

"Mmm. I hate to say it, because his arrogance is so vast, but Phillip's breakthroughs are legitimately galaxy-changing. With him – and me – in hand, the Coalition has now cornered the market on cutting-edge wormhole technology. You will soon have capabilities completely unheard of. The universe is a chaotic and strange place, isn't it? Your faction could become the most powerful in the galaxy, entirely because your ship happened to be in the right place at the right time. Though you could lose that advantage just as easily, when the Barony comes for me. Or the Federation of Sol comes for Thales. Or the Creuss come for us all."

Felix blinked. "Why would the Creuss come for us?" Thales had mentioned the Creuss had wormhole tech already, but Shelma's concern sounded more immediate.

"You have no *idea* what you've gotten into, do you?" Shelma said.

"Tell me," Felix said.

"Thales isn't showing up in your database searches because he was originally a citizen of Jol-Nar, and Hylar systems are not as easy to infiltrate and penetrate as those of other factions. The twin planets are populated mainly by Hylar, of course, but there are a smattering of other species present – the Universities aren't as cosmopolitan as the Coalition, but we value knowledge and learning above all else, and Phillip is the last son of a long line of scholars and researchers. He was still called Phillip back then, but he went by his real surname, Caruthers, not Thales."

Ah, the man's real last name – that would have been more helpful before, since they were getting the dirty details about the man's life now, but still, Felix made a mental note.

"Phillip lived with his parents in a house grown of coral, partially above the surface, partially submerged. Never quite in or out – that's the story of his life. Phillip demonstrated brilliance from an early age. We play a strategy game called Tides, one of the most sophisticated games in the galaxy, and Phillip is the only human who has ever attained master rank – which he did when he was only thirteen. On the strength of that showing, and his test scores, he earned a place in the physics department in our great city, Wun-Escha. He spent four years there, never breaking the surface, and the entire time he wore protective gear that allowed him to dwell at those depths underwater – he refused physical adaptations that would have allowed him to live beneath the waves more comfortably. Some considered that refusal eccentric. Others thought he was a bigot, a human supremacist in the midst of the Hylar, but those who got to know him well realized he had contempt for humans, too. He had contempt for everyone who wasn't him."

Felix nodded. "That much hasn't changed."

"I was the one exception to that contempt, for a while. We met in an advanced lab, working on improvements to starship engines. He watched me work for a while, and then said, 'You're not a complete idiot like the rest of them.'

"'You charmer,' I said. 'No wonder you're the most popular boy in school.' He laughed and said he didn't need to be popular: 'I'm smart, and that means I'll be rich, and once I'm rich, I'll be as popular as I want.' I asked him how he expected to get rich in academia, which seemed to be the path we were both on.

"He said 'Bah'– actually said the word, like a human in a historical sim. He told me he was *human*, in case I hadn't noticed: 'I'll never become Headmaster, and if you aren't the one running the Universities, someone *else* will always tell you what to do.' He said he'd had enough of taking orders from inferiors when he was a child. His parents weren't as smart as he was, but somehow they got to decide what was best for him? That outraged Phillip. He fled their house as soon as he could, only to find he'd traded one bunch of authorities for another. Now he had to answer to professors, advisors, committee heads, all of them standing in his way."

"They were also the ones teaching him, supporting him, giving him opportunities, weren't they?" Felix said.

Shelma's skin tinged softly blue; was that amusement? "Phillip has a tendency to discount the importance of advantages that don't come wholly from within himself. He certainly discounted the value of my help often enough. He told me he didn't intend to suffer under the yoke of oppression and so forth forever. His plan was to do his own research, invent something the galaxy would clamor for, sell it for an emperor's ransom, and then, finally, take charge of his own fate. I told him that sounded good, but until he became master of the galaxy, maybe he could help me with the energy-flow problem we were working on? Back in the early days you could still poke fun at him, a little, if you were careful."

Felix smirked. "Oh, I don't know, I poke fun at him pretty often now."

"Yes, but he probably wants to murder you for it, captain." Shelma undulated in her tank, her large eyes looking beyond Felix, perhaps into the past. "We got along, strangely enough. I could keep up with him intellectually, which he appreciated, and when he began to rant and rave, I tuned him out – he was my own personal white noise generator. We also complemented one another as research partners. He was always better at the theoretical side of things, while I'm an engineer at heart – oh, I've made conceptual breakthroughs too, but I'm happiest when I'm tinkering, adjusting, and making the practical applications actually work, a process that is seldom smooth or easy. Those kinds of challenges thrill me. For Phillip, the only reason to move beyond the theoretical is because it's easier to sell a product than the conceptual outline for one." That blue tinge again. "Maybe that's why he needs me now. He might have hit the limit of what he can build alone."

Maybe we can do without Thales entirely, Felix thought.

Shelma gestured aft. "I'm fairly sure the engine powering this vessel is based on one Phillip and I created during our partnership. Our improvements are still the state of the art. We both received offers to work for the state shipyard, running their propulsion department as co-heads, but Phillip refused, because anything we created there would be property of the Universities, just like the design for this engine is. We received a generous bonus for the engine's development, but Phillip railed about the injustice of having his work 'stolen' – if he'd received even one tenth of one percent of the price of every unit sold, after all, he'd be wealthy enough to buy a small moon. He wanted to do *independent* work, he said."

"What would he even do with a moon?" Felix said. "He's barely emerged from the lab we gave him. He lived in a shack on Cobbler's Knob. He seems to spend most of his time inside his head. Vast wealth would be wasted on him."

Shelma said, "It's true, he's a scientific ascetic in his way. You need to understand, the money is just insulation. A way to put himself above caring about the needs or opinions of anyone else. With enough money, he'll never again have to put himself in someone else's power. I was happy enough with the career advancement our work offered me, so I went to work for the shipyards, while Phillip took his bonus and set up his own lab. He found investors, too, though I'm sure it galled him to have even that much accountability, and he continued to work on propulsion systems, this time with the promise of a share in the profits... but he didn't manage as well on his own. He made little incremental improvements, enough to keep his investors from dropping him, but nothing seafloor-shaking. The gossip among my colleagues was that Phillip was one of those prodigies who peaks early and then burns out. Such people often become fringe figures, railing against an unfair system and espousing horrible political views, which everyone agreed would be a natural fit for Phillip. I wasn't so sure – I thought he was just *bored*. Small improvements didn't interest him. He was always about revolutionary change. Phillip abruptly shut his lab a few years after it opened, having failed to become rich, and he largely withdrew from society."

"If only he'd stayed withdrawn," Felix murmured.

Shelma ignored him. "After about a decade – during which I thrived at the propulsion lab, I might add, and *did* make significant improvements – he suddenly published a slew of papers, a few in respectable venues, but others just released onto the net, presumably because they couldn't pass peer review. He was attempting to achieve the ultimate aim of conceptual physics, a theory of everything that could reconcile the contradictions between general relativity and quantum theory, and he was publishing his intermediate steps. Some of the papers *were* promising, but others were either flawed, or inadequately explained. Phillip never had much patience for making things clear to those he considered his intellectual inferiors, which, as you might have gathered, is everyone. He would occasionally show up at a conference, usually to stand up in the audience and decry some other scientist he considered ill-informed or misguided."

"He really does make friends wherever he goes, doesn't he?"

"We had a drink once at one of those conferences. I asked a couple of clarifying questions about his latest paper. He told me being a cog in the University machine had made my mind 'smaller than ever.' I didn't see him again for a while. After that flurry of activity, he went dark again for several more years. His parents died, he locked himself away in their coral house, and no one knew what he was doing, besides spending his meager inheritance on living expenses. I kept an ear out for news of him, because of our old relationship, and I heard he'd sold the house and used the proceeds to buy a second-hand spaceship capable of long-range travel. No one knew where he was going. No one was especially sorry to see him go. Years passed, and we all assumed he'd settled somewhere, or met with misadventure."

Thales was a cause of misadventures, not the victim of them, Felix thought. "He came back, though."

"Two years ago," Shelma said. "He just showed up at my office. I was running the whole engineering department at the shipyard by then. It was a good position, plenty of perks, but it had been ages since I'd so much as laid a pseudopod on a wrench, and I often looked around and wondered how it was I'd come to *manage* engineers instead of being one. That's why I was amenable to his offer. That, and the fact that he was almost humble. He said, 'Shelma, I need your help.'

"He *needed* my help! During our collaborations, he'd only grudgingly accepted my presence, calling me 'an adequate sounding board' and 'more socially acceptable than talking to myself' and 'a competent grease-monkey.' He found the latter endearment quite funny, since he was the primate, not me. I found it less amusing, but, as I said, I was good at tuning out his more objectionable qualities. I was flattered despite myself at his approach, and asked him what he needed. 'I've been studying wormholes,' he told me.

"I wasn't surprised. He'd always been interested in those. He thought understanding their nature was essential to understanding the universe. We can use wormholes to traverse vast distances in space, but we don't really understand how they function. There are various competing and mutually incompatible theories, none of which Phillip found satisfactory. If he could figure out how wormholes worked, he always said, *really* worked, that would provide a key insight and maybe even unlock the theory of everything. I asked how a theory of everything was going to make him rich – or had he changed his mind about the value of academic accolades these days? Formulating such a theory would be good for a permanently endowed reefdom in the theoretical physics division, even for a human."

The thought of Thales shaping young minds made Felix shudder.

"Phillip said I was being ridiculous. Didn't I see it? A natural side effect of a total understanding of wormholes would be the ability to *create* them. I did my best not to laugh at him. I just said, 'That's impossible.' Back then, I thought the rumors that the Creuss could create wormholes were just stories – part of the legend of the galaxy's greatest bogeymen. The Creuss are energy beings, after all, with a strange relationship to matter, so I thought there were other explanations for their ability to show up in places where you wouldn't expect them. But Phillip told me he'd gone out and studied the Creuss, met some of them, observed others, and that he'd seen them do it – open a wormhole where no wormhole existed before. Once he knew for sure it could be done, he devoted himself to figuring out *how*. He told me he'd nearly cracked it. He was just ... having trouble with the practical side. 'You need your old grease-monkey back,' I said. He actually looked ashamed! He told me he'd always meant it as a term of endearment –

"'I was a lot cruder and crasser in the old days', he explained. More sure of himself and his own importance. He'd come to realize he couldn't do it all on his own. He flattered me, too – said, 'I've tried to work with other engineers, but they lack your vision and your understanding of the deeper science.' He told me he'd secured funding and had a top-notch lab. He looked around my office, and I saw a flash of that old contempt. 'Could I really be happy here?' he asked, 'overseeing new strategic initiatives, when I could be tentacles-deep in the guts of a machine that would alter our fundamental understanding of space-time and make us rich'?"

"It's a pretty good pitch," Felix admitted.

"And I was tempted, captain! But I didn't trust an apologetic Phillip. I asked who was funding him. He told me it was a wealthy human in the Federation of Sol. I asked what his patron planned to do with the technology, if we managed to create it, and Phillip said, 'He's in shipping. I imagine he's going to demolish his competition.'"

"Oh, sure," Felix said. "And the inventor of the plasma

rifle was just interested in using it to kill flies. No obvious military applications at all."

Shelma went bluish again. "I wasn't an academic, captain, not really. I worked in the shipyards, which means I worked with the military, which means I fully grasped the implications of the work Phillip proposed. Even if he *was* funded by some civilian businessperson, I knew the tech would eventually end up in the hands of the military, and then it could be used against *my* people. I told Phillip I was interested. It took a bit of organizing, but I took a leave of absence from the shipyard and went with him to his lab, on a remote moon, and we got to work. I mostly went to... assess him. I thought maybe Phillip's reach was exceeding his grasp again. It wouldn't be the first time. But if he *was* close to perfecting practical wormhole technology, I wanted to be there when he did it. Not because I was intrigued by the technical challenges and the opportunity to work on truly transformative science, though that didn't hurt – but because if anyone had that kind of tech, I wanted to make sure my people had it too... or had it first. I could watch his work, contribute enough to keep him happy, but hold him back from creating a working prototype. When the time came, I could give the technology to my people, who have a long track record of using new technology responsibly. Phillip doesn't understand patriotism, or loyalty, to individuals, or governments, or species. He doesn't comprehend any bond that isn't based on self-interest, which is disturbing, but it also makes him predictable. He wouldn't expect me to join his team in order to slow down or limit his research, because he assumed I wanted wealth and glory too."

"An impressive declaration of patriotism and loyalty to your homeworld," Felix said. "Which makes me wonder how the hell you ended up on a Barony of Letnev station?"

Shelma was quiet for a long moment. "Because of what happened after the Creuss found us, captain."

CHAPTER 12

Felix, Calred, and Tib sat together on the bridge, all deep
in their own thoughts. The viewscreens displayed darkness
and a smattering of distant stars. They were hurtling through
space on a trajectory generated by the ship's computer
specifically to stymie any extrapolations the Letnev might
have made about their route or destination. Evasive
maneuvers were easier because they didn't know their actual
destination yet. Thales said he had to consult with Shelma
before he explained their next steps, and Shelma said she'd
been through a traumatic experience and needed to rest
before she talked to Thales about anything.

"The Ghosts of Creuss," Calred said, breaking the silence.
"I have a cousin who saw one, once – the Ghost was just
strolling through a bazaar out in the Ilanan system, dressed
in that weirdly ornamental armor they wear. All the vendors
and customers ran away, because even the ones who didn't
know it was Creuss knew it was dangerous… or wrong,
somehow. The Creuss didn't seem to notice everyone
flee. A street kid watched it through a crack in a wall, and

he said the Creuss went to a stall and touched a bunch of the rugs. How can they feel anything when they don't have bodies, and their hands are armored? He said the Creuss picked up one of the rugs and threw it over its shoulder. It left something sparkly on the counter of the stall – a jewel that glowed with its own inner light. Some idea of payment, everyone figured. The merchant had the jewel mounted under glass and proudly displayed it, called himself 'rug-merchant to the Creuss.'"

"Was that good for business, or bad?" Tib asked.

"My cousin didn't say. She was more fixated on the fact that two weeks later, the rug merchant was dead from a previously unknown form of cancer, and half the customers who'd visited the stall needed extreme oncological treatments. The gem didn't trigger any radiation sensors, but there was *something* wrong with it – something that caused the flesh to corrupt itself. The rug merchant's family buried the gem in a hole deep in the desert, in a casket lined with lead. I imagine it's still there. The opposite of a buried treasure."

"Ghost stories," Felix said. "Lots of people have them. Usually second- or third-hand, though. You can't take them too seriously."

Tib said, "I heard one that was first-hand, supposedly. Felix, do you remember that ambassador from the Yin Brotherhood, Errin, the one we met at academy graduation?"

Felix nodded. The Yin always disturbed him. They were clones, genetically identical, and religious zealots – everything about them was antithetical to the individualism at the core of the Mentak Coalition. "I do."

"I was talking to him at the reception that night, and he claimed he'd been part of a delegation the Yin sent to the Shaleri Passage. They were hoping to found an embassy there, if you can believe it, and open some kind of formal trade relations with the Creuss. The Yin are masters of the biological sciences – what could they possibly offer a species that doesn't even have bodies?"

"Forget that," Felix said. "What could they hope to get in return?"

"A cure for Greyfire," Calred said. "They're always in the market for *that*. They've exposed embryos to every known form of radiation, hoping the consequences would modify the genes in some useful way. Maybe they thought bathing their unborn in the light of an inside-out star in the Passage was worth a try."

"Errin didn't get into all that," Tib said. "He just told me the Creuss welcomed them and met them on a space station – a replica of a station from Yin space, apparently, probably identical down to the last rivet, but completely new, like it had just been built the day before, specifically for that meeting. Errin said it still smelled of fresh welds and hot polymers. The Yin were disconcerted, understandably, but the Creuss were polite, very formal, spoke their language perfectly, and offered them food that could have been served on any Yin outpost – but Errin did say the food was all exactly the same temperature, just this side of cold, like it had been fabricated or extruded instead of cooked. The Yin tried to talk business, and the Creuss asked questions and made statements, but the stuff the Ghosts said didn't seem to have any connection to what the Brotherhood said

– just random utterances. The ambassador remembered a few of the questions the Creuss asked – they said, 'Why is a frog?' and, 'What is the strategic importance of the color you call blue?' and 'Your armor is soft. Should we make soft armor too?' Pretty baffling, but the Yin attempted to answer as best they could. As far as the ambassador could tell, their answers didn't make any impression at all – there were never any follow-ups, never any sense of understanding."

"Sounds a lot like talking to Thales," Felix muttered.

Tib went on. "The ambassador's theory was that the Creuss weren't communicating at all – he thought they just had random phrase generators built into their armor, to create the illusion of conversation. After a while, the Creuss all turned and left, right in the middle of their nonsense dialogue. The ambassador and the rest of the delegation sat there for a while, waiting for the Ghosts to come back, but then the station started to disintegrate around them – the artificial gravity failed, rivets started to pop out, plates started to separate on the interior walls. No alarms went off, and there were no warnings, nothing you'd get on a normal station when the infrastructure started to fail. The Brotherhood delegation rushed back to their ship and managed to get on board before the whole station turned into a debris cloud."

"The station exploded?" Felix said.

"No, it just came apart, the ambassador said. Not violently. More like all its joins and welds failed at once. They thought maybe it was a threat, but the Creuss didn't make any further contact at all, friendly or hostile or otherwise, so the Yin withdrew beyond the Passage. That was the last time the Brotherhood sent a delegation to the Ghosts, as far as Errin knew. He said they counted themselves lucky to get out alive."

"We're drifting away from the current disaster," Calred said. "Why don't you tell us Shelma's ghost story, captain? What did *she* see?"

Felix stared at the darkness between the stars. "She didn't see the Ghost personally. Only Thales did. She got to the lab after the Ghost was gone, but she saw the consequences. Their whole lab was destroyed. Everything, from equipment to furniture, was reduced to fragments so fine they might as well have been sand. She said you couldn't tell what had been glass and what had been metal without examining the debris with a mass spectrometer. The lab building was totally unscathed, the walls unmarked, the floor not even scuffed, but everything else was just multicolored sand. The data they'd stored offsite drove computers insane when they tried to access it – that's the word she used, 'insane.' Their terminals wouldn't respond to commands in the expected ways, and after a few minutes the data just overwrote itself with nonsense."

"Why is a frog?" Calred said softly.

"Thales didn't give her a lot of details about the Creuss he met," Felix said. "He told Shelma a Ghost appeared in the lab, looked around, and said, 'You must not fracture the void.' Before Thales could reply, he blacked out. When he woke up, everything was demolished, and the Ghost was gone. Shelma showed up moments later."

"What did they do?" Tib asked.

"This is Thales we're talking about," Felix said. "They had

a big fight. Shelma said the visit from the Ghost should be considered a stern cease-and-desist notification from a patent holder concerned about infringement on proprietary technology."

"Ha," Calred said. "I like the way she thinks."

"Thales said their lab getting destroyed was just a temporary setback, and that they'd just have to be more careful about security next time. They hadn't hidden their research, really – they sent updates to the people funding them, occasionally spoke to other experts about thorny problems. They never came out and said 'we're building wormholes,' but someone paying attention might have pieced it together. Thales told Shelma they should just implement new security measures and carry on with their work under assumed names – that's when he stopped being Caruthers and became Thales."

"What work, though?" Tib said. "I thought all their research was turned into sand?"

"It will shock you to learn Thales is eccentric," Felix said. "He likes hard copies. He printed things out, because he liked to spread his files around him on the floor or pin the papers on the walls. Having the data arrayed around him in physical space allows him to better comprehend the whole and visualize new connections. That was one of the reasons he left the Universities of Jol-Nar, apparently– it's hard to sort piles of paper underwater."

"What a strange man," Calred said. "That explains the file boxes we recovered from the human ship. I wondered why he had pounds of dead trees when a couple of data sticks would do."

"Thales still had copies of their research, then?" Tib said.

"Most of it, yeah, tucked away under his bed. Their first model prototype for what Shelma calls the 'activation engine,' was reduced to sand, but they still had schematics."

"Did Shelma go along with his plan?" Tib asked.

"She did not," Felix said. "She told him to go to hell, gave her regrets to their Federation investors, and went back home to run the shipyard. Except when she got to work, her office was just like the lab. Everything was reduced to sand, drifting in the currents. She went to her house, and it was the same. That's when she got scared. She thought the Creuss were following her, making sure she knew she'd crossed a line. She moved, but things in her life kept glitching. The University would lose her records – she said at one point the system insisted she was deceased, and another time it listed her as a minor in need of state guardianship. She did her best to clear up the errors, but so much of life in an advanced society is mediated by technology." Felix shook his head. "She went to the Headmaster and told him about everything that happened, and asked for help and protection. The Headmaster refused and told her that, as far as he could tell from looking up her records, she was not a citizen of the Universities of Jol-Nar, and she should remove herself from Hylar space."

Tib whistled. "That's shitty."

"Huh," Calred said. "I ran a search when you gave me the Caruthers name, and still didn't turn up much beyond the bare facts of his birth and citizenship. Maybe the Ghosts manipulated his records too."

"There were people who knew Shelma personally,

though," Tib pointed out. "She ran the shipyard for years. Does she think the Creuss erased memories or something?"

"She didn't go that far," Felix said. "She thought the Headmaster knew more about the Creuss than she did – that all the higher-ups do – and decided it was better to cut Shelma off than risk annoying the Ghosts."

"Maybe the people who run things have a better understanding of how terrified they should be of the Creuss," Cal said.

Felix nodded. "Shelma said when she told the Headmaster the Creuss had taken action against her right there, on Nar, the Headmaster basically banished her."

"But the Letnev gave her a new home," Tib said. "*They* aren't afraid of Ghosts, are they?"

"They won't admit they are, anyway," Felix said. "The Letnev think they're better than everyone else, including the Ghosts, who don't even have *bodies*. Shelma didn't particularly want to work for the Barony, but they reached out and offered her a place, and protection, and security."

"How did Thales know where to find Shelma, anyway?" Calred said. "He indicated he'd heard about her imprisonment through some kind of scientist whisper network, but now we know nobody talks to him, and if there's one thing the Barony is good at, it's secrecy."

"That's where Shelma made a tactical error," Felix said. "She reached out to Thales through a back channel he'd set up in case she changed her mind about joining him. She told him about the offer of protection she'd gotten from the Barony, to see if he'd join her. He told her he was confident in his ability to protect himself, thanks. But he learned enough from the communication to track her down."

"Intelligent and unscrupulous is a terrible combination," Calred said. "I know they're founding virtues of the Coalition, but still."

"Shelma told me one other thing," Felix went on "She said she was stringing the Letnev along, pretending to make progress on the activation engine, but secretly ensuring they'd never have a working prototype. She didn't want to risk another visit from the Creuss."

"Do you think we have the Ghosts on our ass?" Calred asked.

"It's been more than a year since Shelma joined the Barony," Felix said. "Longer than that since their lab was destroyed. Maybe the Ghosts lost track of them in the meantime. Maybe they got distracted. Maybe it was only ever one Ghost, with some weird obsession, and they've moved on to a different form of entertainment. They're Ghosts. We don't understand why they do anything, so how can I predict what they'll do now?"

"Felix," Tib said. "*Do you think we have the Ghosts on our ass?*"

Felix sighed. "I'm definitely afraid we do."

"I had an interesting conversation with Shelma today." Felix perched on the edge of a work table in the rooms Thales had taken over for his lab.

"That squid does love to hear herself bubble on. Did she tell you all my deep dark secrets?" Thales poked at a tangle of wires with a screwdriver. He hadn't shaved or showered in some time, and his company was unpleasant even when he wasn't smelly and disheveled. Felix wondered if Thales was merely oblivious to matters of hygiene, or if he was trying to create a personal forcefield of foulness.

"More pathetic than deep and dark, really," Felix said. "She made you sound like a sad outcast who never lived up to his early promise."

"I'm still upright and breathing, captain. I have plenty of time to live up to plenty of things. And at least I *showed* early promise."

"She told me about the Creuss, Thales."

He stopped poking at the device, slowly lowered the screwdriver, then turned to face Felix, his face blank. "Did she?" His voice was carefully neutral.

"Is it true? Did you actually see one of the Ghosts, face to face?"

Thales scowled. "Ghosts! What an idiotic name. The Creuss are energy beings – sapient entities composed of coherent light. They don't *have* faces. No biological creature has ever seen a Creuss in its true form. Their bodies aren't stable outside the twisted physics that exist within the Shaleri Passage anomaly. The Creuss I met was wearing armor, like they always do when they interact with meat-creatures like us. The armor is usually humanoid in shape, but there's no reason it should be. Maybe they're mocking us. The one I met had a helmet like a mantis head, decorated with ornamental knotwork. It wasn't as big or imposing as you might think – it was slim, lithe, and the armor moved as smoothly as flesh. The Creuss have done amazing things with materials science, which is interesting, since as energy beings–"

"Thales, I'm more interested in the fact that the Ghosts of Creuss *destroyed your lab*."

"Yes!" He balled his hands into fists and shook them in the air. "That's the proof, captain! I was *close*! I never told Shelma this, but before the Creuss came, I was beginning to worry – what if their wormhole technology could *only* be replicated in the Shaleri Passage? There are bizarre space-time anomalies there, the same sort of anomalies that allow stable wormholes to exist, but on both a grander and more intricate scale. In the Shaleri Passage there are dark places, folds, dips, pinpricks, funnels, corners you can see around – corners that can see around *you*. Places where light misbehaves and entropy spontaneously reverses itself. I visited the Passage in my travels, and came out alive, which makes me part of a small and select group. *That's* where the Creuss do their science, under those bizarre conditions, and I thought – perhaps something about that Shaleri Passage allows their tech to work. Maybe you can only open wormholes from there, or with a machine *constructed* there, or with energies drawn from that place?" He grinned. "But then the Creuss came, threatened me, and destroyed my lab. There's no reason they'd do that, unless I was on the verge of a breakthrough. Their intervention was proof I was on the right track!"

"Shelma says the Ghosts might be coming after us, Thales."

"Oh, nonsense." Thales waved his hand like he was shooing away flies. "Shelma just frets. The Creuss think they scared us off. If they were still worried about us, they wouldn't have stopped at one act of vandalism."

"The Creuss did pursue Shelma, Thales. They followed her all the way back home and ruined her life."

"Paranoid ravings. If anything happened to her at all, the Barony probably did it, to scare her into joining them. The Creuss never bothered me in Cobbler's Knob."

Maybe that's because Shelma was the one making the real breakthroughs, Felix thought.

"If you're scared of the Creuss," Thales went on, "I have a simple solution: we just have to build a working prototype. Once we have wormhole technology, the Creuss won't have any reason to hurt us – it'll be too late to stop us then. The genie, as they say, will be out of the bottle."

"You're assuming the Ghosts will respond logically–"

"Go tell your boss you're afraid of Ghosts, then," Thales snapped. "Well? No? Then stop this pointless whingeing. I need to talk to Shelma. Surely she's rested by now?"

Felix wanted to say a lot of things, but as much as he hated to admit it, Thales was right: there was no point. The Coalition wasn't going to rescind Felix's orders because of rumors about the Creuss. The sooner he finished this mission, the sooner he could stop worrying about Ghosts. "I'll check on her," Felix said.

CHAPTER 13

Felix didn't sit when he visited Shelma's quarters this time. He stood with his back against her closed door, looking up at the ceiling, as if lost in thought. "It occurs to me, and I'm just thinking out loud here, but, if you're willing to bring your skills to the Coalition… could we do without Thales? My superiors are only interested in him because he claims he can generate wormholes for us. If you can do the same thing…"

Shelma changed color, her body flushing to a deep orange. Felix had picked up that red coloration meant "angry" or at least "annoyed," but the fine points of Hylar body language were still outside his skillset. "In the realm of engineering, I can do anything Phillip can do, better. I admit he's brilliant, and I never would have created his conceptual and theoretical framework, but that framework has been built. I know how to implement his theory. At this point, he needs me to continue – I don't need him."

"My only concern is, you'll do to us what you did to the Barony. String us along without making real progress."

"I understand your worry, but don't see what I could do to assuage it, even if I were motivated to do so. I've been honest with you, which is more than Phillip ever was. At this point, I think it's inevitable that wormhole technology will be developed. Phillip was right – once people know it *can* be done, they'll figure out how to do it. At least, this way, I can try to guide the process and protect my people. I'll need a promise, in writing, from your highest authority, that this technology won't be used for acts of aggression against Jol-Nar or its allies."

The idea that such a document would hold up if the political situation shifted the wrong way was touchingly naive, or maybe she was just trying to make herself feel better and tell herself she'd done her best. "That sort of thing is rather above my pay grade, but I can contact my superiors."

"Do that. If you can agree to my terms, then, yes. You can lock Phillip in a cell while I get on with the work. Just don't set him free. His mind is a weapon, and he holds grudges."

"His mind is a sewer I'm sick of swimming around in." Felix left her quarters and went to call his boss.

"Thales is banging on Shelma's door," Calred said over the comms.

Felix swore. He was still bouncing his signal through the numerous layers of encryption and obfuscation necessary to safely contact Jhuri. "Can you send a drone to drag him off?"

"She opened the door. They're talking. Should I intervene?"

As long as Shelma didn't say, "Ha ha, they're firing you and hiring me," what was the harm in letting them talk, really? Surely Shelma knew him well enough to avoid antagonizing him unnecessarily. Just then the connection clicked in, and Jhuri's face filled the air over Felix's desk.

"Just keep watch, and if they start to argue, break them up," Felix said.

"I assume you aren't talking to me," Jhuri said.

"Sorry, sir." Felix closed the ship channel. "I have an issue I can't resolve without exceeding my authority." He explained, without getting into specifics that needed to stay deniable, that they'd "rescued" the "prisoner" – and that she was requesting certain assurances before she'd consent to work with the Coalition. He told Jhuri about the Ghosts, too – both the visit to the wormhole lab, and the stories Tib and Calred had shared.

"Tell this Shelma whatever she needs to hear," Jhuri said. "Tib Pelta can forge whatever documents are necessary."

Felix winced. "We can't work with her in good faith?"

"She's an unwilling defector from the Barony, and by joining the Barony she already betrayed her homeworld. So, no. I'd say good faith seems rather inadvisable. If it's any consolation, we're on friendly terms with the Hylar, so it's possible you'll inadvertently tell her the truth."

"Ah. Right." Felix didn't like it, but he understood it. "But what about the Ghosts?"

"Oh, what's that thing you humans do, when you go spend the night in the woods for recreation?"

"Er, have outdoor sex, sir?"

"No, captain. I was thinking of campfire stories. I've heard variations of that disassembled space station story half a dozen times – sometimes the ambassadors are Yin, but sometimes they're Naalu, and sometimes they're *us*. As for the merchant and his deadly jewel, if you question Calred, I think you'll find he heard it from a cousin's cousin's friend, and that curiously there's no actual planet, let alone city or quarter, specified in the story. They're legends, Felix, and I suspect Thales is just taking advantage of those legends for his own purposes. He probably screwed up an experiment and destroyed his own lab and blamed it on the Ghosts. He hasn't been a paragon of honesty so far."

"That's true, sir, but–"

"But what?"

But I am afraid of Ghosts, Felix thought. Which wasn't something he could say to his superior. "Nothing, sir. How do you feel about us sidelining Thales in favor of Shelma?"

"Get us working wormhole tech, captain, and no one will care how you did it. Assign your personnel however you see fit. But keep Thales around. Ideally, don't let him *know* he's been sidelined. You may still need him. Shelma wouldn't be the first defector to overstate her own value."

"Yes, sir." Felix had known, deep down, that getting rid of Thales completely was unlikely, but without hope, what did you have?

He shut down the communication and answered a pulsing priority call from Calred. "What is it?"

"It's Shelma," Calred said. "She's having a seizure or something."

They didn't have a ship's doctor – the ship *was* the doctor, with an automated medical suite and a database filled with the data necessary to treat a variety of injuries and illnesses for all the species that lived in the Mentak Coalition, even the rare ones like the odd Ember of Muaat, male Naalu, unhived Sardak N'orr, or renegade Yin.

By the time they wrestled Shelma's clearly malfunctioning exo-suit tank into the sick bay, though, it was too late – she floated lifeless in her sustaining fluid like a specimen in a jar in a medical museum.

Felix punched a wall, hurting his knuckle, then turned and pointed his finger at Calred. "What did Thales do to her?"

Calred frowned, then pulled up security footage and sent it to the nearest screen. "Thales went to her door," he said, narrating what Felix could see for himself. "She opened the door. He stood there talking to her for a while. She didn't invite him in. After a couple of minutes, he left."

"What did they say?"

Calred fiddled with his gauntlet, and the video started over again, this time with audio. "Are you excited to work together again?" Thales said.

"You know I find the work interesting. I still have the same reservations I did last time, but the work itself seems inevitable, and the Coalition is no more objectionable than the Barony was."

"Just remember, Shelma, you're working for *me*. I'm still the lead on this project."

"Ha." Her tank bubbled. "I always let you think that, didn't I?"

They didn't have a clear angle on Thales's face, but Felix could sense his scowl. "Shelma–"

"I'm tired, Phillip. Can we do this later?"

"You know what has to happen next, Shelma. You know what we need. I saw your files. I saw the *absence* in your files. You came to the same conclusion I did."

"I don't know what you mean."

Thales reached out, touching her above one of her suit's manipulator arms – like a friendly hand on the shoulder, except nothing like that at all. "Yes, you do. You tried to obscure the problem, to hide it from the Letnev, but it's a glaring hole in your otherwise thorough breakdown of the engineering problems. I'm talking about the *power source*, Shelma. There's only one reason you'd omit mentioning the power source. You know there's only one place we can get it. One place we can *steal* it."

"I don't know what you're talking about, but if you have to steal something, it's good you have a pirate crew on your side," Shelma said.

"It's a shame you made such a mess of your job at the shipyard, or we could use your connections to get the source more easily."

"I was targeted by the Creuss–"

"That's your story, yes." Felix could hear the man's smirk. "I know the truth. You went back home and found they'd given your job away. You made a scene. They asked you to leave. Ghosts. Ha. The only ghost is your dead career–"

"You have no idea what you're talking about." Shelma shut the door in his face, and Thales shrugged and walked away.

Ugh. Had Shelma lied to Felix, too, or was this just more mind games from Thales? "Play it again," Felix said. "No sound this time." He watched, then said, "There. When Thales touches her. Did he do something? Put something on her armor? Insert something? Manipulate something?"

"The resolution isn't good enough to tell," Calred said. "But if he did... A suit malfunction could have killed her, absolutely. The suit certainly isn't working now – it doesn't even turn on. Maybe her filtration system failed, or there was an electrical fault. I saw her spasming on the feed. We'll have to see what the ship says after the autopsy."

"Thales killed her." Felix was suddenly, absolutely, sure.

"I don't like the man any more than you do," Tib said, "but why go to all that trouble to break Shelma out of the Barony station just to murder her?"

"He's got her files. He's got her prototype. Maybe that's all he needed."

Tib considered, then shrugged. "It's possible, but it still seems like going the long way around. Stealing her files would have been *much* easier than stealing her, too."

"So let's find out," Felix said. "Take her body to the infirmary. Can the ship's computer examine her and determine cause of death?"

Calred said *hmm*. "Ships with bigger crews usually have a medical officer on board to handle such things, but I imagine the automated systems can do it, if I can figure out how to configure the tests. The results might take a while if the cause was something unusual, though."

"We've got time," Felix said. "I'm going to talk to Thales."

"Just talk, though, right?" Calred said. "We're down to just the one wormhole scientist, and I think undersecretary Jhuri would be upset if someone gave him brain damage."

"I can control myself," Felix said.

•••

"She's dead," Felix shouted. "We went to all that trouble to rescue her, when she didn't even want rescuing, and now she's dead!"

"How regrettable." Thales didn't look up from tinkering with the prototype they'd taken from Shelma's lab. "She was a capable engineer. Still, her death isn't entirely tragic – it has certain clear advantages."

Felix had a bit of a temper as a teenager. He'd worked hard to get it under control and to channel his flashes of rage into energy to fuel his ambitions. This time, though, that energy was too much to contain. He flashed across the room, spun Thales around, and slammed him into the bulkhead, pinning the man against the wall by his throat. "You're *happy* she's dead?"

Thales gurgled, and Felix eased his grip enough to let him talk. "I didn't say I was happy, captain. I said there were advantages." He tried to shove Felix away, but the captain didn't budge. Thales exhaled heavily into Felix's face, then said, "I realize the state of economic theory in the Mentak Coalition is primitive – that's because you steal instead of actually producing anything of value – but in the rest of the galaxy, there's a concept called 'supply and demand.' With Shelma gone, the supply of scientists capable of creating working wormhole technology has been reduced by half, while the demand remains constant. That means *my* value has doubled. I was already worth ten of you, Duval. Now I'm worth twenty."

Thales was remarkable, in his way. He'd insult you to your face while your hands were literally around his throat. Felix let him go and took a long step back, to reduce the temptation to strangle him some more. "With Shelma dead, you have a monopoly on wormhole technology? That's your advantage?"

Thales rubbed his throat and scowled. "It's not a true monopoly, since the Creuss can do it too. But since they won't sell their technology, they don't matter much in practical terms. Otherwise, yes, of course. I couldn't leave Shelma in the hands of the Letnev. She might have duplicated my work – with their resources, she might have gotten there first! Then where would we be? Being second to market just drives prices down. New technology is most advantageous when it's asymmetric. If *one* faction can open wormholes, they can dominate the galaxy. If two can... there's an old term for enemies who possess equally powerful technology: 'mutually assured destruction.' That kind of situation leads to gridlock, no progress, no *winning*. My technology is valuable *because* it's unique."

"You didn't need or want Shelma's help. You just wanted to make sure she couldn't help anyone else. You used me."

"You *exist* for me to use. That's your purpose." Thales went back to his work bench, apparently content that Felix was no longer a threat. "That's why you were assigned to this mission. It's true, I didn't *need* Shelma, but she might have been helpful. I'd hoped to collaborate. She was hardly amenable, though. I'm sure you saw our conversation. Her death is a setback, and a shame, but it's not insurmountable."

"I know you killed her, Thales. You murdered your own friend, maybe your *only* friend, just to make another few credits."

"Three untruths in one sentence! That's impressive error

density, even for someone as consistently dense as yourself, captain. Shelma and I weren't friends. We were colleagues. We had a certain amount of respect for one another's capabilities, I suppose. I didn't murder her, either. Her death was probably caused by a fault in her exo-suit – you probably damaged the mechanism during your messy rescue attempt. Either way, it's a pity. As for the third error… it's not about *money*, captain. It's about changing the galaxy. About being the *man* who changed the galaxy."

"After my ship performs an autopsy, do you think it will confirm accidental death?"

"I'm only making an informed guess," Thales said pleasantly. "But I imagine I'm correct in the broad outlines." He didn't seem worried, which meant he knew the autopsy would show no wrongdoing, or else he was so convinced of his importance that he thought it wouldn't *matter* if they could prove he'd murdered the Hylar.

The problem was, if Thales was the only person in the galaxy who could create wormholes on demand, he really *was* that important.

"When this is all over…" Felix began, and then stopped. He couldn't think of any threat he'd be allowed to follow through on, and he hated to make empty ones.

"When this is all over," Thales finished, "I'll be rich, and you'll be promoted, and we'll never have to see each other again. Now, if you'll excuse me, I should look over the rest of Shelma's files. I doubt they'll be any use, but you never know. Meanwhile, *you* should call your masters and tell them you crippled the Barony of Letnev's wormhole technology program and pillaged its resources for yourself.

You people love pillaging. I'm sure you'll get a pat on the head." Thales waved a dismissive hand, and Felix left, because another wave of rage was building within him, and this time he might not stop at pushing the man against a wall.

We should have shoved Thales out an airlock when we had the chance, he thought.

CHAPTER 14

"Where are we going?" Severyne demanded.

"I love it when you get that tone." Azad lounged in her quarters – pretty cushy by Letnev standards, as they'd belonged to the commandeered ship's first officer, but they could pass for a solitary confinement prison cell anywhere else – and looked up at Severyne, who stood in the doorway, doing her best to be imposing and severe. Azad could be respectful when the chain of command made it necessary, but Severyne wasn't part of that chain of command, was she? And being insolent with her was much more fun. "Come sit beside me. Craning my head back to look up at you is giving me a cramp. I don't want to end up all stiff-necked like you." Azad sat up and scooted over on the bunk, patting the thin mattress.

Severyne entered, turned, and sat down. She kept her eyes front as Azad slouched against the bulkhead and looked at the Letnev woman sidelong. "We have limited time, Azad." Severyne clipped off her words. "I've followed your course settings so far, but I demand to know our ultimate destination."

"What will you give me for it?"

"You have your life, the promise of freedom, and my agreement to give you the Hylar scientist when we capture her. What more could you possibly want?"

"A little kiss?"

A muscle in Severyne's jaw twitched.

Azad grinned. "I'm just kidding. I'll take lives, and I'll take the spoils of war, and I'll coerce confessions, and I'll blackmail assets to turn them to my cause… but I only enjoy kisses when they're given freely."

"How nice to learn there are limits to your depravity."

"I thought you'd find it comforting. All right, I'll tell you where we're going, and as a bonus, I'll even throw in why. When we captured Thales and scooped up his files, I had my squad's analyst do a quick look through his data. She had cognitive implants that enhanced her pattern-recognition, that kind of nerd stuff, so she was able to collate a large amount of information quickly. She found something interesting in the reports he sent to his old investor."

"You mean the human businessperson who funded their original lab?"

"That's the one." The funding for Thales and Shelma's lab had actually come from the Federation of Sol's black ops military budget. The affable "investor" they'd taken meetings with was just a useful idiot the covert branch employed when they needed a plausible front, and Azad had read all the reports before she even started this mission. "Going over those reports, I noticed a weird omission –

Thales never once talked about a power source. It seems like ripping holes in space-time would take a lot of juice, doesn't it? But he never even sketched a drawing of a fusion reactor. That got me curious." It had actually gotten the analysts curious, and they'd asked Azad to help them satisfy that curiosity. "I flipped through the rest of his files, looking for anything pertaining to power, and there it was – a notebook with page after page, full of exclamation points and circles and underlines. Turns out, yeah, their design needs a lot of power – more than you could get from a reactor of conventional size, even the ones that power warships. You'd drain a war sun just warming up their activation engine. Using conventional energy sources, you'd have to turn a whole planet into a power plant, and something like that's not exactly practical or portable."

"I assume Thales found a solution?"

"Sort of, but it's one of those solutions that generates a whole new set of problems. Thales had a power source in mind, something experimental and well-guarded, and he was pulling his hair out because there was no way he could get his hands on it, and couldn't think of a plausible alternative. Apparently, your friend Shelma told him about it – an experimental energy source, very portable, that taps into so-called 'dark energy.' You know what that is?"

"It's the theoretical energy source that causes the universe to expand," Severyne said.

"I knew you were smart. Dark energy is limitless, or damn near, but it's also theoretical – nobody's figured out how to plug a starship into the engine that moves the stars. Back when she was running the shipyards, though, Shelma had connections in the blue-sky R&D division–"

"The what?" Severyne interrupted.

"Blue sky – oh, right. Where you're from, you never see the sky. I don't know what the equivalent idiom is in the Barony. It means no limits, wide open."

"Ah. We say 'endless dark.'"

"Who says it's not a beautiful language? So, anyway, Shelma knew people in the endless-dark research and development division, and they told her they were working on a device that taps into the dark energy field that's present all around us. Thales was excited about that, and his notebook was full of attempts to figure out how such a thing would work – he figured if he couldn't get his hands on the power source, maybe he could reproduce it. He didn't have much luck, though. Too far outside his area of expertise, I guess. When he gave up on cracking the problem himself, he started trying to figure out how to steal the one the Hylar were working on. He scrawled the names of various powerful people and factions – even the Nomad, can you believe that? – who might have the resources to break into the Universities of Jol-Nar. One of those names was the leader of the Mentak Coalition, so Thales ended up with partners he was thinking of joining up with anyway. Funny, huh?"

"You think they are headed to Jol-Nar, to steal this power source?" Severyne said.

Azad slouched deeper. "They must be. The Coalition won't let them ride around in circles in space forever. Those pirates are going to want results, and that means they need the power source. So let's go to Jol-Nar and wait for Duval and his crew to show up." She tapped the side of her head. "Then I'll get a ping off Phil's tracker, we'll swoop in, kill the pirates, recover our scientists, and go our separate ways. I can even use their ship to go home, once I hose off the bloodstains."

"You make it all sound so simple and straightforward."

"I always try to keep my plans simple. Do you know why?"

"I'm sure you'll tell me." Severyne sniffed.

"Because plans almost always fall apart, and if you keep them simple, at least you didn't waste too much time on something that doesn't work anyway. That's OK though. The part where the plan fails – that's where things get interesting."

"My life has been entirely too interesting of late," Severyne said. "I'll set a course for Jol-Nar."

"You might want to hold off on that." Azad looked around at the cheerless bare bulkheads and low ceiling, designed to make subterranean control freaks feel slightly more comfortable in the vastness of outer space. "Before we go to squid city, we need to switch ships."

"Switch. Ships. This is the *Grim Countenance*, a state-of-the-art Barony warship, the finest vessel in our system–"

"About that," Azad interrupted. "Don't you know it's lousy operational security to have a ship this nice patrolling some strategically insignificant mining planet? A ship this nice makes people wonder what's down there that's worth protecting – or what's on the supposed weather station in orbit. My analysts figured out where you were keeping Shelma because they got curious about this ship."

"I raised the same objections!" Severyne said. "I was overridden by the station director."

"Smart and tactically sound too. Be still my heart. So, yes, the *Grim Countenance* is a great ship, and I'm sure it could blow Duval's *Temerarious* into radioactive dust, but that's not our goal, so this ship is more gun than we need."

"You want us to proceed with *fewer* armaments?"

"I'm just saying, something with fewer guns would still get the job done. The problem isn't the armament, though. The problem is, this is a Letnev ship. It's covered in spikes and shit, Severyne."

"Our distinctive ship design strikes terror into the hearts of all our foes, and inspires respect in our allies–"

"You don't need to read me the brochure, Severyne. I'm not insulting your culture's aesthetics. I like big spikes as much as anybody. I'm saying, what happens if the Hylar see this ship slide into their system? They're going to get curious, and when we don't have a good explanation for our presence besides 'We're here to kidnap a human and a Hylar,' the squids are going to get annoyed. If this were a less distinctive ship, the kind you see sold secondhand all over from the Federation or the Coalition, we could fake a transponder, maybe do a little creative welding to change the silhouette, dirty the place up a little, and no one would be able to tell the warship *Grim Countenance* from the long-range merchant freighter *Sunny Smile* or whatever. But… spikes and shit."

Severyne groaned. "I requisitioned the best ship. My only thought was pursuing and destroying Duval's vessel, not infiltration. If I'd realized–"

"It's not your fault. You don't do covert ops. Prison guards aren't spies. Different skill set." Azad scooted a little closer to Severyne on the bunk. "I can teach you some of what I know, if you like."

Severyne scooted an exactly equivalent distance away. "First of all, I don't intend to make a habit of activities like this, so your tutoring won't be necessary. Second, why would you want to teach me anything?"

"For the time being, on this op, you're my partner. I go out in the field and do dangerous things with dangerous people for a living. I often have to team up with people who might betray me at any moment – local assets with divided loyalties, or opportunists who don't stay bought. You and I, amazingly, have a unified purpose: we both want the same thing, and we need each other's help to get it. That provides us with a rare opportunity to build trust. Also, I'd like you to be good at 'activities like this,' since my survival could depend on you at some point."

"I will consider what you say. What do we do about acquiring another ship? I cannot return home without the *Grim Countenance*, so selling it or trading it is out of the question."

"I know a guy," Azad said. "I think I can work something out."

Severyne's grim expression brightened infinitesimally.

Azad suppressed a sigh. She was almost certainly going to have to kill Severyne at some point. Her superiors wouldn't like it if she missed the opportunity to take the Barony out of the wormhole competition. Conversely, there was no way an agent of the Barony would let a

Federation operative take Thales, for the same reasons – Severyne would, inevitably, try to betray her, too. In a way, killing Severyne when the time came would be self-defense. Azad had already murdered one woman she liked this week, and she didn't look forward to doing it again.

She was cute, though. Azad had never even kissed a Letnev. Not a good idea, with the whole having-to-kill-her thing, but there was no harm in looking and appreciating, right?

Severyne was entirely too aware of the heat of Azad's body, so close to hers on the bunk. Did humans have higher body temperatures than Letnev? Severyne had never spent much time around humans – certainly not this close to one who was wearing so little clothing. Azad seemed to think a thin tank top and loose pants were appropriate attire for everything. Severyne could see Azad's *shoulders*, and her collarbone, and her biceps, and... Their species weren't *that* different, physically, and Azad's skin was dark and seemed somehow burnished, not like the bland paleness Severyne had observed in the other humans she'd met. Azad had a smell, too, a sharp mixture of sweat and something else, something uniquely *her*, that Severyne found strangely appealing.

Nothing mattered but the mission. Severyne focused her mind like the beam of a welding laser on the issue at hand. "You have 'a guy.' Is that meant to reassure me?"

"He's Hacan. Runs a scrapyard out near Vega Major. Lots of ships pass through there, mining vessels and freighters and so on. He buys used ships, fixes them up, and sells them on. Now, I don't want to shock your sensibilities, but he's been known to make deals that aren't strictly legal. Sometimes people bring him a ship for sale, and he doesn't always check the provenance as carefully as he should."

"He is a thief," Severyne said. Thieves were despised in Letnev culture. Life in the caverns of their homeworld was hard, death just one bad harvest away, and those who chose selfishness and personal gain over the good of their society were shunned. Of course, stealing from other species didn't count; if you weren't Letnev, you weren't exactly people, anyway.

"I don't know, he drives a hard bargain, but by and large I've found him – oh. I see what you mean. In most places, *receiving* stolen goods is a different offense than stealing them in the first place, but sure, basically, say he's a thief. More importantly, he has a great inventory of ships and he owes me a favor. He can get us a less distinctive vessel and hold onto the *Grim Countenance* without a lot of pesky hangar fees, or any records that we docked with him."

"How expensive are these ships of his? I have to submit my expenditures for approval–"

"Don't worry about that." Azad waved it away breezily, as she waved away so many things. Severyne hated that she found Azad's confidence appealing. The human wasn't *that* much older, but Azad had spent her years acquiring practical experience, while Severyne had spent most of hers in classrooms and lecture halls. Severyne's grasp of textbook tactics was excellent, and in theory she knew how to suppress prison riots, secure a station, and protect VIPs, but the first time she'd needed to put any of that knowledge into practice, she'd lost her prisoner. Maybe she *could* learn something from Azad. There were many areas where Severyne had largely theoretical knowledge – areas that could benefit from further practical experience...

She realized her eyes were lingering on the hollow at the base of Azad's throat, and slowly, deliberately, she turned her gaze away. Was it the transgression of finding a human attractive that made Azad so alluring? Severyne had long feared she had a streak of contrariness hidden inside herself, and Azad brought it out. "I hope this doesn't take too long. Duval has a head start already."

"Oh, I think we'll be all right. Duval has to steal something from the starship propulsion laboratory of the Universities of Jol-Nar. That's not something you just stroll in and *do*. He'll have to do research, make plans, figure out some angles. He'll probably have to source materiel, maybe even recruit more confederates – even if he's a criminal genius and does most of his thinking on the way to the Hylar system, we've got a couple of days."

"I desire a swift conclusion to this mission."

"Aw, Sev. Here I was thinking how much I enjoy spending time with you."

Severyne stood and stepped away. "Send me the coordinates for your guy."

Azad sketched a lazy salute, lounging across the bunk and grinning.

As the door closed behind her, Severyne felt a pang of regret. Azad was an interesting person. Infuriating, but interesting. It was a shame she'd have to kill the woman. She couldn't let the Federation of Sol get their hands on wormhole technology. If she did, her superiors would have her executed, so, in a sense, killing Azad would be self-defense. That didn't make her any happier about it. Severyne decided, as a gesture of respect, to pull the trigger herself, rather than ordering one of her guards to do it.

Then again, with Azad dead and gone, Severyne wouldn't be plagued by these increasingly intrusive *thoughts*...

CHAPTER 15

"Apparently we need to break into an experimental research and development laboratory in the Universities of Jol-Nar, steal a prototype power source, and get away without being arrested or killed. Does anyone have any suggestions for how we can accomplish that?" Felix looked from Tib to Calred. To think, he'd once found sitting on this bridge with his crew relaxing. Of course, back then his biggest problem had been fielding calls from colonists who wanted him to use the ship's impressive sensor array to find a lost sheep. (He'd done so once, naturally, because he'd had nothing else particularly pressing to do.)

His crew was silent. Felix said, "I'm sorry. That wasn't a rhetorical question. I am asking how we do the thing that I just said we need to do."

"If Shelma hadn't died, I'm sure she'd have useful information," Tib said. "She used to run the shipyard, so she had connections in the experimental labs. She could have sketched us floor plans, maybe even told us about security measures. I wish Thales had brought up stage two of his plan before her unfortunate 'accident.'"

"No use weeping over broken eggs," Felix said. "Can we do the same thing we did on the Letnev station? Fake our credentials, pretend to be a delivery ship, get close, sneak in?"

Calred shook his head. "My cousin is very angry with me, so she won't be offering us any more assistance along those lines. Her company lost their contract with the Barony, and it was a *big* contract. Speaking of which, I promised I'd make it up to her by securing them an equally lucrative arrangement with the Coalition. Didn't you sleep with the chief supply clerk for the Lucanis system once, Felix?"

"There's a reason it was only once," he said.

"Ah, well. Until I make things right with her, we won't be able to borrow any schedules, authorizations, or manifests, so we wouldn't pass inspection. Sorry."

Felix sighed. "It's not your fault. Once we're covered in glory and flush with success and the Table is handing out rewards for our exemplary accomplishments, we'll see about setting up your cousin with a good contract."

"What if we fail?"

"Oh. Failure would probably mean incarceration or execution by the Hylar, and in that case, you'll be well beyond your cousin's wrath."

"I am comforted," Calred rumbled.

Felix drummed his fingers on the arm of his captain's chair. "I noticed one interesting thing in the dossier you compiled about the head of the research and development lab," he said. "There was that little fluff piece that mentioned his collection of alien artifacts. He likes mysterious objects of mysterious provenance from mysterious places, so if we had such an artifact, and made an appointment, maybe we could get into his office, which is in his lab, so he could take a look?"

"It's a shame we don't have any mysterious artifacts handy," Calred said.

"I bet we could come up with something," Tib said. "Or at least a convincing facsimile."

"We'd need to be convincing facsimiles ourselves," Felix said. "The kind of adrenaline junkie deep-space explorers who stumble on unknown alien tech don't travel in ships as respectable as the *Temerarious*. We'd need to show up for the meeting in a smaller long-range craft, something beat-up and pitted with micrometeoroid impacts, scarred by weird energy weapons wielded by uncontacted alien cultures, that sort of thing. Where can we get a plausible ship?"

"I know a guy," Calred said.

"A cousin?" Felix said.

Calred shook his head. "He's Hacan, but we're not *all* related. I know him from some work I did for the Coalition. You know I spent time in the asset distribution arm of the pirate service?"

"You sold stolen goods to fences, you mean," Felix said.

"I did. And our favorite fence when it came to converting stolen ships to currency was a gentleman named Sagasa the Disciplinarian."

"That is not a very welcoming name."

Calred grinned. "'Disciplinarian' is a title used by members of a certain Hacan religious order – specifically the monks in charge of making sure none of the initiates stumble into heresy, or shirk their duties. Sagasa is an apostate these days, though he was devout when he lived in the desert. The way I heard it, he was so devout and incorruptible that when an acolyte ran away from the order, they sent Sagasa to track the cub down, even though their order eschews exposure to worldly things. Once Sagasa got on his first starship, though, he realized he liked worldly things. The order sent a couple of people to bring *him* back, but that didn't go well, and the order decided to let him go. Sagasa kept using the title in his new life, because it sounds scary – but it also sounds like he'll only punish you if you give him a reason. That pretty much fits the way he does business. Sagasa and I are on good terms. He can get us a plausible ship, probably one some genuine adventurers died in, and he'll let us dock the *Temerarious* in his shipyard until we're back."

"Perfect," Felix said. "We can figure out the details of our plan on the way. Where's Sagasa based?"

"Not too far out of our way," Calred said. "His scrapyard is out by Vega Major."

"I have already given you a crucial element necessary to complete your plan," Thales said. "Now you ask more of me? I am not a crafter of trumperies. Would you have me sew a monkey's torso to a fish's tail and claim it's a mermaid? Glue antlers to a jackrabbit's head and call it a jackalope? Put wings on a snake and display it as the mythical Aaalu? You are distracting me from my work, captain."

The rooms Thales had taken for a lab no longer reflected even the relaxed military order that characterized Coalition ships. Now the walls were covered in printed pages and sketches from Shelma's files and Thales's own, and he'd gone even further, drawing on the actual bulkheads in places. The floor was dotted with cairns of stacked papers, and there were coils of wire, clumps of crystal, and assorted machine components on every surface. Felix recognized one of the ship's repair drones, upside-down, its carapace open and half its parts removed. There was a pile of blankets and cushions in one corner – according to Calred, who monitored the security cameras, the scientist slept there, taking short naps every few hours in lieu of longer cycles before snapping awake and continuing to tinker with Shelma's torpedoshaped device: the activation engine.

Felix felt a headache coming on. Talking to this man was bad for his mental and physical health. "Your *work* is opening wormholes, and you need this power source to do it. We can't buy it, because it's not for sale – officially, it doesn't even exist – and if we're going to steal it, we need your help."

"I already helped."

"We need *more* of your help," Felix said.

"You're pirates. I'm a scientist. I don't need your help to calibrate a neutrino detection array. Why do you need my help to steal something?"

"This isn't piracy. This is burglary, if we're lucky, and robbery if we're not."

Thales looked up briefly. "There's a distinction?"

"Piracy is going out on a ship and stealing something from *another* ship. Sometimes, you steal the other ship while you're there. Burglary is entering a place illegally with the intent of removing something that doesn't belong to you. Robbery is stealing something from another person directly, usually with threats of violence, or *actual* violence."

"I suppose every field of study has its own terminology. Burglary and robbery are outside your skillset, then?"

"I didn't say that, but part of doing a job like this is making use of expert assistance." Flattering Thales couldn't hurt. "You're an expert on alien technology, aren't you? So help us fake something that looks plausible enough to catch the director's interest."

Thales put down his tools and scowled. "You need something that will pass for an alien artifact of unknown provenance. Something that has properties, or purports to have properties, that the head of experimental research and development at the University will find interesting, and want to see in person. I'm sure I can come up with something, though I may need some source material to create it. There's nothing on *this* ship that would pass for a component of an alien device."

"Fortunately, we're headed for a huge junkyard," Felix said. "It should have all the weird trash you could ever want."

"No doubt you'll feel very at home there," Thales said.

"Because I'm trash, you mean?"

"That was my implication, yes."

"Do you remember our conversation about how you need to be less terrible all the time?"

Thales chuckled, and it was a low, nasty, oily sound. "I thought we understood each other, captain. You've proven you'll do whatever I ask, if it's necessary for my project. That even if you suspect me of murder, you'll obey your superiors and give me what I want. In light of those facts, I think we can dispense with all that nonsense about courtesy."

"Do you really want to see how far you can push me, Thales?"

"I'm a theorist first and foremost, captain, but I'm also an engineer, and it's useful for engineers to know the tolerances of their equipment."

Felix stared at him. "I'm your equipment, am I?"

"You are one small component in a machine I am creating – a machine that will transform the galaxy and shift the balance of power, and in favor of your nation. You're a *vital* component, captain, rest assured. I couldn't do this without you. There's no shame in serving your role properly. Let me know when we've reached this junkyard of yours, and I'll solve your problem." He turned his back. Felix was dismissed.

Felix looked at a heavy wrench on a nearby table. He could pick it up, swing it hard, cave in the man's skull, and ruin all that remarkable gray matter. Of course, he wouldn't do that, but it gave him a warm feeling to know he *could*.

I never used to daydream about murdering anyone, Felix thought. Thales was such a terrible person, he was making Felix into a worse one, like his terribleness was contagious. Or even radioactive.

Vega Major wasn't a particularly nice place to visit. The planet had beautiful rings, but those rings were infested by mining ships and surrounded by orbital habitats to support the miners – which meant, at least, that there were plenty of bars and other entertainments available, though they were a bit grease-stained and grimy. The surface of the planet was habitable, technically, but its seas were inhabited by vast numbers of unintelligent giant squid. There were colonies down there, but the colonists required a high tolerance for eating squid and, potentially, being eaten by squid, if they strayed too close to the water.

The sister planet, Vega Minor, was a nicer place, and home to a respected company, the Vega Propulsion Corporation. (Felix asked if there was maybe an experimental power source *there* they could steal instead, but Thales said they didn't have anything suitable, and then went off on a long rant about how the corporation had cheated him on some engine component he'd devised.) The stilt-cities that dotted the shallow seas there were home to thriving populations drawn from all over the galaxy, and the one time Felix had visited, he'd thought the place would fit right in as part of the Coalition.

Alas, they weren't going to Vega Minor. They were on the far side of Vega Major instead, approaching what looked like the aftermath of a horrific space battle. A vast cloud of floating wreckage filled their viewscreen, with hundreds of ships of all descriptions floating in various states of destruction or disrepair. There were Mentak cruisers, Federation pickets, Letnev thorn ships, even – "Is that a Muaat *war sun*?" Felix stared.

"It's almost half of a Muaat war sun," Calred said. "Last time I was here, Sagasa was bragging about winning the contract to scrap it. Someone else won the other half – the Embers didn't want to give anyone the whole thing, lest they try to get it up and running again. All the armaments were removed, of course, but still. It's an impressive hunk of metal, isn't it?"

Felix whistled. The Coalition had big terrifying weapons platforms too, of course – all the major factions did – but the Muaat war suns set the gold standard for horrifying military overkill. He'd never seen one of them this close up, and had always assumed that if he ever did, it would mean he was about to die.

When they got closer to the debris cloud, it became more obvious this wasn't a graveyard, but a recycling center. Drones floated everywhere among the wrecks, blowtorches sparking, saws spinning, articulated arms plucking and sorting components into carts that looked small in comparison to the ships around them but were actually the size of houses.

A bored voice spoke over the comms. "Welcome to Sagasa Scrap and Salvage, we make old things new again, how can we help you today?"

"I'd like a meeting with Sagasa," Felix replied.

"The Disciplinarian is very busy today, I'm afraid–"

"Tell him I have a large black ops budget I'd like to spend on him," Felix said.

A moment's pause. "The Disciplinarian doesn't take new clients of that sort without a referral."

"Tell him Calred the Hacan is part of the crew," Felix said.

A long pause. "From Moll Primus?"

"That's the one," Calred rumbled.

"One moment please." A longer pause. "Proceed to dock B and follow instructions."

Their ship interfaced with the Sagasa Scrap and Salvage docking system, the Disciplinarian's computers guiding them on a safe path through the field of wreckage. From a

military perspective, this place was incredibly defensible –
any force that tried to get to the station at the center of this
mess would have to navigate the debris field, and a lot of
those ships still had working fuel and propulsion systems,
which meant a lot of them could be easily turned into
bombs. Calred said once you got deeper into the debris field,
some of the ships weren't wrecks at all, but fully functional
warships, disguised as junk. Attack could come from any or
all directions, in there. "I'm glad Sagasa is on our side," he
muttered.

"Ha!" Calred laughed from his security station. "Sagasa
is on his own side. He'll make deals with anybody and
everybody. He says we're all equal in the eyes of the divine,
so who is he to discriminate?"

"I can't wait to meet him," Felix said.

CHAPTER 16

"I hate ocean planets." Severyne gazed through the viewport at the looming shape of Vega Major, and the gentle curve of Vega Minor beyond. "All that water, none of it fit to drink. Wasteful and inefficient. There is darkness and depth and pressure, yes, if you go down far enough, but then, those depths are so often full of teeming monsters."

Azad stood beside her. "On the other hand, there's lounging on the beach, maybe someone attractive rubbing lotion on your back, you swim in the warm water, it's got upsides."

"There are species who consider such activities pleasant, I know, but the relentless sun is my own vision of horror."

"So you sit under an umbrella, or wear a big hat. You'd look good in a big hat, Sev. Much better than you do in that flat cap with the little brim and the silver stars on it you were wearing when we first met. You can sip fruity boozy drinks out of hollowed-out examples of the very same fruit that's blended up in the drink. Surely you can appreciate *that* – it's efficient, right?"

Severyne's lips twitched. She very nearly smiled. "You must think the Letnev a joyless people. It isn't true. We simply take pleasure in things that your species, as a whole, does not. I find joy in competence, and order, and important work done well."

"Sure, all that stuff is great," Azad said. "But have you tried getting drunk and sleeping with a stranger?"

Severyne resolutely ignored that. "I assume this cloud of wreckage is our destination?" The screen lit up with hundreds of targets, ships all ringed in green to show the system didn't consider them current threats.

"Welcome to the scrapyard of Sagasa the Disciplinarian. Biggest and best junkyard in the sector."

Severyne narrowed her eyes. "I see Letnev ships among his inventory. How did he come by *those*? We decommission our own vessels in the Barony."

"You're looking at the far end point of battlefield economics, Sev. The Barony gets into the occasional fight, doesn't it? And, contrary to what your national propaganda says, you don't win *every* engagement. After a battle, the winning side recovers what they can, but usually they have to rush off to kill some other people someplace else, or they need to resupply, or they're chasing down survivors, or they got beat up badly enough themselves that they need to limp home for repairs both medical and mechanical. There are teams of freelance scrappers who pay closer attention to politics than most politicians do, so they know where battles are likely to break out, and they hang around. After the surviving forces withdraw, the scavengers go in, and they gather what's worth selling."

Severyne had never really thought about what happened in the aftermath of a space battle. Logistics wasn't her area, and neither was military engagement; she worked in what was sometimes called "inward-facing" security. "They loot battlefields and sell the spoils to people like Sagasa?"

"Only the junk." Azad leaned on the curving black rail in front of Severyne's chair, a posture that thrust out her rear end in Severyne's direction in a rather distracting way. "Salvage that still works gets sold to mercenaries, or local forces, or sometimes they sell it back to the military that lost it in the first place, at a price that's *slightly* cheaper than sourcing new stuff from a factory would be. The scavengers also perform other, ah, crucial functions. Delivering mercy, and the like."

"That sounds like a euphemism. We don't like euphemisms in the Barony, Azad. We prefer to view the world as it is."

"They kill the dying, Sev. Space battles are different from terrestrial ones – they tend to be a lot more all-or-nothing, because if your ship gets destroyed, *you* get destroyed, so there are fewer wounded, overall. Fewer doesn't mean zero, though, and there are always people lingering with significant bits of their anatomy missing in the aftermath, and no help on the way."

"The scavengers *murder* battlefield survivors?" Why had Severyne's required courses on military engagements not covered this material? Probably because the Barony didn't like admitting to losses of any kind.

Azad said, "Oh, not always. Only the ones who are too far gone. They patch up people who can be patched up without too much trouble, and get them back home, for a price. Most factions will pay for the safe return of officers, and for grunts... well, ideally their return gets lumped into a purchase of weapons and supplies. If you're an outside contractor or a mercenary though? Forget it. Nobody's paying to get you back."

That was disturbing, but Severyne knew the military had to make difficult decisions. "Freelancers are summarily executed?"

"No, you're not thinking like a scavenger," Azad said. "Try again."

A test, then. An intellectual exercise. Severyne had always excelled at those. It was translating them to practical application that was proving harder than she'd ever anticipated. "If the point is to extract maximum value, turning what others view as waste into profit, and there are survivors who cannot be converted into money, they must instead be converted into... labor? The scavengers enslave them?"

Azad turned and gave her a smile. "Very good. Really it's more like indenture, because that's almost as good as slavery, and you get fewer rebellions from within and sapient rights complaints from without. If the scavengers save your life, and nobody pays them for the trouble they took to save you, you can always work off your debt. The pay is reasonable, and they treat their employees well, overall. Plenty of people choose to stay on even after their debt is paid, and some of them settle into scavenging for life. It's dangerous work, salvaging battlefields – there's always lots of unexploded ordnance that might explode when you touch it, flying debris that can puncture your suit or your lungs, things like that. There's a lot of, let's say, turnover, so new recruits are always welcome. Honestly, though, after you've barely survived a battle, being a salvager seems pretty safe in comparison."

There was something about Azad's voice. "You speak as if from experience."

"I've spent a good chunk of my career as a deniable asset – nobody pays for *my* safe return. Either I make my own way home, or I don't go home at all. I spent six months working for a salvage outfit that found me stuck in a crumpled escape pod tube in a wrecked ship after an engagement went bad. That's when I met Sagasa, actually."

"You have had a rich and varied life, haven't you, Azad?"

"I like going new places and meeting new people." She winked. "Just think, if my mission had gone more smoothly, and I'd snatched up Thales without getting all tangled with Duval and those pirates, you and I would never have met. Wouldn't *that* be a tragedy?"

"If you hadn't failed in your mission, Duval would never have attacked my station and put my life in danger, and I would be in my quarters right now, sleeping, instead of going to meet a criminal Hacan in a junkyard."

"Life does take some unexpected turns, doesn't it?" Azad said.

A voice over the comms said, "Welcome to Sagasa Scrap and Salvage, we make old things new again, how can we help you today?"

"Tell the old crook his favorite scrapper Amina just

brought him a top-of-the-line Letnev warship," Azad said.

"*What?*" Severyne gasped.

The station at the center of the debris cloud was a tangle of metal bolted together from castoff habitat modules, with entire scrapped ships welded into the middle of corridor rings. "It looks like a work of very bad art," Felix said.

"The station started out as a standard modular system, but over the years Sagasa has embellished the place," Calred said. "I know it *looks* like a haphazard garbage heap, but it's built solid, and the placement of those ships isn't random – they're placed at set intervals, and their weapons systems are still intact, and pointed outward."

"This is like a warlord's fortress," Felix said. "Does Sagasa really expect to be attacked?"

"Scrap and salvage is a cut-throat, low-margin business, and when you add in the Disciplinarian's not-strictly-legal activities… a man like him can make a lot of enemies. The Vega Corporation doesn't love having a hub of slime and criminality so close to their headquarters, either. Sagasa has repelled an assault or two over the years. He repelled them robustly enough that not many people have tried him since."

"I'm glad we don't have to steal anything from *here*," Felix said.

"Indeed. Stealing from Sagasa would doubtless result in disciplinary action."

They docked with the station and headed down to the airlock, Felix in the lead, Cal a step behind on his left, Tib in the back, clearly wishing she was invisible. (Calred said sneaking around Sagasa's station wasn't advisable. The

Disciplinarian would be annoyed if he found out.) The interior of the ship did away with the scrap-heap motif, the corridor walls and floor made of smoothly polished metal, with discreet cameras dotted everywhere – but not so discreet you'd fail to notice them if you looked, which was presumably the point. Sagasa wanted you to know you were being watched, and watched by a professional.

A Winnaran in an elaborate jeweled headdress waited for them in the corridor beyond the airlock, hands clasped behind him. "Do you have any weapons to declare?"

"Not on us," Felix said.

The Winnaran seemed unconvinced, and pointed a handheld scanner at them each in turn before nodding. "This way." He turned smartly and led them down a twisting maze of corridors, and as they made it closer to the heart of the station, they encountered several reinforced doors with recessed gunports. Those doors didn't open right away, and the Winnaran waited patiently at each one, clearly used to this level of security. Eventually their little group reached a cavernous waiting room that Felix recognized as the repurposed bridge of a Coalition dreadnought; that gave him a weird sense of pride. The stations and seats had been stripped out, replaced by large pots of lush green climbing plants that wound around the stripped frames of tactical panels and navigation screens. The overall aesthetic was like being in a spaceship that had crash-landed in a jungle some years before.

The door that would have led to the captain's ready room on a functioning ship was flanked by a pair of guards wearing armored exo-suits so elaborate that Felix couldn't guess the species of the beings inside. In addition to the plasma and kinetic weapons built into their suits, the door guards also held more primitive weapons – wooden poles with elaborately curved and recurved spikes of bronze on the heads.

"The Disciplinarian has a sense of theater, doesn't he?" Felix murmured.

"Oh, just you wait," Calred replied.

The Winnaran gestured for them to sit on a metal bench that was only partially covered in vines. Felix expected to be offered refreshment, but instead the secretary (or whatever he was) just said, "You will be called," and left the bridge.

Felix looked at the guards. "Hi there," he said. "Having a good day?"

The guards might as well have been statues.

"They don't do small talk," Calred said. "It would ruin their whole sense of menace. You might as well try to strike up a conversation with a particle cannon."

"I bet he would," Tib said.

"I just try to make meaningful connections wherever I go. It's called networking. It's the key to diplomacy. You could both learn–"

The doors to the ready room slid open, and a burly, hairy humanoid bustled out, muttering to itself and adjusting a brown cloak. He was a Saar! Felix didn't think he'd ever met one of that species. The Saar kept to themselves so thoroughly that you could forget they were part of the galactic community at all. Didn't most of them live out in an asteroid field somewhere, among the rubble of their exploded home planet? They probably had a pretty vast and ongoing need for ships, in that case, so they must be a great market for Sagasa. The Saar took no notice of Felix and the others as he stomped by and away.

Felix half rose, but the guards lowered their pikes, crossing them over the open doorway, and then the doors slid shut again. Felix sat back down, and the guards moved their weapons to vertical.

"The Disciplinarian likes to take a breath between meetings," Calred said. "He centers his mindfulness or whatever. I'm pretty sure it's just a show-of-power thing. Make it clear to us we're penitents, and he's the one granting an audience."

Moments later, the doors slid open, and a voice beyond barked, "Come."

They went in, Felix in the lead, only hesitating a moment as he passed the imposing armored guards, but they didn't even twitch. The ready room was as lush and green as the waiting area, but dominated by a large desk made from artfully welded-together starship parts, surfaces polished like the rest of the station.

The Disciplinarian sat behind the desk in a chair that was really more of a gleaming metal throne, high-backed and elaborately decorated with vines made of twisted wire stems and gold-foil leaves. Strange choice of décor, overall, for someone from a monastic order in a desert… or maybe Sagasa's arid background explained why he liked growing things here in the different desert of space.

Sagasa was flanked by a pair of unlikely guards, or attendants, or recording secretaries, or who knows what. On his left stood a Naalu, though "stood" probably wasn't the right term for what a man-sized serpent with arms did. Rested on its huge scaly tail? He… it had to be male, since the Naalu were a matriarchal culture, and you'd never see a female working for a Hacan or anyone else. Naalu could read minds, or sense intentions, or detect lies, depending on who you asked, though some people said it was just the females who had that power. There were a few Naalu in the Coalition, but Felix hadn't met any. He decided to be scrupulously honest, just to be safe.

A N'orr crouched on the Disciplinarian's right: a looming nightmare of chitinous claws, a head made of hideous triangles, a mouth surrounded by dripping mandibles, the whole thing balanced on entirely too many spiky legs. Felix wasn't bothered by spiders, but spiders weren't usually taller than him, with mouths big enough to engulf his head. There were a few unhived N'orr in the Coalition, Felix knew, descended from prisoners on the original penal colony, but he wondered how this one had ended up here. The N'orr didn't have a hive mind, despite popular misconceptions, but they didn't prize individuality either, and so their species didn't produce many outcasts or rogues or wanderers.

"Just you wait," Calred had said. The Hacan definitely knew how to make an impression.

There was one chair, suitable for humans, on the other side of the Disciplinarian's desk. It was made of wood-textured plas, had one leg visibly shorter than the others, and the back support was held together with wire and industrial tape. As if the power imbalance wasn't stark enough already, but any edge you could get in a negotiation was worthwhile. Felix decided he'd stand.

The Disciplinarian gazed at them. He was older than Calred by at least a few decades, his mane nearly white, his eyes steady and dark, his muzzle marked with scars. He wore an elegant buff-colored robe worked around the neckline and sleeves with a vine motif, and even seated, he gave off a sense of strength and mass and gravitas. His eyes settled on the security officer. "Calred. May the sun warm your back, brother."

"May blood redden your claws," Calred said with equal formality.

The Disciplinarian smiled broadly. "It's nice to talk to someone with manners. I had a Saar in here a minute ago, and he actually spat on the floor!" He inclined his head toward the N'orr. "Counselor An'Truk here wanted to spear him through the thorax but I said, 'Maybe spitting is a compliment in their culture.' It's important that we all get along, eh? Look at you three, all working together on a starship. The *Temerarious*. You're supposed to be patrolling a colony system, Captain Duval, yet you arrive at my humble scrapyard boasting of a covert operations budget. Have you been under *very* deep cover, or is this a recent promotion? Given the presence of Calred, who I know to be a steady sort, I will omit the third possibility – that you're lying or delusional."

Felix inclined his head in an acknowledging nod. "We are on a mission. I can't tell you much about it."

"That's fine. I deal in tangible things, not information. Information gets too close to politics, and I value my reputation as a neutral party who plays no favorites. How can I help you with this mission I don't want to know any details about?"

"We need to borrow a ship," Felix said. "I'd also appreciate it if you'd let a scientist we're traveling with paw through some of the more exotic wrecks out there."

"All things are possible," Sagasa said, "if the price is right."

CHAPTER 17

The *Grim Countenance* was assigned to docking port YB-2. Azad stood next to Severyne on the bridge, watching the station grow in the viewscreen as they approached. "That docking port can't be sequential," Severyne said. "How many airlocks does this misbegotten scrapheap of a station have?"

"Oh, lots," Azad said airily. "The Disciplinarian tries to park everyone where they can have a bit of privacy. Sometimes people don't want to be seen visiting. And there's always the risk that he'll have visitors from both sides of some conflict dropping by at the same time. Sagasa is steadfastly neutral, and doesn't like fuss or conflict." She paused. "What I mean to say is, he doesn't like conflict *here*. He loves conflict elsewhere. I suspect he even funds the occasional rebel alliance or splinter political faction, knowing his small investment will reap big returns in salvage later. But maybe not – he always claims he stays out of politics, and it could be true. Not *everyone* lies constantly, but Hacan can be tough to read, even for other Hacan, let alone a humble swabbie like me."

"You shouldn't have told him he could buy our ship," Severyne said, not for the first time. "We are *not* selling him this ship."

"I know, I know," Azad soothed. "We're going to work all the details out when we get in to see him. I just had to snag the guy's attention. We're going to *borrow* another ship, for a nominal fee, and leave him the *Grim Countenance* as collateral. He'll take the deal, because if we come back, he makes a little money, and if we don't come back, he gets a Letnev warship, and that's worth a *lot* of money. Alternatively, we can offer him a lot of money in the first place, no collateral necessary, but I'm trying to help out your expense report situation."

"Your plan is acceptable. I dislike the suggestion that we won't return, however. We will come back, and we will be triumphant."

"Ah, right. The Letnev spirit. Never admit even the possibility of defeat, right?"

"What benefit can there possibly be in imagining one's failure?"

Azad shrugged. "Overconfidence has brought down a lot of generals, Sev."

"Better to be overconfident than to doubt one's capabilities."

"Now, there I agree with you." She slung her arm over Severyne's shoulder, and the Letnev squirmed away with a deftness and grace that surprised Azad. Had Severyne trained as a dancer? No, ridiculous, Letnev didn't dance. What, then? That movement had been more than merely natural. Azad kept talking as if nothing had happened.

"Some people think I'm overconfident – do you believe that? When really I just have clear-eyed self-regard and a complete understanding of my own abilities." Azad knew that was a little pompous, and was hoping to needle Severyne a little.

Instead, the other woman said, "The presence of excellence often disturbs the inferior."

Oh, I like you, Azad thought. She hated her a little, too, but that just made things more fun. If Azad had wanted a simple life, she wouldn't have joined covert ops.

They went to the airlock, and into the station. A Winnaran with a gaudy jeweled thing on his head looked at them all snooty and said, "Any weapons?"

"A Letnev military officer is never without her sidearm," Severyne said.

The Winnaran pushed a button, and a drawer slid out of the wall. "Place your weapons in this locker. You may retrieve them on your way back."

"It's OK," Azad said when Severyne stiffened. "This isn't a shooting place. It's a money place."

Severyne glared at the Winnaran, then put her sidearm in the drawer. Azad did a little twirl to show she was unarmed – she was wearing a close-fitting top and shorts, so she couldn't hide much of a weapon, and hadn't bothered with the ones she could – but the Winnaran scanned them both with a handheld device anyway before saying, "This way."

"Let me do the talking when we get in there," Azad said.

"That is acceptable, as long as you say the right things," Severyne replied.

"OK!" Felix held up his hands. "I give in. You are the better negotiator. It's not my money, anyway. I just have to fight hard enough to keep my supervisor from yelling at me afterward. We have a deal."

"Fine," the Disciplinarian rumbled. "You don't care if I starve. And why should you? I am only a Hacan, and you – you are a human, most favored race of the galaxy. Though it grieves me to take such a loss, we have an agreement."

Felix cleared his throat. "Do you think you could, ah, invoice us for two percent more than we actually agreed? Just as a favor?"

"A favor?" The Disciplinarian looked at the N'orr, then looked at the Naalu, then looked back at Felix. "I don't know this word."

"He is describing a transaction where only *one* person gets something," Calred said.

"That doesn't sound right," the Disciplinarian said. He was clearly enjoying himself. "I will invoice you at two percent more, in exchange for one percent more. Calculated after the addition of the two percent, of course."

"But – that's – never mind. It's fine. It's good. Excellent." A Coalition officer who didn't skim a *little* was suspicious, so Felix had to get something, but the Disciplinarian was better at this sort of thing than he was.

"The exchange rate is really not in your favor today, unfortunately," Sagasa said. "Speak to my secretary on your way out – he's in the waiting room now, escorting my next appointment. He'll take your payment. Then you can pick up your new ship and let your scientist scrounge around in an unidentified vessel we bought years back from some long-range scrappers. My experts say it's millennia old and doesn't match anything in any known historical database. I bought the thing because I was intrigued, but as I said, there's nothing of any value there – what isn't fused into glass is completely inert, and I couldn't even sell the parts, since they aren't compatible with any known propulsion system."

"As long as there's weird stuff in there that looks really weird," Felix said.

"I am sure there is a good reason you need something like that. I am pleased that I have neither the need nor desire to know that reason. Good day, my friends."

Felix gave a little salute and turned away. That could have gone worse, he thought. This might even work. The doors slid open before him, and he led the way out of the office.

There were two people sitting on the bench they'd recently vacated, a human and a Letnev, and the Winnaran secretary loitered nearby. Felix nodded his head in a friendly greeting and smiled one of his default charming smiles – which froze on his face just as Calred said "Huh," and Tib said "Uh-oh."

She was wearing workout clothes instead of terrifying mercenary armor, which explained why he hadn't recognized her right away, but the human was Amina Azad, the operative who'd gotten the drop on him (before Tib got the drop on *her*), who'd subsequently escaped the custody of a raider fleet flagship, and who had apparently somehow tracked them *here*. But why ambush them in the waiting room? Why not hide in the debris field and –

Wait. The Letnev woman with her. *She* looked familiar too. She was the head of security from the Barony research facility. What was her name – Several? Severus? Severyne.

"That is an odd couple," Calred said, and then Severyne lost her shit.

She leapt from the bench with a roar, slapping her hand against her hip. For a moment she looked utterly bewildered, as she realized whatever weapon she'd reached for wasn't there. Felix was suddenly very grateful for the Disciplinarian's security measures.

Severyne was undaunted. She decided to take the direct approach, rushing at Felix and shouting what were presumably insults in her native tongue. Felix was OK not knowing exactly what she meant; he got the general idea. The Winnaran tried to restrain Severyne, but she did some fancy hand-to-hand combat thing, and the man was suddenly on his ass, looking around in a daze.

Felix tried to dodge out of her path, but he bounced off one of the guards, who was yelling too, and waving his halberd or whatever that thing was around. The other guard stepped forward to block the Letnev's attack – and she jumped, grabbed the polearm shaft in both hands, twirled around it, and kicked the guard in the knee.

The kick had absolutely no effect – the "knee" was an armored hydraulic mechanical joint, so it probably hurt the kicker more than the kickee, even through Severyne's shiny black boots – but the Letnev kept moving. Somehow her angle and momentum (and, possibly, the guard's shock at being attacked by an unarmed person half his size) allowed her to yank the polearm smoothly out of the guard's hand.

Now she was armed. With a bit of wood that had a pointy thing on the end, true – it was hardly a pulsed-energy rifle – but she was highly motivated. Felix could understand that.

He'd blown up her house and probably gotten her in a lot of trouble.

Felix jumped out of the way when she jabbed at him, only dimly aware of the rest of the fuss going on around him: the guards were trying to aim their weapons, but the secretary was stumbling around, dazed, in their field of fire. Severyne wasn't an easy target, dancing and spinning and whirling her polearm, progressing gradually toward Felix. She would have sliced him up, except she had to keep dodging the guards. Then the Naalu came slithering into the room, and the N'orr scuttled through, and the place was plunged into even deeper pandemonium. The Disciplinarian came out of his office, bellowing, "Stop this! Everyone stop *now*!" to no particular effect.

Felix did a diving roll to avoid a slash from Severyne's polearm, and ended up next to the other guard, who still had his ceremonial weapon. "Little help?" he said, and grabbed the weapon from a surprisingly unresisting hand. He swung the pole up and blocked one of Severyne's blows.

"So," he began, then stepped back as she jabbed at his face. She wasn't much for small talk either, apparently. Felix had done some fencing at the academy. This was not very much like fencing really, but there were a couple of commonalities: it was all about timing and distance. She was pressing the attack, and he couldn't change the tempo – she was coming at him furiously, and he was constantly on the defensive, barely blocking her blows, which fell hard enough to make his hands numb. She was backing him into an ivy-covered wall, so distance was going to be in short supply soon, too.

Beyond Severyne, Felix saw Azad sneak up behind Tib, and tried to shout a warning, but his cry was lost in the general shouting. Azad punched Tib in the back of the head and shouted, "How do *you* like it?" and then the N'orr snatched them both up in complex unfolding limbs. Calred was waving his arms around in front of the guards, who were trying to get a clear shot at Severyne, probably, but were, in the process, also taking aim in Felix's direction.

Felix tripped on a vine, lost his footing, and fell backward. Severyne stepped up to him and raised the polearm in both arms, spinning it so she could drive it down point-first into his body like a spear. Oh, this was going to *hurt* –

A huge paw plucked the weapon from her hands like it was a toothpick from a cocktail glass. The Disciplinarian grabbed Severyne by the back of her neck and lifted her bodily off the ground. She kicked and writhed and hissed furiously, and he gave her a little shake, at which point she stopped, hanging limply in his grasp, breathing hard.

"You have been very bad," the Disciplinarian said.

"That was some impressive hand-to-hand action," Azad said to Severyne. The N'orr crouched behind her, its front limbs on her shoulders, their serrated edges just brushing the sides of her neck. The Naalu stood behind Severyne, his own hands pressing down on her shoulders firmly. Felix thought they looked like interspecies couples posing for pictures at a Coalition formal military ball, except they all looked miserable.

As if she'd read his mind, Azad went on, saying, "We should go dancing sometime, Sev. I can only quibble with your choice of time and place to *deploy* your hidden skills–"

"Shut up," Severyne said. "You, Sagasa. I will give you my Letnev warship and all the money in my discretionary account if you turn these criminals over to me."

"Oh, babe," Azad said.

"You mean us criminals?" Felix was sitting in a chair – a decent one, brought into the office for the occasion – beside Calred. Tib was also seated, pressing a medpack to the back of her head where Azad had punched her. "*Us*? Criminals? You – you criminals!"

The Disciplinarian slammed his hands down on the desk. "I will negotiate almost anything, but I will not negotiate that. Can you imagine what would happen to my business if word got out that I sold visitors to my yard to their enemies? No one would come here any more. That means you'd have to offer me more money than I would make in the rest of my career before I'd even *consider* it." He paused, then lifted an eyebrow. "Are you? Offering me that much? Probably a few percent of the annual gross domestic product of the Barony would cover it, I think. I'd have to do some calculations."

"That is beyond my current resources. But if you hand them over, we can reach an accommodation–"

Sagasa sat back down. "I don't offer credit without collateral under the best of circumstances, and these aren't those." He swiveled his gaze. "You are in my bad books now, Amina. Why did you bring such a rude person to my place of business?"

"Call it a crime of passion, Sagasa. Duval's Devils are the deadliest bunch of renegade pirates and slavers in the sector

– they kidnapped Severyne's mother and husband and baby and sold them to the Embers of Muaat as a discount fuel source–"

"Oh, come *on*," Felix cried.

The Disciplinarian sighed. "Amina. You amuse me, as always. But I am not currently in a state in which I crave amusement. I abhor violence in my office, and my waiting room is next to my office. My secretary sees two fingers when I hold up one. Your associate cut down one of my plants. There will be consequences." He turned to Felix and his crew. "I apologize for the inconvenience. As recompense, I will give you that extra two percent on the invoice at no charge."

"That's very generous," Felix said.

Sagasa shrugged. "It's fine. They're going to pay for it." He gestured to Azad and Severyne. "I think our business is concluded, or nearly so. You can be on your way."

Felix cleared his throat. "The thing is, they're going to immediately chase us and try to kill us again, so…"

Sagasa chuckled. "Not *immediately*. Believe it or not, this Letnev isn't the first person to behave recklessly upon encountering someone they dislike on my station. We have a policy: we hold the aggressor in a secure room for a minimum of three hours. That gives those transgressed against time to get *out of my system*. If you want to fight after that, I don't mind, because you'll be doing it elsewhere. I suggest you make haste."

"We, ah, have to do that thing, though, with the stuff, before we go–"

The Disciplinarian nodded. "Of course. An hour for that

should be sufficient? I'll hold these naughty sapients for four hours, then."

"What thing with what stuff?" Azad said. "What are you even doing here, Duval?"

"We're just leaving." Felix sketched a salute to Severyne. "That was good spear-work. I hope we never meet again. And I am sorry about your people back on the station. We meant to leave more quietly than that."

"Human scum." Severyne looked like she wanted to spit, but she was better at containing herself now, with the Naalu's hands pressing down on her shoulders.

Calred and Tib said their farewells to Sagasa, and they all filed out.

"Duval's Devils," Felix said as they passed through the waiting room. "Kind of has a nice ring to it."

"I don't know," Tib said. "'Human scum' suits you pretty well too, don't you think?"

CHAPTER 18

The Disciplinarian escorted them to his brig personally, with one of the heavily armored guards along, just in case they got squirrely. Azad was a little worried Severyne *would* do something rash – again – but the Letnev woman seemed lost in her own thoughts.

Azad had to try. "Sagasa. Be reasonable. Just give us an hour. We barely even broke anything."

"You were the aggressors, Amina. We have rules here. You can leave in four hours. If you hurry, you can catch up with them… if you can figure out where they're going."

"Two hours. I'll bring back their ship for you as a gift after we capture them. It's a Mentak Coalition cruiser! Top of the line!"

"Maybe ten years ago it was."

"Still. It's a good trade, huh, for a couple of hours? You'll have to give me another ship in exchange, I can't *walk* out of here, but I'll take one of those junkers you can't offload."

"Would you like to stay for eight hours?"

"You jump from four to eight? That's a bit much. I thought you were a master negotiator."

"When one negotiates from a position of strength, one can be a bit unreasonable."

They reached the brig – not that it was really a brig, because this was a privately owned scrapyard, not a military ship or a local jail; those were the kind of places where Azad usually got locked up. There were just two cells here, the low-tech kind with metal bars, but the locks were too complicated to pick, especially with no tools except her teeth and fingernails. Low-tech was better than high-tech, in some cases. None of Azad's implants would do her any good here.

The guard opened the first cell door, and Azad stepped inside. He had to shove Severyne, who didn't stumble, but almost danced in as she caught her balance. That grace again. The cage door clanged shut, and the Hacan and his guard turned to leave.

Azad reached through the bars and snapped her fingers. "Hey, Sagasa, before you lock us up, can we at least talk *business*? We came here for a reason, and it wasn't getting into a fight with Duval's Devils."

The Hacan turned. "Ah. In all the disarray, I forgot you had a proposal. I am willing to hear it, if you still wish to proceed, because business comes first, but I hope you're prepared to be charged a penalty for making me get up from my chair."

"Severyne is really sorry about that. You know how the Letnev are. Hot-blooded and impetuous." Azad thought she could *hear* Sev grind her teeth behind her.

"That is indeed their reputation throughout the galaxy," the Disciplinarian said solemnly, and then chuckled. "You *do* amuse me, Amina. What did you want to sell, and more importantly, what do you want in return?"

They haggled and argued, and the Hacan pointed out more than once that Azad was in no *position* to argue, given that she was locked in a cell on a space station that might as well be his own sovereign nation... but Azad would never let a little thing like having no leverage stop her from advocating for her own interests. Eventually they reached an agreement: they'd get a fast and unobtrusive ship, in exchange for a not-that-modest financial consideration, and the *Grim Countenance* as collateral.

Once he was gone, Azad turned to Severyne. Her feelings had grown rather more complicated. She'd enjoyed teasing Severyne, liked her company, and found her attractive, but all that was just mental amusement. Seeing Severyne fight like that, her grace, her absolute conviction in the face of impossible odds... now Azad liked her, thought she was attractive, and *admired* her. She began to reconsider her stance against sleeping with people she might have to kill. Maybe there was a way to keep Severyne alive, and, if not, she could at least die with a happy memory, right? She put her hand on the Letnev's shoulder. "I know this seems bad, but really, we're not any worse off than we were before."

Severyne said nothing, staring at the wall beyond the bars, her forehead creased. Azad had seen that little line there before; it could be annoyance, hate, or deep thought, but it was definitely cute.

Azad put her back against the rear wall of the cell and settled in. It wasn't too disgusting a cell, as far as private dungeons went. She'd seen worse. "We made contact with the enemy and it didn't go our way, but that's just the way it is sometimes, and we're both alive. We didn't get eaten by Counselor An'Truk, we didn't get our arms ripped off by the guys in the exo-suits, and in a couple of hours we'll be on the trail again–"

"Your tracker didn't beep." Severyne's voice was even more devoid of emotion than usual.

"What's that?"

"This tracker in your head, that tells you when Thales is close. It *didn't beep.*" Severyne stood up from the bench, her hands balled into fists. "We were docked on the other side of a space station from him, he was *right there*, and you didn't know it!"

"They must have found the tracker and disabled it," Azad said. "I didn't think they would, but it wouldn't be the first time I underestimated Duval and his crew."

Severyne shook her head. "There was never any tracker at all, was there?"

"That is also a possible interpretation of the available information. Listen, Sev, don't be mad. I couldn't tell you the truth, because back then you didn't know me, but now you can see the truth: I don't need a tracking device, because I know Thales. I researched him thoroughly before my mission. Haven't I anticipated where he'd be *twice* now?"

"Once!" she shouted. "You predicted he'd come to *my* facility, and then you predicted he'd go to the Universities of Jol-Nar, but you did *not* predict that he would come *here*!"

"I must have known it *subconsciously* though." She tapped

her forehead. "There's a lot going on in here, all the time. I do wonder why they came here. Must be part of their plan to infiltrate the Universities."

"I am leaving you here." Severyne turned and stormed away, as far as you *could* storm in a cell that was only three meters square.

Azad cleared her throat. "Are you sure? The thing is, if you leave without the *Grim Countenance*, I'm going to have to take your ship for myself. I'll *have* to, because I have a mission here too. If you leave *with* the *Grim Countenance*, you have the same problem you had before: sailing a heavily armed Letnev ship to the Universities, and getting all the wrong kinds of attention in the process."

Severyne scowled. Oh, that line on her forehead. "I will simply warn the Hylar that they are the target of a gang of thieves."

"OK, let's game that out." Azad crossed her legs and leaned back. "Let's say they believe you. Let's say they believe you so much they agree to arrest Duval and company before they even commit a crime, with no proof apart from your word. Then the Hylar will have Duval in custody, along with Thales and Shelma. The Hylar aren't huge fans of the Barony. They aren't going to hand their prisoners over to you. They're big believers in due process, and their trials take forever, so even if you work out some kind of extradition agreement, which would be an impressive feat, it'll take ages. Or do you see it differently?"

Severyne didn't answer.

Azad made her voice softer. "Haven't I been helpful, Sev? Let me continue to help."

She could see the Letnev's practical side warring with her anger. In a human, the balance could have shifted either way, but Letnev culture was about suppressing the emotional in favor of the practical. "No more lies," Severyne said finally. She turned to look down at Azad. "Do not mislead me. Do not omit things. Be honest. I cannot make plans unless I am aware of all the factors."

"No lies at all? That's a pretty big tool you're taking out of my toolbox, Sev, but all right. For you. I am sorry I wasn't straight with you before. That thing about the tracker, it's the same way I had to tell the Disciplinarian some bullshit to get him to meet with us. I had to tell *you* some bullshit to get you to take me with you."

Severyne sat back down. "I understand your reasoning. We need speak of it no further."

Apology accepted, then. Azad managed not to grin. "Hey, I was really impressed by your moves back there." Severyne looked at her sharply, and Azad held up her hands. "Honestly! If Sagasa hadn't stepped in, you would've had Duval's heart on a stick."

"I trained for more than *just* sitting behind a desk," Severyne said. "I excelled at hand-to-hand combat training, and was invited to take advanced study. I noticed that you struck a blow of your own, against the hideous little creature who killed my sniper."

"I really hate her. I hate Duval more, because his face is so smug, but yeah, Tib Pelta is up there on the hate list."

Severyne seemed to struggle with something. Finally she said, "I must apologize. I behaved impetuously. If I had remained calm, we might have turned that chance meeting to our advantage. Or, at least, not suffered this delay. This is my fault."

"You did fine," Azad said. "In most circumstances, when you encounter your enemy at a moment when neither one of you expects contact, you *absolutely* move just the way you did – hit first and fast and hard. You can settle the whole situation right then, most of the time."

"At first I wanted to capture him," Severyne said. "To force him to give me Shelma. Then I thought, I could kill him and force his *crew* to give me Shelma. Insofar as I thought at all."

"I admit, when we first met, I thought you were a basic bureaucrat, and that if your workstation so much as got messy, you'd melt down. But you showed real badass instincts back there, Sev. It just happened to be a situation where a good offense *wasn't* the best idea, but that's not your fault."

"You have said this word, badass. I do not know it."

"It's the highest compliment I can offer, Sev. It means you're a lot like me."

"I am not at all like you," Severyne replied, but Azad noted there was no little hateline on her forehead that time.

Felix was babysitting Thales as he scrounged through the mysterious alien vessel, because Tib and Calred refused to spend any time with the man. When Felix tried to pull rank, Tib said, "I was *injured* in the line of *duty*," and Calred just pretended he couldn't hear Felix, making obviously fake static noises into his comms. That was gross insubordination, even by Mentak Coalition standards, but they'd all had a trying few days, so Felix let it go.

This ancient wrecked vessel didn't have any life support, and it had probably never supported their kind of life anyway, so Felix and Thales were in environment suits. The ship was an unsettling place, full of twisting dark corridors with walls that must have been some kind of metal or plastic, but that had an organic, swirled texture, like fingerprints. The corridors changed size gradually, sometimes contracting so small they had to go on hands and knees, other times dilating to nine or ten meters high. What kind of creatures would be comfortable in such a vessel? "This place is creepy," Felix said, shining his light into yet another empty corner of yet another empty and oddly proportioned room.

"*Still* afraid of ghosts?" Thales said in his comms. "I thought we went over that. Ah, here we are. An engine room. I bet there's something suitable here."

The new chamber was the biggest yet, and it was, at least, less bare – there were dangling cables and wires; things like gearwheels, except they were triangular; a huge crankshaft that floated, unconnected in the lack of gravity; and various smaller bits of machinery, variously sprouting blackened crystals, surrounded by transparent globes, or with overlapping loops of material that made Felix's head hurt when he tried to trace all their intersections. "A completely unknown species built this thing, so long ago your ancestors weren't even in jail yet," Thales said. "Those creatures made this ship, they traveled in it, they abandoned it or wrecked it, and some wandering idiots found it millennia later and towed it back here because they thought it might be worth a credit or two. It all makes you feel insignificant, doesn't it?"

"I guess we are pretty small, measured against the vastness of everything," Felix agreed.

"What?" Thales said. "No. I mean, it must make *you* feel insignificant. Which you are. *I'm* not insignificant. I'm the man who invented wormhole technology. No one in the galaxy will ever forget *my* name, unlike the pathetic fools who built this thing. I was musing on my own immortal greatness, captain. Do try to keep up."

"Right. How foolish of me."

"Even a fool has his uses." Thales picked up one of the crystal-encrusted things, a device or component about the size of two fists put together. "This should do. It doesn't look like anything I've seen before, and a matching scan through the available databases doesn't turn up anything similar."

"The Disciplinarian said it's worthless, though."

"Oh, probably – it certainly seems inert. But it *is* genuinely alien, and it's unlike any other artifact that's been publicly logged. Mere novelty is not enough, on its own, to interest Director Woryela, but that's where the fakery comes in. I'll use this as the basis to create something truly enigmatic and alluring."

"Woryela?"

"The person you're going to *scam*, captain. Head of the experimental research and development division, propulsion section. You should really read those dossiers Calred compiles for you."

"I know his name," Felix said. "I didn't realize *you* did."

"Oh, I used to work at the Universities. I'm not up on all the latest gossip, but I know the major players." He turned toward Felix. "We should go. It's disturbing to have this

Azad woman so nearby, even if she is in a cell. She has a tendency to escape those, as I recall?"

"She probably could escape. I don't think she will, though. She doesn't want to piss off the Disciplinarian."

"How did Azad find us? You assured me there were no tracking devices on Shelma or myself."

"There was one on Shelma, but we neutralized it. We didn't detect any on you, and we did a pretty deep scan. The thing is, I don't think they *did* find us. They seemed as surprised as we were."

"It's a big galaxy, captain. To suggest that our meeting is coincidence rather strains credulity."

"It *is* a big galaxy, yes, but it's not that big a sector. In this particular region of space, there's only one person you go to if you need an untraceable ship, and that's Sagasa. They're after us, and clearly needed something from Sagasa to help catch us. I wish I knew what."

"I'm sure your brilliant military mind will unravel the puzzle," Thales said. "Or, more likely, there was a tracking device, and you just missed it."

"Your confidence means everything to me, Thales."

CHAPTER 19

Felix and Tib floated in space in the cloud of wrecked ships, inspecting the exterior of the vessel Sagasa had loaned them. Calred was on the *Temerarious*, helping Thales pack his notes and equipment, which he understandably refused to leave behind.

The *Endless Dark* was a far smaller vessel than the *Temerarious*, meant for longrange travel and exploration, not battle. This little ship had gone a long way and come back whole, though the same couldn't be said about its original crew.

"I think it looks like a bird wearing a tiara," Felix said.

"That tiara is all its sensors. You want a lot of sensors in a ship meant for exploring, captain."

"I know what it is. I just think it looks stupid."

"The *Temerarious* looks like a fat fish with tusks." Tib put her hands on either side of her mouth and hooked fingers into fangs.

Felix snorted. The *Temerarious* had a big belly of a cargo hold, and its fore cannons *were* a bit tusk-like. "I always say our ship reminds me of a shark, but that's just me being poetic. Now that you mention it, I can see the similarity to a walrus. While I'm complaining, what about this *name*? '*Endless Dark*' is a little bit ominous for a ship meant to go out into deep space and come back with riches, don't you think?"

"You're just uncultured, captain," Tib said. "'Endless Dark' is a Letnev idiom. It means the same thing my people mean when we say 'unbroken canopy.'"

"Oh. Well. That clears it up."

"I think you'd say 'the sky's the limit?' If you're Letnev, endless dark is a *good* thing, just like for my people, an unbroken canopy means you're safely under cover of the trees as far as you can see, and free to go where you like without fear."

"Oh. Thanks, Tib. That makes me feel better."

"That's the most important part of my job as first officer. Do you want to check the interior, and I'll finish looking over the exterior?"

Felix concurred and went into the ship. They had to look the vessel over quickly, just keeping an eye out for major, likely-to-kill-them-all-in-transit-level problems, because they were on a ticking clock. Severyne and Azad would be coming after them in just a couple of hours. He didn't think the Disciplinarian would tell the duo which way Felix and his crew had gone, or in what kind of vessel, but Azad had somehow tracked his crew here, and they might pursue them to the Universities, too. *Just what you want in a heist: extra time pressure.*

The interior of the ship was cramped by the standards of

the *Temerarious*, but they'd manage, and the life support, engine, and other functions all checked out green. There wasn't much in the way of weaponry on board, but where they were going, weapons wouldn't help much anyway.

"It looks good in here." Felix sat in the cockpit. There was a little plastic figurine of a Xxcha in war armor glued over the control panel, which he recognized as a character from an adventure sim popular a decade before. A stab of melancholy went through Felix as he looked at that little personal object, put there by a crew that had set out for adventure and riches and had come back, diminished, to sell the remnants of their dream to a scrapper. He looked out the bulbous viewport at the dead ships hanging all around him and suppressed a shudder. A lot of broken dreams ended up here. "How do things look on your end, Tib?"

"I don't see any great big cracks in the hull," Tib said. "I'd like to check things over more thoroughly, but I don't think we'll die as soon as we turn the engines on or anything."

"This ship went all the way to the fringes of the galaxy and made it back," Felix said. "That gives me comfort."

"That's completely irrational, but I'm glad it makes you feel better, captain."

"I just mean, if the ship has worked this long, it's probably fine, right?"

"Everything works, right up until the moment it stops working," Tib said.

"I'm trying to remain optimistic here. Go get Thales and Cal, would you?"

"Aye aye."

Felix powered up the ship. Once he was confident

the systems were humming properly, he stripped off his environment suit and sat down in the cockpit again to lay in a course.

Sagasa had assured him the ship had been thoroughly cleaned and bathed in sanitizing light, but there was a small, dark smear on the side of the navigation console. It looked distressingly like blood. Another little personal touch left behind by the former crew.

Optimism, Felix thought.

The *Endless Dark* didn't really have a bridge, so once they were underway the crew met in the galley, which was just about big enough for the four of them, if they didn't mind their elbows touching; this ship had originally held a crew of three.

Calred dished out bowls of nutritious protein glop, and Felix dutifully ate. Mostly what he wanted was sleep and a shower. Those would come next. He slurped the last bit of slurry off his spoon and said, "This is an official mission briefing. Sagasa was kind enough to provide us with fake identities, belonging to real explorers who, in reality, are still out there somewhere exploring." *Or dead.* "I'm Heuvelt Angriff, swashbuckling outcast scion of a wealthy family, spendthrifting my inheritance on expeditions to uncharted regions of space. Tib, you're Dob Ell, my loyal family retainer and all-purpose adjunct and helpmeet."

"I'm your what now?" Tib said flatly.

"I know, I know, but it was tough to find ID that made sense for a crew made up of a couple of humans, an Yssaril, and a Hacan, OK?"

"Who am I, then?" Calred said.

"You're Ferocious Naadin, deep-space guide for hire, Hacan of a thousand talents."

"I like it."

"I hate mine even more now," Tib said.

"Swashbuckling. Loyal. Talented. Ha," Thales said. "Who am I, then? An applecheeked maiden you rescued from space pirates?"

"You're nobody. Sagasa got you a flimsy ID, but it doesn't have to stand up to scrutiny – you're just a passenger we picked up on Vega Minor, and we're transporting you to your next destination for money. We don't know you, or anything much about you. You'll be staying on the ship, so the Universities won't take as close a look at your ID anyway."

"Calred is staying on the ship too," Thales pointed out. "And *he* got a fancy bespoke identity."

"Yes, but Calred would have felt left out if I didn't include him," Felix said.

"You don't care if *I* feel left out?"

"We would all prefer to leave you out, Thales," Tib said.

"I'd like to leave you out in the desert," Calred said. "Perhaps tied to wooden stakes."

Thales showed his teeth in what could not accurately be called a smile. "The contempt of simpletons is as good as the praise of geniuses." He stood up. "I'm going to go finish faking your wondrous mysterious artifact, unless you need me to sit and listen to further prattle?"

"Go on," Felix said.

The whole crew relaxed when he left. "Is he *really* going

to walk free and be wealthy when this is all done?" Tib said.

Felix sighed. "If he delivers wormhole tech to the Coalition, they'll probably put up a statue to him in the Plaza of Heroes on Moll Primus."

"He's a murderer," Calred said. "We know it, and we might even be able to prove it."

"Several of our most illustrious ancestors in the Coalition were murderers."

"That was then, and this is now," Tib said. "Thales had us kidnap Shelma just so he could kill her and steal her stuff."

"The Coalition has a whole raider fleet devoted to killing people and stealing their stuff."

"That's not fair," Calred said. "The raider fleets only kill people who make trouble or can't follow instructions. Thales is something else entirely."

"I don't disagree with you," Felix said. "I'm just saying what the Table of Captains will say to justify shrugging off any allegations we bring them."

"He only wins if he succeeds," Tib said.

"I know. I've thought of sabotaging things too, for the pleasure of seeing Thales fail. But what he can offer is too important to the Coalition."

"His success would be good for us, too," Calred said. "We'll have more promotions and bonuses than we know what to do with if we bring this thing home."

"That's why I haven't stabbed him in the neck yet, personally," Tib said. "My selfinterest is stronger than my him-hate."

"That's the Mentak Coalition way," Felix said.

"I'll be glad when we're done with the part where we earn

our rewards," Calred said, "and get to the part where we can start enjoying them instead."

Felix sent a message to the Universities, knowing it would probably take a while to navigate the necessary layers of bureaucracy to reach director Woryela. He used all the key phrases that Thales fed him: "previously unknown technology," "unidentifiable chemical signature," and, "produces energy without a discernible source," the last to appeal to the director's professional as well as personal interests.

He included some pictures and video of the crystal-studded machinery; the crystals glowed pale blue now, thanks to something Thales had done, but insisted wasn't poisonous or radioactive. Felix also sent a bunch of graphs and charts of diagnostic data that meant nothing to him but that Thales assured him would make any Hylar scientist drool, or whatever the squid equivalent was. "We have a paying passenger at the moment, so we don't have time for endless meetings," Felix's message concluded, "but if we can have an initial meeting with someone high up – the head of the propulsion lab seems like the obvious choice – who can determine whether what we have is valuable, we can make a deal. If you're too busy, we have a contact in the Barony who's willing to see us next week. We're in your neighborhood, though, and we're eager to recoup the costs of our expedition as soon as possible." He hoped that last bit added the right note of desperation to make Woryela think he could snag a bargain.

Then Felix went to sleep, for the first time in what felt like days, as the *Endless Dark* cruised through its namesake.

The ship roused him a couple of hours out from the Jol-Nar system. He'd missed their passage through the wormhole on their route – Calred had handled the transition – which struck him as funny, considering the overall nature of their mission. He yawned and checked the system, where he found a reply from Woryela himself: "We're very interested in appraising your find. I can spare a little time tomorrow morning if you can make it to Wun-Escha," with an invitation to digitally accept the appointment.

Tomorrow morning. Felix checked the local time and groaned. He had to wait another fifteen hours before they could meet. That was probably considered swift by academic standards, but right now it felt like eternity. He accepted the appointment, then met with Calred and Tib. "I don't like it. Azad and Severyne will have plenty of time to catch up with us. Are you *sure* there isn't a tracking device on Thales?"

Calred sighed. "I did everything short of a cavity search, and I only skipped that because it's not necessary with my scanning equipment. There's nothing inside that man he wasn't born with, except gallstones. Azad and Sagasa clearly knew each other from some past business. She was probably just there to buy a ship to chase us with, or weapons to kill us with."

"They *had* a ship, though – Severyne said she'd trade the Disciplinarian a Letnev warship in exchange for us. Why trade down?"

"Why did *we*?" Tib said. "Those thorny Letnev ships are distinctive. Maybe they wanted to be more subtle."

Felix pondered, then opened comms. "Thales, is there

any way Amina Azad could know we're heading to the Universities of Jol-Nar?"

"Of course there's a way," Thales said. "She didn't strike me as much of an intellectual, but she had some time with my files, and she may have looked over them."

Felix closed his eyes. "You're saying your files mentioned the need for this power source?"

"I did say that, and see no need to say it again. I'm *working*." The channel closed.

The crew sat in silence for a moment, then Tib said, "There are only two of them. Three of us. We've got the numbers."

"Severyne will have others with her," Felix said. "She's a supervisor, so she's going to be supervising people. Guards from her station, who will be eager to see us again, since we left a few of their colleagues dead back there."

"I'm worth two of any of her guards in a fight," Calred said.

"Let's hope she only brought two, then," Felix said. "We might be OK. They don't know what ship we're in. We're under assumed names. The Hylar system is bustling. We'll be tough to find."

"Unless they go straight to the experimental propulsion lab," Tib pointed out. "Which is exactly where they will go, if they read the files, which we have to assume they did."

"We'll just have to be extra vigilant," Felix said.

"Oh, well. *That* will make a nice change from our current atmosphere of total relaxation," Calred drawled.

"Give me some good news," Felix said. "Tell me the ship found proof that Thales murdered Shelma."

Calred tapped his fingertip on a tablet. "The ship is

running screens, and has ruled out one-hundred-and-sixty-two known toxins, poisons, and chemicals so far. There are lots to go."

"You're free to go." The Disciplinarian's Winnaran secretary opened the cell door. His headdress sat askew because of the lumpy bandage fastened to the back of his skull.

"Your head injury was regrettable," Severyne said. "You should not have attempted to restrain me."

"That was not an apology," he said.

"It sure wasn't." Azad stood from the bench and stretched. "But she's from the Barony. It's about the best you're going to get."

They followed the Winnaran along the station's corridors. "We have to hurry," Severyne said. "We need to get my sidearm, gather my guards, board whatever heap the Disciplinarian has seen fit to saddle us with, and burn as fast as we can for the Jol-Nar system. With luck Duval and his devils will still be there, and if not, we can try to pick up their trail–"

"I was thinking about that, while you were napping," Azad said. "I know you're all hot to chase after them, and I get it, but how about if instead, we don't?"

"What are you talking about? Our very lives and futures depend on recovering Shelma and Thales!"

"I don't know about 'lives.' I'd have to go rogue, and never return home, but the Federation navy invested a lot of effort teaching me how to disappear completely, and I have marketable skills, so I'd survive. I'd prefer not to live that way, though, and at this point, it's gotten personal – I *do* want to settle my score with Duval and his sucker-punching sidekick. I'm not saying give up. I'm suggesting we approach the problem in a different way."

"What did you have in mind?" Severyne asked.

"I'm still working out the details. Let me work out some more of them." She trotted ahead to walk beside the secretary. "Hey! Let me talk to you for a minute. Remember me from last time I was here, when we made that little side arrangement? Maybe we can help each other again..."

CHAPTER 20

The twin planets Jol and Nar hung in the viewscreen, blue spheres against the black, shining in the light of their local star. "I've never been here," Felix said. "But it's your home. Are you sad you won't be landing?"

Thales sat in the co-pilot's chair. He grunted. "Not really." He gazed quite fixedly at the planets in the viewscreen, though, Felix noted. The man wasn't totally incapable of human feeling; he'd just buried whatever good impulses he had beneath meters of resentment and grievance and grudge. "I grew up on Nar. The waters are warm enough to swim in without freezing your testicles off, which is more than can be said about Jol. There's even an archipelago – off-worlders call it the Reef; you couldn't pronounce the Hylar name for it. My family spent a lot of time there, since it's one of the only places hospitable to air-breathers. Some of my only good memories are from those days."

Felix tried to imagine Thales having a happy day at the seaside with his family. It was like trying to imagine a moray eel reciting poetry. Still, this side of the man was interesting, and might even yield useful information, so Felix kept listening.

"I began my studies in Nuun-Dascha – that's where I met Shelma. The greatest city on Nar, and the whole place is a school, really, surrounded by businesses and workers who support or provide for the scholars."

"What's the city like?"

"It's ancient. Not made for human comfort. There are great coral towers, though, dating from the days when the Hylar had to hide from predators, before they mastered the seas, and because humans like having roofs, the off-worlder dormitories were in those towers. I counted as an off-worlder, though I'd spent my life in the Jol-Nar system. The halls were cramped, with corridors designed for creatures who don't have bones. The locals never made much of an effort to provide for the comfort of other species. The idea was, we were lucky to be allowed to study at the greatest institution of higher learning in the galaxy, and if we didn't like it, we were welcome to go elsewhere. The hell of it is, they were right – the Universities are unmatched, at least in the sciences, which are the only fields of study that actually matter. Oh, there are embassies and businesses with domes and such that hold atmosphere, but those are meant for dignitaries and tourists, not students." Thales seemed to realize he'd been talking for a while, because he scowled. "None of that matters. You aren't going to Nar, anyway. You're going to Jol. A world of frigid seas, with a few islands no one would want to live on. The city *you're* going to is Wun-Escha, and it is admittedly more welcoming for off-worlders, since it's the seat of government, where the

Hylar leader the Headmaster lives, and they get so many diplomatic and trade delegations from elsewhere. There's a whole section of the city with an atmosphere hospitable to humans and several other species of airbreathers. You won't even get a momentary sense of what my life down there was like."

No one can possibly understand my suffering – the cry of every aggrieved adolescent, even Felix himself, once upon a time... But like most people, he'd grown out of it. "Why doesn't Woryela work in the other city, if that's where the schools are?"

"Plenty of scientists work for the experimental propulsion lab, captain. I did myself, once upon a time. But it's not an academic setting in the way you're thinking – it's better to think of it more as a military installation than the sort of training academies or scholastic institutions you're familiar with."

"I was a lot happier about stealing something from a university than a military base, Thales."

"I'm sure you were. I've given you everything you need, though. More than you need. Woryela's office is near the labs, and there are only a few places the power source could be. Once you're with him in the office and you deploy my surprise, you'll have all the time you need for your slippery friend to search for the power source."

Felix nodded. Thales had come up with a good idea, he had to admit. Woryela was one of the Hylar who could breathe air for weeks at a time, and he was meeting them in his office, where the atmosphere was conducive to their biology as well – visiting researchers came there from all over, after all. The mysterious alien artifact now had a small reservoir inside, and when Woryela handled it, it would disperse a sedative and dissociative gas designed to work on the Hylar – he'd pass out, and wake up an hour later with no memory, or at best a confused one, and by then, Felix and Tib would be long gone.

Felix had found the idea of using gas absurd – "Won't we be underwater?" But Thales had called him an idiot and said Woryela would doubtless meet them in a room with air: "He won't risk examining a potentially delicate alien artifact in a submerged zone. Water can be too damaging. Woryela is the sort of Hylar who can breathe the same air you do, too, so he won't be in a tank or anything – those are cumbersome and avoided when possible. I *have* thought this through."

Felix had other concerns, though. "Are you sure the gas won't affect us?"

"Did you steal a Hylar's nervous system at some point?"

"Not the last time I checked."

"Then you'll be fine. The gas may not smell very nice, but it won't hurt you."

"OK. How do I look?" Felix was wearing adventurer garb: black tactical pants and a vest covered in pouches, his head topped by a battered broad-brimmed hat he thought looked rather dashing.

"Like an idiot, but like the kind of idiot you *should* look like."

"Good enough."

Director Woryela sent a shuttle to pick them up, and Tib

and Felix sat together, strapped into their respective seats, as they plummeted bouncily through the atmosphere. Felix hadn't felt planetary gravity in a while, and it was more intense than the artificial kind. His lower back ached. When had *that* happened? That seemed like something that should happen to people older than he was.

Felix felt the splash when they hit the water, and heard a hum as the engines kicked in. From orbit to the bottom of the sea. Quite a journey. "It's exciting, visiting the Hylar homeworld. One of the great cities of the galaxy, down there below us somewhere."

"If you say so," Tib muttered. "Who am I to disagree? I'm just a humble loyal retainer." She wore a version of Felix's outfit, with a rucksack strapped to her chest. The bag contained the fake artifact and the other thing Thales had made for them.

"I haven't even asked you to polish the silverware or pour me some tea. You're getting off easy. Honestly, I think of our staff like *family*, don't you know. Let's take a look at the view. Shuttle, let's have some windows, please."

Rectangles all around them went transparent, or rather, created a convincing illusion of transparency; they were screens connected to external cameras. Felix had expected to see schools of brightly colored fish, vast coral structures, or maybe a kelp forest; instead there was just dim, murky water, and as they descended, their surroundings became indistinguishable from darkest night. "Oh," he said. "No light down here."

"Space is brighter than this," Tib said. "Ugh."

"Shuttle, what's underneath us?"

This time the whole interior of the shuttle went transparent, like they were in a glass bowl. Darkness surrounded them. "Wow. Shouldn't we have some kind of safety gear? Life vests or air tanks or something?"

"At this depth, if we got out of this shuttle, our lungs wouldn't be able to expand against the crushing pressure, and we'd promptly die, so no, there's not much point in safety gear."

"You are very bad for morale, Tib."

"We loyal retainers do what we can."

After a while, lights glimmered beneath them, dim and far away, like distant stars. "That must be Wun-Escha."

"Or else the bioluminescent bulbs of deep-sea predators trying to lure prey into their nightmare maws."

"Or that," Felix said.

The lights gradually brightened, revealing domed structures and organic coral towers, and soon they passed other vehicles, smooth and streamlined and aerodynamic – or, Felix wondered, was it aquadynamic? Their shuttle zipped along, and Felix was surprised at how fast it moved, now that he could gauge their progress by the city whipping past beneath them. They sailed between two towers, and through windows (he hoped very thick ones), Felix could see off-worlders, living and working in their pockets of air so far below the world above. How strange it would be, to live in a place like this... but then, was it any stranger than living in space, like he did? Space and the sea were both vast and inhospitable and rather chilly environments that would kill you if you didn't have the right equipment. At least down here there weren't micrometeoroid impacts or radiation.

Though in space there weren't toothy underwater predators, and you might suffocate, but you wouldn't drown. There were always trade-offs.

The shuttle docked at a sprawling but low facility, a series of cylinders and domes hugging the seafloor. "I thought the lab would be bigger," Felix said.

"I think it's mostly underground."

"Oh, good. I was thinking we weren't far enough down yet. We'd better get suited up." They fastened on their helmets and checked their air supplies.

The doors hissed open, revealing a – well, not an *airlock*. A water-lock? Some system to equalize the pressure with the submerged areas beyond, anyway. They stepped into the cylindrical chamber, and once the ship was closed behind them, water slowly filled the space. The heaters in their environment suits clicked on to compensate.

Once the lock was filled with water, the outer door opened, revealing a clean white room. A Hylar, slightly smaller than Tib, waited for them, floating in the faintly green-tinged water and holding a glowing tablet in one thin pseudopod. Felix had gotten so used to Shelma in her exo-suit that it was strange to see a Hylar unencumbered. "Mx Angriff?" she said on their open comms channel. "And Mx Ell. Let me help you." She offered them each mobility packs that strapped onto their suits, and showed them how to use the controls to adjust their buoyancy and propel themselves forward and back with jets of water. Felix spun himself around in a circle at first, but got the idea fairly quickly. She attached visitor passes, little round badges in bright orange, to their chests with some adhesive. "Keep these visible at all times. They'll allow you to leave the facility once the meeting is over."

"You won't be escorting us out?" Felix said.

"It's a busy day," she called. "Don't worry, the badges will only open the doors necessary to lead you back to the shuttle, which is programmed to return you to your ship after you board. The badges also track your location, of course, so there's no danger of you getting lost in here."

Felix glanced at Tib, who shrugged infinitesimally. They had restricted access and this was a place full of security doors, but they'd expected that. Tib would figure out a way to work around the problem. Felix hoped.

"Come along. The director carved out an hour for you, and that hour has already started." The Hylar approached a round door, which opened to reveal a textured tunnel with walls of white coral. Branching corridors appeared at irregular intervals, some open, others sealed with formidable-looking metal doors. There were no windows, and Felix was grateful he didn't have claustrophobia, as the tunnels were made for Hylar physiology, and fairly tight for someone his size.

They reached a security checkpoint with a guard – a Hylar bristling with needle-like extensions that must have been weapons – and floated through into a sea cave lit by bioluminescent orbs stuck to the walls. Their guide turned and left them without a word, and a Hylar at the center of the room glanced up at them and said, "Wait." She was operating three terminals at once with six pseudopods.

Why does no one ever offer me refreshments? Felix wasn't sure how that would work underwater, but still, it would have been a nice gesture. And I thought we were already late for our very brief appointment?

After a few moments, the receptionist paused in her work, in response to no stimulus that Felix could detect, and said, "Director Woryela is waiting for you. Go on up."

"Up?"

Tib nudged Felix and pointed up. The ceiling was a shimmering circle. They adjusted their buoyancy and rose, breaking through the top of the pool into air. They clambered out into a sort of conference room, though one where the floor was dotted with other pools, presumably giving access to other parts of the facility.

A Hylar perched on a stool behind a long table, wearing a sort of headband that held a complex array of lenses on adjustable arms. "Welcome! You can take off your helmets. The air in here can sustain you."

Felix removed his helmet and set it on the table, sniffing cautiously at the briny but breathable atmosphere. "Thank you, ah, Director Woryela?"

"Indeed! And you are Heuvelt Angriff and Dob Ell!" His artificial voice was booming and hearty. "Back from the depths of space with bountiful mystery! How I envy you, dauntlessly exploring the vast unknown!"

Felix had expected a calm and measured academic, or a humorless bureaucrat, but Woryela was positively jolly, and he wasn't sure how to respond.

The Hylar could tell. "Not what you were expecting, eh?" he said. "I always get that – too much energy, too much verve, for someone in a position like mine. But I got here because I'm good at my job, not because I'm good at playing politics. What was my job, do you know?" That look must be Hylar for "expectant."

"Ah, propulsion?" Felix said.

"That's right, Heuvelt, may I call you Heuvelt? I always get mixed up on human honorifics. I come from *propulsion*! Before I moved into the technical side, I was a test pilot. I used to spend more time in the void than I did in the ocean, strapping untested technology to a seat and launching myself as far and fast as I could. Experimental propulsion is the most exciting discipline we've got, as far as I'm concerned – anything that can propel a starship faster than any other starship has ever gone before also has a good chance of exploding or turning your body inside out. There's no substitute for that kind of thrill. That's half of why I met with you, and cleared a whole hour – the artifact is interesting, of course, and if it does half what you say, we'll pay well for it – but it's really for the chance to spend time with other people who *understand*. That's a real treat. The people who work for me, they're good at what they do, the best in the galaxy, but I never get to talk to the rocket jockeys any more. That life never get old, does it? I miss those days."

"We, ah, appreciate you having us," Felix said. "It's true, there's nothing like feeling the hum of a starship accelerating as you blast into the uncharted. That's what Dob and I live for." A sudden impulse seized him. "I heard rumors you were working on harnessing wormhole technology here, though – that would make most forms of propulsion pretty redundant, wouldn't it?"

The Hylar shook his head. "Wormhole tech, perpetual motion machines, mind uploading and digital immortality

– there are always rumors that we're about to achieve those, but we're not. All that stuff is impossible, and, I for one, am glad, because overcoming engineering challenges is a lot more fun than waving a magic wand and poof, every difficulty is overcome."

"They say the Creuss can open wormholes, though," Tib said.

"They say the Creuss can kill you in your dreams, too. They say the Creuss can turn into mist, and if you breathe that mist they can possess your body and use you like a puppet. They say lots of things." He swiveled on his stool. "I won't say making wormholes is impossible. Once upon a time, there were Hylar in these seas who didn't even know there *was* a surface, let alone anything beyond – the ocean was their whole universe. They didn't know we had a sister planet, or that there was such a thing as outer space, or a whole community of intelligent alien species. Now, there are Hylar all over the galaxy. But I will say, I think we're as far from having wormhole technology right now as those ancient Hylar were from building their first starship. We've had a couple of researchers over the years who thought they'd cracked the wormhole problem, but they never convinced me, and they don't seem to have accomplished much without me. In the meantime, I'm happy enough with what we *can* do. But maybe you brought me something impossible today! Shall we take a look?"

CHAPTER 21

Felix nodded to Tib, who opened the airtight carrying case she wore across her chest, removed their "artifact," and placed it in on the table.

The Hylar picked up the crystal assemblage with delicate pseudopods, and some of the lenses on his face rearranged themselves. "Interesting. These crystals could be part of the original specification, but they're more likely caused by chemical leakage, or the side effect of some process gone wrong. This glow looks like... huh. It appears to be a simple luminescent gloss, of the sort that fades over time. This paint isn't nearly as old as the rest of this object appears to be – in fact, I recognize it as a variety produced here on Hylar. People paint it on their windows during the Festival of Luminous Depths." He looked up at them, his eyes magnified by the lenses. "Gentlepersons, I hope you haven't wasted my time with some amateurish attempt at a hoax–"

The device abruptly cracked open, breaking into two unequal halves, and a tightly rolled piece of paper slipped out. "What's this? A message from the ancient aliens, written conveniently in a language I can read? Really, Heuvelt and Dob, this is disappointing." He unrolled the paper and stared at it, lenses telescoping.

Felix looked at Tib. What the hell was going on?

"'Courtesy of Phillip Caruthers,'" Woryela read. "What, that man who published those absurd papers about a theory of everything? What is the meaning of this –"

Gas began to hiss from the sundered device, and Felix instinctively held his breath. Thales had claimed the artifact wouldn't hurt them, but he also hadn't mentioned his plan to include a personal note for the director. Felix waited for Woryela to slump over and pass out, but instead the Hylar gasped and writhed, limbs spasming wildly, knocking the artifact off the table. Woryela fell off the stool and looked up at them, lenses askew, eyes somehow pleading. He tried to crawl to the door, then shuddered all over again, and slumped.

Tib knelt and looked the Hylar over. "He's not unconscious, Felix. He's dead."

Of course he was. Felix clutched his helmet. "Thales. He *used* us, and we – Tib, we just assassinated a high-ranking official! We committed murder!"

"We were used as murder weapons, anyway." Tib scooped up the artifact and put it away in the case. "Wrestle with the implications later, captain. We need to finish the mission and get out of here."

Of course. Bad as this was, getting caught wouldn't make it any better. Felix found the note from Thales and shoved it in a pouch on his suit. No reason to leave any evidence behind.

"You stay here," Tib said. "I'll go look for the power cell. We've come this far." She opened the bag and removed a small spherical device, half matte black, half crystal. It was, Thales claimed, a perfect replica of the power source they were stealing – not functional, of course, but with a mess of fused wire inside that might fool the engineers into thinking the device had merely malfunctioned, at least for a while. The original plan was, Tib would take the real cell and replace it with the fake one, and when Woryela woke up in a confused daze, no one would even know a robbery had taken place.

Tib searched the director's body until she found a badge and held it up. "Our key to victory. Let's hope the plans Thales drew up are accurate. I don't want to get lost down here." She peered into different pools, finally settling on one in the far corner that should lead to the deeper labs, then put on her helmet and dropped out of sight.

That left Felix, sitting there with a cooling body, desperately hoping the receptionist wouldn't decide *now* was the time to offer him a drink, that no emergency would occur that required the director's urgent assistance, and that no Hylar heads would pop out of any of the pools of water all around him. He put on his helmet and listened to his own heavy breath in his ears.

Felix wondered what slight, real or imagined, the director had committed against Thales. Woryela had called the man a lunatic – an assessment that seemed more accurate the longer Felix knew him. That comment Woryela had made, about people who'd come to him over the years talking about wormhole technology – was that about Thales? Had he tried to get Woryela's support and failed, been laughed out of the office, and nursed a grudge for all these years?

How long before Thales tried to kill Felix? Maybe never. Maybe he didn't think Felix was important enough to kill. That thought should have been more comforting than it was.

Tib reappeared, from a different pool this time, and spoke on a private comm channel. "We're all set. The layout was just like Thales described, and the power cell was in one of the first places he suggested I look."

Felix was impressed. "That didn't take you long."

"I only saw one Hylar, and they didn't see me. There were security doors to deal with, but this got me through all of them." She held up Woryela's badge.

"Maybe we should hold on to that, in case we have trouble getting out," Felix said. He tried to focus on the logistics of getting safely away, so he wouldn't focus instead on the coil of rage and hate he felt for Phillip Thales. Thales may have killed Shelma himself, albeit with Felix's unwitting help, but this time, like Tib said, he'd actually used Felix as a murder weapon.

Felix and Tib stepped into the pool, adjusted their mobility units, and submerged. The receptionist glanced up, surprised, as they floated down. "Done already?"

Felix realized they hadn't used up their hour. This had been both easier and far more horrifying than he'd anticipated. "Our ancient alien artifact is a hunk of useless junk," Felix said. "At least the director broke the news to us gently. He said at least now he had a free half hour to catch up on his reading."

"Oh, that's too bad," she said. "He was so excited to meet you. Better luck next time."

"We appreciate it." Felix and Tib exited the room into the tunnel beyond, giving a little wave to the spiny guard, who ignored them. Their visitor badges gave them brief audible directions, leading them through the rounded tunnels back to their shuttle. The trip back seemed to take much longer than the trip in. If the receptionist popped her head into the conference room and found the director unresponsive, would the facility get locked down? Would Felix and Tib be tried for murder in the slow-but-inexorable court system of Jol-Nar? Would anyone believe them if they named Phillip Thales as the mastermind and claimed to be unwitting pawns? *We're not guilty, Headmaster, we're just gullible fools?*

They reached the shuttle without incident. Once they boarded and strapped in, Felix said, "I just realized: if the real Heuvelt and Dob ever come back from their trip, they'll be wanted for murder."

"Maybe Sagasa can sell them new identities," Tib said. "I'm more troubled by the fact that we're *actual* accessories to the crime. This can't go on, Felix. We can't just keep helping Thales fulfill his various vendettas. He's going to send us to kill some editor who rejected one of his papers next at this rate, claiming he needs his kidneys to build a filtration system or something."

"I'm going to… I don't know what, Tib. Speak sharply to him, I guess. What can I do? Jhuri won't let me summarily execute the man. I can't even hit him in the head without risking damage to his valuable brain."

"I'm just registering my displeasure, captain."

"It's noted. And shared."

They were near the surface of the ocean – light beginning to faintly shine from above – when the shuttle stopped, paused, and began to descend again. "Crap," Felix said. "Shuttle, why are we descending?"

"Destination changed," the shuttle said blandly.

"Change it *back*," Felix said.

"Authorization required."

"I'm authorizing it!"

"Proper authorization required," the shuttle clarified.

"They found his body," Felix said.

"Yes. Let's hope they haven't canceled his privileges yet." Tib pressed Woryela's badge against one of the shuttle's sensors. "Director-level override. Resume original course, and disable all exterior communications and tracking."

"Complying with route request. Engaging confidential mode."

"That's all it takes?" Felix said.

Tib shrugged. "The person we killed is a director-level member of the Universities of Jol-Nar, captain. He reported directly to the Headmaster. Until someone down there remembers to disable his access, which isn't something just anybody can do anyway, this shuttle thinks we're him. Since we shut down the shuttle's comms, they can't seize control of the shuttle again anyway."

"So once we get to orbit, we're free and clear?"

"No. Once we get to orbit, we get chased by Jol-Nar forces."

"Oh."

"We'd better call Calred and have him pick us up someplace else."

Felix opened his encrypted channel to the ship and explained the situation.

"I'm going to break his legs," Calred said. "Thales can science without his legs."

"We're going to discuss that option, and others, but first we need to avoid getting captured by the proper authorities."

"I'll turn off the ship's transponder and pick you up at these new coordinates, at an earlier point on the original intercept course. I'll have to skim down into the atmosphere, but the *Endless Dark* can handle that. Then we'll run away as fast as we can. And *then*, the legbreaking."

Once their shuttle rendezvoused with the *Endless Dark*, they set a thermal bomb on a timer inside the shuttle, so it would explode while still en route to its original destination in orbit. Maybe the people on the ground would think "Heuvelt" and "Dob" had exploded, too, and even if no one was fooled by that, at least the devastation would remove any skin flakes or other trace evidence they'd left behind – Felix didn't want the Hylar sequencing his DNA and rifling through databases to find him.

Back on board the *Endless Dark*, Felix peeled off the thin laminate he'd worn over his fingers, which bore Heuvelt's prints, and removed the skullcap and wig that had prevented him from dropping hair follicles that could be traced back to him – all part of the false identity package they'd paid so well for.

Twilight Imperium

Overall, Felix felt good about their chances of getting away with murder, assuming no one caught them on their way out. That only made him angrier at Thales. Woryela had clearly been a nice, conscientious professional, and Thales had killed him just to salve his own ego.

"The shuttle just went boom," Calred said. "Looks like there are security ships converging on that location, scanning the debris field. They haven't noticed us. Our transponder is spoofing a fake name and identity" – that much was standard Mentak Coalition military protocol, often useful on piratical missions – "and I'm going to mingle with some of the trade route traffic, where at least no one will try to shoot us with *large* guns, for fear of hurting profitable innocents. From there, we're off to the big empty, and maybe we can get away clean. Not that I feel very clean."

"You've got the helm, then. I'm going to talk to Thales." Felix stomped through the cramped corridors and found Thales taking one of his naps. He kicked the scientist in the side, and Thales rolled off his bunk onto the floor, then looked up, blinking.

"I take it something went wrong," Thales said, "and you've decided, once again, to take out your own failings on me?"

"Woryela is dead!"

Thales made a face that Felix supposed was meant to be indicative of surprise. "What, since you made the appointment? You didn't meet with him?"

"No, we met. We gave him your artifact, and he read your note, and then it gassed him, and then he *died.*"

Thales stood and ostentatiously brushed himself off. "The note, I confess, was a bit cheeky, but I knew you'd have the good sense to pick it up on the way out, and he wouldn't remember it when he woke up anyway–"

"He isn't going to wake up! He's dead!"

"That is regrettable. I take full responsibility."

"Is that a murder confession?"

Thales gave that exaggerated look of surprise again. "Murder? It was an accident, at worst. My degrees are in physics, captain. I consider myself a capable chemist, but xenobiology is hardly my area of expertise. I based the gas I created on a certain recreational drug that Hylar youth enjoy – I used to manufacture it and sell it during graduate school, to help fund my studies – and while I *did* intend to make it more powerful and fast-acting… oh, dear. I must have miscalculated, and made it too strong." His expression and voice were both perfectly level. "Or else the director had some underlying health problems, unknown to me, that proved fatal in combination with the drug. Or perhaps he was on other medication that interacted badly with–"

"You killed him, Thales. I know it. You know it. Why are you pretending otherwise?"

"You insult me, captain. My work is meant to *improve* life in the galaxy, to usher in a new age, where even the most distant stars can be as close as our nearest neighbors. Think of the new sense of community and galactic harmony my invention will foster. I am a *benefactor*, not a killer."

Felix couldn't believe what he was hearing. "A while ago your big selling point was the way the Coalition could drop raider fleets on our enemies from anywhere without warning!"

Thales nodded. "I adjusted my sales pitch to suit my

audience, but I assure you, my ultimate goals are altruistic. I will be remembered as a hero to the galaxy, captain. Murder accusations would only muddle my legacy. So even if I had deliberately engineered a Hylar-specific neurotoxin, one that would kill and then exit the victim's system without leaving a trace, I'd hardly admit to it, would I? I have my reputation to consider. My legacy. They'll name buildings after me in the Universities when this is done – they'll clamor to claim *they* were the ones who recognized my genius and nurtured my mind." He looked Felix up and down, like he was a machine too broken to bother fixing. "Why would you want to accuse me of such crimes, anyway? Any confession I made would implicate you alongside me." To Felix's absolute shock, Thales patted him on the cheek. "Now be a good boy and run along until I need you again."

Felix punched Thales in the face, knocking him back into his bunk. It felt so good, he punched Thales again when he tried to stand up. Thales stayed down that time, holding his bleeding nose, squinting through an eye that would start to swell shut soon. Felix shook his hand, wincing – punching someone straight on like that was hell on your knuckles.

"You will regret that, captain." Thales's voice was low – even mild. "If you really think I'm a cunning and remorseless murderer, was it wise to strike me?"

"Who said I was wise? I'm just a useful idiot, aren't I? But you're on my ship, in my custody, and the bullshit is done, Thales. You will not use me any more. You can build your machine, and test it, and if it works, we'll deliver it to my superiors, and I'll never see you again. That's it. If you do anything else, I will execute you."

"Your superiors–"

"My superiors think you *might* be useful. You haven't proven it yet. Until you do, you are vulnerable. If I tell them you choked to death on a protein nugget, do you really think Tib or Calred will contradict me? Do you think we can't create footage to match the story, in the unlikely event there's an official investigation into this very *un*official mission?" Felix grinned at him savagely. "If there's one thing I've learned from you, it's how easy it is to get away with murder if you just plan a little. I have been pushed as far as I will be. Don't push me any farther. Just be glad I'm the one who came in here to talk to you, or you'd have worse than a bloody nose and a black eye. Calred wanted to break both your legs, and I was tempted to let him."

"*Finally*," Thales said. "I thought you were as spineless as a Hylar – that the Coalition had saddled me with a jellyfish for a minder. It took you long enough, but you showed a little mettle in the end. I'm moderately impressed."

"I hate you, Thales. You repulse me."

"I'm sorry to hear that. I'm just starting to like you, captain."

The contempt of simpletons is as good as the praise of geniuses. So what did receiving the praise of monsters mean? "What's the next step, Thales? You have your power source. Where do we go from here?"

Thales kept smiling at him in a dishearteningly friendly way. "I'll need a few days to complete the assembly, and then I have a few good test sites picked out–"

"Captain!" Calred called over Felix's comms. "We're being pursued by a ship!"

Felix cursed. "From Jol-Nar? How many?"

"Not from Jol-Nar," Calred said. "I evaded *those*. I evaded us right into sensor range of another ship. It's the Barony, captain."

CHAPTER 22

"This is Severyne Joelle Dampierre of the… I don't even know what this stupid ship is named. Call it the *Garbage Scow.*" The face on the *Endless Dark*'s viewscreen was grim, with a line of concentration vertically centered on her forehead. Azad was sitting behind her, and she waved at the screen. The rest of the crew consisted of masked guards, like those on the Barony station, all holding energy weapons and looking distressingly competent. "Stand down and prepare to be boarded, Duval. You will hand over Phillip Thales and Shelma, and submit yourselves to my authority for trial and punishment in the Barony."

"Severyne–" Felix began.

"This is not a negotiation," she continued. "We will not contact you again. Comply, or we will board your vessel and summarily execute you for resisting." The screen winked out.

"She's still a charmer." Felix was seated in the cockpit, though at the moment the ship was flying itself, executing a series of evasive maneuvers that Calred assured him were doomed to fail. "You have a better sense of this ship's specs than I do, Calred. Think we can outrun them?"

Calred's voice crackled over the shipwide comms. This was a conversation everyone could contribute to, even Thales, if he had anything worth saying. "In this thing? No. Their ship is a cruiser, secondhand, looks like Federation make, but much faster than ours. The *Endless Dark* is built for distance, not speed. We'd beat them in a marathon, but this is a sprint."

"I assume we're outgunned too?"

"An *actual* garbage scow could outgun us. Their ship has three cannons fore and two aft, looks like."

"How long until we're in range of said cannons?"

"They could turn us into very small hot pieces of metal and meat right now, captain. They just haven't."

"They won't shoot us while we have Thales and, as far as they know, Shelma. So that's something. How long before they're in range to board us?"

Cal *hmm'd*. "If they were Coalition raiders, I'd say we had fifteen or twenty minutes. Since they don't have the specialized equipment or training our fleets do, they'll have to get close enough to disable our engines without risking blowing us up. That means... maybe forty minutes?"

"Great. How do we set up an impregnable defense in forty minutes?"

The silence was long.

"Well," Felix said finally. "Do we surrender, or go down fighting?"

"They're from the Barony," Tib said. "Letting them capture us would be worse than dying. Their prison camps are infamous."

"We could offer to trade Thales," Calred said. "In exchange

for our freedom. If Dampierre would take our calls and negotiate. Which she won't."

"I think Severyne has something personal against me, anyway," Felix said. What a depressing way to die. The prospect of going down fighting for the Coalition, sure, that was always a possibility, but fighting for *Thales*? Dying to protect a murderous egomaniac? It was hard to take any comfort in that.

"Aren't you lot supposed to be soldiers?" Thales said. "As you've pointed out, the Letnev won't destroy us. History is filled with stories of small bands of warriors defending against superior forces! Put me in the center of the ship. Rig some booby traps in the airlocks. Find narrow apertures you can defend. This Severyne woman can't have *that* many soldiers with her. Fight back! Protect me, protect yourselves, protect our future–"

"Shut up," Felix said. "They're not going to swing over here on ropes and kick the airlocks in. In forty minutes–"

"Thirty-eight," Calred said.

"– thirty-eight minutes, they're going to get close enough to disable our engines with sufficient precision to avoid accidentally killing us. At that point, our ship starts to coast. They'll overtake us. They'll open up their huge cargo bay doors and swallow us up, like a big fish swallowing a little one. *Then* they'll board us."

"So we defend ourselves then!"

"They'll pump the ship full of gas to knock us out before they board," Felix said. "Or poke a hole to let our air *out*, and come in for us after hypoxia makes us lose consciousness."

"We'll put on our environment suits–"

"Those have limited air, and after they've caught us, they're in no hurry any more. They'll just wait us out. This is field manual stuff, Thales. We *are* soldiers. There are times you fight, even when the manual tells you the fight is hopeless, because where there's life, there's hope, but in this case... not much hope. So." Felix cracked his neck. He was captain, and he was going down with his ship, even though this wasn't even really his ship. He was going to miss the *Temerarious*. Or, well, he wouldn't – the dead had no regrets – but he missed his ship preemptively. Sagasa would sell her back to the Coalition for a reasonable price, at least. "We'll swing around, open fire on them with our piddly little guns, and give them no choice but to shoot back and try to disable our engines. Which, at this distance, there's a good chance they can't do safely – they might hit the core and kill us, which I'm assured is the quickest of all possible deaths. If by some chance they *do* manage a disabling shot, and leave us dead in the lack of water–"

"We scuttle?" Calred said.

"That's the idea."

"I'll prepare to overcharge the reactor," Calred said. "If they swallow us up, they'll get indigestion."

"Wait, are you saying you're going to blow up our ship?" Thales cried.

"And I don't see a reason to say it a second time," Felix said.

"Wait. *Wait.* I can't die here, on the cusp of my greatest triumph!"

"I bet no one in history has ever said *that* before," Tib muttered.

"You said 'piddly guns,'" Thales said. "Why are the guns piddly?"

Felix sighed. "Because this isn't a warship, Thales. If we were in the *Temerarious*, we'd have a fighting chance. But the *Endless Dark* is an exploration vessel. It has weapons, because every adventurer fantasizes about fending off space pirates, or *being* a space pirate, or making first contact with a new species and blowing them up, but they're just small energy weapons. They aren't powerful enough to hurt something like the *Garbage Scow*, at least, not in the time we have – if their ship sat still and let us shoot them for an hour or two, sure, we could put enough holes in them to make a difference, but I doubt they'll be that cooperative."

Thales went *hmm*. "Energy weapons... so the limiting factor is the power supply. Our cannons are powered off the ship's reactor?"

"Big warships have separate power sources for their weapons," Calred said. "This one doesn't. So, yes, I know what you're thinking. We can divert *all* the ship's power to the weapons battery, to make the cannons stronger. It won't help much, though. This ship's reactor is built for long-distance efficiency, not bursts of output. Even if we juiced the weapons up, we'd get double their usual power for a few short bursts, but it wouldn't make any real difference–"

"We do have a separate power source for our weapons, you idiots," Thales said. "You just *stole* one."

Felix looked at Tib, who looked back at him. "Wait. That power cell thing. That's powerful enough to run the guns?"

"It's powerful enough to *rip holes in the fabric of space-time*, you dolts," Thales said. "Yes, it can power your lasers."

Felix's heart sped up. Hope was a powerful thing. "Calred, can you configure the guns to run off an external power source?"

"The lasers are aftermarket additions wired into the reactor here anyway, so yeah, it should be easy, but do you think this will really work?"

"No, but since our other plan is a pointless last stand, it can't hurt to try."

"They'll have us in ten minutes, Cal," Felix said from the cockpit.

"I'm the one who told *you* how long we had, captain, I *know* – there! It's connected! Power is flowing, board is green, available energy is… I don't know, because my diagnostic tool only reads up to nine-hundred-and-ninety-nine petawatts. So, more than that."

"That's… wait… that's…"

"More powerful than a gamma ray burst," Thales said. "More energy output than a star. Yes. That's the whole *point*. This power cell draws on the energy that drives *galaxies* out into the greater dark."

Felix whistled. "You said it was powerful, but I didn't realize."

"The question, of course, is how much power these cannons of yours can actually use," Thales said. "Without melting in the process."

"Cal?" Felix said.

"I'm looking up the tolerances!" Calred said. "Huh. OK. These things are ridiculously overengineered. Whoever equipped the *Endless Night* bought very expensive cannons, way more than they needed. Some salesperson got a good commission that day."

"Probably somebody like Heuvelt, spendthrifting the family fortune," Felix said. "You're saying we can put up a fight now?"

"We can start and finish a fight, captain. Especially since the *Garbage Scow* will not expect us to punch this hard."

"All right then. Let's take out their weapons and their engines."

"Why not life support?" Thales said. "That seems simpler."

"Engines and weapons are on the *outside* of the ship," Tib said. "That's so they can propel the ship through space, and blow up things they encounter in space. Life support systems are buried deep inside the ship, where the alive things are."

"Fine," Thales grumbled. "I assumed the order was due to a combination of weakness and sentimentality. Carry on."

"I wasn't waiting for your permission, Thales," Calred said. "Ready to flip and shoot on your mark, captain."

"Mark." Felix braced himself as the ship stopped short and spun around to face the *Garbage Scow*. Thales squawked over the comms, and Felix muted him. His crew had known to brace for the maneuver, of course. Thales hadn't. Oops.

The enemy ship was hurtling toward them – an immense bulbous vessel, with the black dots of cannons pointing their way.

"Weapons hot," Calred said. "*Extremely* hot. Felix. Can I push the button?"

Felix's fingers twitched, but he put them in his lap.

Sometimes being captain and taking care of your crew required sacrifices, and though he desperately wanted to do the shooting himself, it was Calred's job. "Please. Do the honors."

The viewscreen darkened to near opacity, but even so, the flash of the firing cannons was blinding. For just a moment, their ship was almost certainly the brightest thing in the universe. The cannons pulsed twice more, in quick succession. "That's all three of their fore weapon arrays," Calred said. "If they get anything like the same combat training *we* did, they'll wheel around to aim their aft guns – there they go."

The *Garbage Scow* was invisible through the darkened screen, but their ship's sensors showed its actions on Felix's tactical board. The Barony ship did its own hard spin, and when is engines were in sight, the *Endless Night* fired again, several times in succession, and the glow of the enemy engines went dark.

"That's it!" Cal shouted. "Engines and cannons gone. Good thing, too. Our cannons weren't well maintained and, ah, it turns out, maybe I shouldn't have pushed them to the absolute maximum of their specifications."

"We don't have guns any more?" Thales said.

"We don't have anyone to shoot at any more, either," Felix said. The *Garbage Scow* could still maneuver with its reaction wheels, but those were meant for minute adjustments – it wouldn't be going very far without extensive repairs. "Did you take out their comms, too?" Felix said. "I'd expect Severyne to start yelling at us right about now, vowing revenge and promising doom and all that."

"Maybe she's too embarrassed," Tib said. "She seems like the kind of person who gets embarrassed easily."

"The Letnev aren't very good at failure," Thales said. "Perhaps they just need more practice." He paused. "Well? Don't you people have anything to say to me?"

"Shut up?" Calred said.

"Shut up, you murderer?" Tib said.

"They pretty much covered it," Felix agreed.

Thales huffed. "I'd expect a little gratitude. I just saved your useless lives."

"You did," Felix said. "But only as a side effect of saving yourself. If throwing us into the ship's reactor would have saved you instead, you'd have done that just as readily."

"You're becoming quite curmudgeonly, Duval. You remind me of myself at your age."

"Gross," Tib said. "What's next, captain?"

Before Felix could answer, Thales did. "Next, you take me back to my lab on the *Temerarious*. I'll connect the power source to my prototype. We'll travel to one of the test sites I've identified. I'll switch on my activation engine and change the course of galactic civilization. I'll be rich and famous, and you'll receive largely undeserved promotions and accolades."

"Works for me." Felix switched to a crew-only channel, cutting Thales out. "What do you think?" he said. "Could the end really be in sight?"

"Thales doesn't want us to assassinate anyone else, apparently," Tib said.

Calred said, "Severyne and Azad are floating in a disabled ship, and getting farther behind us all the time. Thales hasn't decided where we're going next, so it's hard to imagine they'll beat us there."

"Maybe this awful mission could actually succeed," Felix said.

"As long as the Creuss don't show up and reduce us to our individual atoms for meddling in their business," Tib said.

"Thank you for that, Tib."

"My pleasure, Felix. A captain with nothing to worry about is barely a captain at all."

They returned to the Disciplinarian's scrapyard, and Felix hailed him on their comms, surprised when the Hacan answered personally. "We brought back the *Endless Night*, undamaged," Felix said. "Well, we broke the guns. But they weren't very good guns anyway."

"I'll bill you for them," Sagasa said. "Did you run into your friends out there?"

"We did."

"Are they dead? Did you destroy the cruiser I sold them?"

"The ship is disabled and adrift, but they're probably alive."

Sagasa sighed. "I wish you'd blown them up. They might still bring my cruiser back, and I won't get to keep the far superior ship they left behind as collateral."

"Were you rooting for *us* to lose, too, so you could keep my ship?" Felix said.

"I never pray for the death of a customer, Captain Duval. I thrive on repeat business. But taking ownership of the *Temerarious* would have eased my grief. Dock at port AZ-5. I'll send someone to do a walkthrough of the *Endless Dark*."

"A walkthrough? Seriously?"

"I'm always serious about business. I need to make sure the vessel is as undamaged as you claim."

"I need to get to work, captain," Thales groused. "I don't want to sit here while some fool examines the paint on this bucket."

"None of us want to spend an extra moment with you, Thales," Felix said. "Cal, take him back to the *Temerarious*. Keep an eye on him while he gets to work. We'll join you after Sagasa finishes looking for dings and scratches to overcharge us for."

"Excellent," Thales said. "Just fetch the power supply–"

"I'm going to hold on to that part," Felix said. "I'm sure you have other things to do first. You can plug it in later, when we're on the way to your test site."

"Why?" Thales demanded.

"Because I don't trust you," Felix said. "There are three crucial components to your success: your brain, Shelma's prototype, and this power supply. I'm not going to let all three of them be in one place at one time unless I'm there too."

"Outrageous. What are you afraid I'll do with it?"

"Shoot Calred in the back of the head and steal my ship," Felix said.

"Like I'd turn my back on him," Cal said.

"Or you might contact Sagasa and offer *him* the deal of a lifetime," Felix said. "Partnering with an independently wealthy businessman would be better for you than working with the Coalition, since Sagasa is motivated purely by profit, just like you."

"You're paranoid, Duval," Thales said. "More and more you remind me of myself–"

"Just go," Felix said.

Amazingly, the walkthrough was just slow, not slow and expensive. Sagasa's Winnaran secretary noted the damaged cannons, but after a thorough inspection of the ship inside and out, declared there was no other damage that would require repayment. "I'm surprised you didn't charge us for wear-and-tear on the engine," Felix said.

"Oh, that's included in the original price," he explained, entirely straight-faced. He presented a hand terminal for Felix's approval, and he authorized the charges. Jhuri was the one paying, anyway. "Thank you for visiting Sagasa Scrap and Salvage," the secretary said. "We–"

"We know," Felix said. "Point me to my ship, please?"

Felix and Tib set off through the station, toward the airlock where the *Temerarious* waited. "A couple more days, Tib, and we're free. This whole mess will be over."

"It has been an ordeal," Tib said. "Do you wish we'd stayed on patrol duty?"

Felix considered. "I don't, really. This is the kind of work I've always wanted to do. We organized a jailbreak, pulled off a heist, prevailed in ship-to-ship combat – it hasn't been boring, and the crew really pulled together."

"I've always trusted you, and I had a good feeling about Cal," Tib said. "But that feeling wasn't ever tested before. Now I *know*. If it wasn't for Thales, and the murders – especially the murders – I'd be happy with this mission. Even with all that, I don't want to go back to flying around in circles any more, using my skills for hide-and-seek."

"We will get promotions after this, if Thales gets his engine working," Felix said. "We'll have our choice of postings. Jhuri will take care of us."

"Maybe we can start thinking about where we want to land after this is all over."

"Shouldn't we focus on the immediate future, Tib?"

"Why would we want to do that?" Tib grimaced. "The immediate future has Thales in it."

"That is an excellent point. I've been on this officer track, working my way up to a command bigger than my best friend and an endearingly insubordinate Hacan, but maybe the covert ops life is more appealing. What do you think?"

"I had to work hard to keep *out* of covert ops, Felix. They always want Yssaril to work as spies. As if that's the only thing we're good for – sneaking around and listening through doors. But what we've been doing out here isn't exactly espionage. We haven't been gathering much in the way of intelligence."

"If anything," Felix said, "we've been rushing around with a regrettable lack of intelligence."

"We're essentially the personal get-shit-done-squad for undersecretary Jhuri, at the moment," Tib said. "That gives us connections, support – of a sort, anyway – and a lot of novelty. We could do worse than to continue in this capacity, if Jhuri wants us."

"I don't know if Calred would want that kind of gig," Felix said. "*His* dream is to run the weapons board on a dreadnought."

"I'm sure Jhuri would ask us to steal a dreadnought at some point, if this mission is any sort of indication."

"Don't say that. This mission isn't over yet, and I don't need any more challenges today."

His comms opened, and Calred's voice shouted, "Felix! We have a problem!"

"Don't we always?" Felix said.

"Not like this!" There was something strange about Cal's voice, and it took Felix a moment to recognize the tone, because he hadn't heard it from Cal before.

The Hacan security officer was afraid.

CHAPTER 23

Severyne was nervous about how nervous she *wasn't*. She should have been more worried. She was, after all, in the midst of violating all Barony best practices, on a deniable mission that could very well end up with her execution, and she was currently trusting her fate to the criminal skills of the most annoying human in the galaxy – a human who also inexplicably made Severyne's palms sweat and her heart beat faster when she stood too close, which she did *all the time*.

Instead of cold fear, though, Severyne felt exhilaration. Why? She'd sent her entire complement of guards – without any supervising officer! – off to the Jol-Nar system in a cruiser she'd purchased from a Hacan crime lord. Her guards were in pursuit of the fugitive *she* was meant to be pursuing. By all rules and regulations, Severyne should have been there too, running the operation. But after they reached the *Grim Countenance*, Azad had said, "Let's be real. We're not going to catch Duval's Devils out there."

"Why do you say that?" Severyne demanded.

"We don't know what kind of ship they're in. We don't know how they're planning to steal the power source – strongarm robbery, some sort of confidence game, bribing a technician to smuggle it out to them, or something I haven't even thought of yet. I'm not a fan of the Coalition, but when it comes to parting people from their property, the Mentak have *skills*. Without knowing their plan, we don't know their timeline, where they'll strike, or when they'll leave. Jol-Nar is one of the hubs of galactic civilization, so it's not like Duval and company will stand out against the usual traffic. We'll be looking for one specific grain of sand on the beach."

"Don't mention beaches," Severyne muttered.

"Now, when chasing them was our only option, going to Jol-Nar and hoping to catch them coming or going was our best bet," Azad said. "I'm lucky almost as much as I'm good, after all. But now we don't have to chase them: we can sit here and wait for them, because we know they're coming back."

"You're sure the information you received from the secretary was reliable?" Severyne said. "I don't understand why he would help you. Surely Sagasa places a premium on discretion in his employees?"

"Oh, totally, but that Winnaran *hates* Sagasa's ass. One time he overhead Sagasa tell a client he liked to hire Winnarans because they're a 'naturally servile race' that's 'only happy when they have boots to lick' and that they've been 'looking for a new emperor to serve for centuries, and who's more imperial than me?' He could still quote that years later. So now, for a price, the secretary is willing to slip people info about Sagasa's clients, as a way of proving his own independence. We did some business last time I was here, and we just did a little more business today, though you paid for it."

"How did you discover this Winnaran's tendency toward duplicity?"

"In my line of work, Sev, it pays to talk to people. That's the first step toward developing an asset."

"Am *I* an asset, Azad?"

"You certainly have many notable ones," Azad said.

"You will not deflect me with your innuendos," Severyne said.

"Here I thought I was flirting."

"Are you manipulating me?" Severyne said, more quietly.

Azad put her hand on Severyne's shoulder, briefly. "Only insofar as I'm always manipulating everybody. You and I have goals that align, so there's no need for a bunch of bullshit. The only problem we have is figuring out how to achieve those goals. I have strong opinions, and I will make every effort to bring you around to my way of seeing things. Fortunately, you have a bright analytical mind, so as long as my ideas are good, I have confidence you'll agree with them – and if they aren't good, you'll make them better."

Severyne was flattered by the compliment, though she didn't want to feel flattered. "We know, if your source is to be trusted, that Duval left his ship here for safekeeping, and that he intends to return for it. Your plan is to lie in wait on his ship and ambush them."

"That's it exactly. Why rush around to Jol-Nar when we

can just sit here and get our scientists *and* the power cell delivered into our hands?"

"I can see one reason why not," Severyne said. "What if they fail? What if their daring heist is a disaster, and Duval and his crew are captured by the Hylar, along with *our* scientists?"

"That would be unfortunate," Azad said. "I'm not sure us being in orbit around Jol or Nar would make it any less unfortunate."

"Nevertheless. We will dispatch my guards to Jol-Nar in the ship Sagasa has loaned us, where they will wait on the outskirts of the system, close enough to monitor comms traffic. If there *is* a disastrous crime, there will be news reports, yes? The Hylar have very poor information control, as I recall."

"If you mean they have a mostly free press and that their news doesn't consist entirely of government propaganda, then yes, their information control is poor as piss."

"Excellent. I will put my squad leader in charge, with strict and specific orders. If there is any suggestion that Duval and company have been arrested, he will send a message to us, and we will formulate a plan to liberate Shelma and Thales. I will have my guard station whatever garbage vessel Sagasa has for us along the most direct return route for Duval's ship, so even if our enemies do succeed in their mission, my people will have an opportunity to disable and capture Duval's vessel on their way back. It is *always* wise to have contingency plans in place."

"I like it. Don't send them on the most direct route, though. Have the computer compute the best route from

Jol-Nar to evade and mislead pursuers, and station your people somewhere along that trajectory. Even if Duval isn't literally running from the cops when they leave Jol-Nar, they'll be careful when they depart."

"You think like a criminal, Azad." Severyne did not mean it as a compliment, but the human grinned.

"See, you've improved our plan already. Belt and suspenders is a good idea, when you have the resources to deploy both. I have to admit, I hope your crew *doesn't* catch Duval, though. I want to snag him personally."

"All that matters is the outcome," Severyne said, though secretly she agreed.

"I have one little refinement to suggest. On the off-chance that Duval encounters your guards but manages to evade them, we can make sure they're *really* taken by surprise when they get back. All we need to do is record a little video of you being threatening and imperious, and I *know* you're good at that."

Now they were sneaking through an airlock to break into Duval's ship, preparing to lay an ambush. There were so many variables in play that Severyne could not possibly account for them all. But instead of terror, she felt only exhilaration. Perhaps a life in station bureaucracy *wasn't* the most fulfilling possible future for her. "I may have misjudged myself for my entire life," Severyne said out loud.

Azad glanced at her. "It's never too late to figure out who you really are, Severyne."

She scowled, annoyed at herself for revealing her inner state. "How are you going to gain access?"

"Oh, the external controls for the airlock can be operated

in a couple of ways. There are transponders in the ship's environment suits, of course, to allow re-entry from spacewalks and whatnot. But there's also a backup system that's keyed to biometrics, to allow people to enter from stations. This door should open for any member of Duval's crew."

"We are not Duval's crew."

"True, but we've been up close and personal with them. These doors are pretty forgiving, since people might be trying to board in a hurry while getting shot at and stuff, so you don't have to get your retina scanned while singing three verses of 'The Sun Shines over Jord' and having your blood drawn – you just gotta show the ship real quick that you're you. When I smashed that little Yssaril bitch over the back of the head, I made sure some blood and hair stuck to my fingers." She dipped into her pocket, and then smeared her fingertip over a sensor. The airlock door unsealed. "Ta da."

"You couldn't have known you were going to need Tib Pelta's genetic material to open a door," Severyne said.

"Hey, I like planning for contingencies too."

"Do you have *my* hair in your pockets?"

"No, Sev, I have not collected any of your genetic material. We're partners, not adversaries. I don't need to use you. I work with you."

"You are a very convincing liar. I can see why you are moderately successful in your chosen career."

"I'm the best there is at whatever it is I feel like doing. Shall we explore our new ship?" They stepped into the airlock and on into the vessel itself. "I was wondering, why didn't you send the *Grim Countenance* out on your contingency mission?"

"And risk losing a ship of the Barony? The garbage scow Sagasa foisted on us is more than a match for the small vessel Duval took, if your treacherous Winnaran is to be believed. The superior firepower of the *Grim Countenance* is hardly necessary."

"Ha, fair enough. Better hope that garbage scow comes back, though, or Sagasa is going to claim the *Grim Countenance* as his collateral."

"We will solve that problem if it arises." Severyne wrinkled her nose at the state of the Coalition vessel as they inspected it. There were dirty dishes in the galley, personal items at workstations on the bridge, and wrapped pallets of emergency supplies in almost every bit of unused space. "Is this a ship of the Coalition fleet or a cargo vessel?"

"I think they did relief missions back in the colonies. Look, in here, it's some kind of lab."

"Is there anything of value here?"

Azad poked through the bits of wire and sheared pieces of metal scattered on the bench and shook her head. "Looks like they took everything with them when they left. Makes sense. You don't want to leave that kind of tech lying around unattended. Let's keep looking around, though."

They found Duval's cabin – Severyne was tempted to urinate on his bed, but decided that would qualify as conduct unbecoming a Barony officer – but she did pick up a bottle of liquor and was about to smash it on the wall when Azad plucked it from her hand. "Hey, that's Coalition gin. There's this botanical on Moll Primus, sort of like a citrusy version of a juniper, I can't really describe it, and they use its needles to infuse the booze – we're going to keep this and celebrate our success later."

"Fine. But I wish to desecrate this space somehow."

"I'll wipe my butt on his sheets later or something. Let's move on."

They found Shelma's body not long after.

CHAPTER 24

First, Azad noticed the exo-suit tank, tucked into the corner of a storage space. She didn't know what it was, but Severyne's reaction told her it was something important, and bad: the Letnev stiffened, and then emitted a sort of keening wail. "Where is the medical bay?" she snapped.

Azad, who had the basic schematics for a whole bunch of different ship models filed away in her head, didn't ask questions; she just led the way. The medical bay was gleaming and sterile – there were automated systems in place to keep it that way, even on a Coalition ship – and Severyne was clearly familiar enough with the basic layout to pull up the information she needed. She consulted a terminal, then went to a wall full of rectangular panels of various sizes and pressed the smallest one.

The panel hissed, then slid open with a gout of icy vapor, a drawer extending into the room. There was a Hylar body on the rack, pseudopods curled up, body shriveled in the cold, various sensors connected to her. Was the ship conducting some sort of diagnostic, perhaps to determine cause of death? There was no obvious sign of injury.

"Shelma is dead." Severyne's voice, always icy, was now absolute zero.

"I'm so sorry, Severyne," Azad said.

"I will be executed for this."

Azad winced. Sev was probably not wrong. "You don't know that. There are still ways you can turn this around."

"*What* ways?" She spun, fists clenched, and glared at Azad. "My sole mission was to recover Shelma! As long as I brought her back, we could cover up everything else, and life would go on. My director would have *hated* me, and I would have had to transfer to another posting at some point if I hoped to advance, but my life would have continued. Now I will be on record as overseeing a catastrophic security breach, and failing to redress that breach. I am dead. I am walking, and talking, and dead."

Azad took a step toward her. "We still have Thales. *He's* not in a drawer here, and if he was gone, Duval wouldn't be rushing around making moves. Your lot tried to recruit Thales, too, so…" She trailed off.

Severyne laughed. "So what? Do we cut him in half? Or do you propose to share custody of the man? A joint project between the Barony and the Federation? We'll make wormholes and explore the universe together? You were going to betray me and try to take both of the scientists and all their files *anyway*. Now that there's only one scientist, you want to share?"

"You were going to betray me, too," Azad said quietly. "It's the business. We work together until we don't. But now I don't have to betray anybody, and neither do you." Relief flooded through her. There was a way through this. "Sev, why don't you come with me?"

The Letnev blinked at her. "What are you talking about?"

"You said it yourself. If you return to the Barony empty-handed, you're dead. So stay with me instead. Help me complete my mission. Don't go back."

"The director will send people to find me. They have ways of tracking down rogue officers."

"If you defect to the Federation, we can protect you."

Severyne shuddered. "You want me to join the *humans*?"

"Is that worse than joining your ancestors?"

"You will have to give me a moment to think about that." Azad laughed.

Severyne took a deep breath, then closed the morgue drawer. "I will consider your offer. In the meantime, my personal mission has changed. It is no longer possible to recover Shelma. Instead, my new objective is to destroy Felix Duval. To ruin his life as thoroughly as he has ruined mine."

"Well, hey," Azad said. "We're standing on his ship. That's a pretty good start–"

"You have made overtures toward me," Severyne said abruptly. "Were they sincere, or were you merely mocking me?"

Whoa. Having your life destroyed could do a number on anyone's sense of self and priorities, but that was a pretty abrupt turn, even by catastrophe standards. Unless Severyne had been interested all along, and now that her old life was over, she was willing to loosen up certain strictures…

Oh. Or it could be for another reason. "They were sincere,

but I didn't think you'd take me up on them. Listen, you're under a lot of strain. I don't want you to do anything you'll regret later–"

"Letnev do not allow themselves regrets," Severyne said. "We only move forward. Let us go." She turned and stalked back toward Duval's cabin.

Azad watched Severyne go and ran a complex mental calculation. She had no particular need to kill Severyne now, that was true, which opened up the way for a different kind of relationship… but Severyne had even *more* incentive to kill Azad. That was the only way she could lay claim to Thales, after all, and halfway redeem herself with her superiors. Azad figured this sudden desire for carnal connection was about thirty percent terror-induced arousal (that was absolutely a real thing, as many eve-of-battle assignations over the years had proven to Azad's satisfaction). The other seventy percent was an attempt to get Azad to let her guard down – to make her think Severyne had feelings and affection for her, so she wouldn't see the gunshot to the back of the head coming.

Azad made her decision. Sure, it violated her rule, but transgression made it more exciting in a way, didn't it?

She was used to people trying to kill her. At least this way, they'd both get some enjoyment out of being alive first.

Afterward, Azad stretched like a cat and turned over in Duval's bed – the captain's quarters had the best bunk, which was nice – and looked at Severyne's face. The Letnev woman had the slightly stunned expression of someone who'd just tried, for the first time, something that would become their new avocation, passion, or addiction. "Nice, huh?" Azad said.

Severyne turned her head, looked at Azad for a moment, then looked back at the ceiling. "I am not inexperienced. At the academy, sometimes … well. The nights in the dormitory were cold, and there were few ways to warm up. But humans *do* run hotter than Letnev, it seems."

"Could be that's just me."

Severyne's expression shifted to seriousness. "We should prepare ourselves for Duval's return."

"Oh, even if they went to Jol-Nar, committed the theft in five minutes, and came straight back, we'd still have hours."

"Nevertheless, I desire no further surprises. We need to fully seize control of the ship's systems."

"Look at you, going from all pleasure to all business. Fine, I'll put my pants on." Azad kissed Severyne's cheek and rolled out of the bunk. It was still safe, to a high degree of certainty, to turn her back on Severyne; the Letnev still needed her. But once they subdued Duval and had Thales in hand, then Azad would have to get properly vigilant.

That was fine. Vigilant was pretty much her default state.

Severyne sat in the captain's chair on the bridge while Azad hacked the ship's systems. "What's funny is, the intrusion tools I'm using are *made* by the Mentak Coalition. It's no good being a pirate captain if you can't take control of captured vessels, so they've got a whole suite of techniques for spoofing authorizations and cracking encryption. But because the Coalition is full of people with rather flexible moral systems, those tools didn't stay proprietary for long

– they got sold on the black market, and Sol got their hands on one, reverse engineered it, made some tweaks so the tools could attack Coalition safeguards too, and here we are. A nearly universal spaceship key. And… there. Welcome, Captain Severyne, to the good ship *Temerarious*, now yours to command."

"Wait. You're giving me the priority authorizations?"

"You're the one sitting in the big chair. I'm much better at running weapons anyway. The ship is ours. Now we just wait, for word from your people on the garbage scow, or for Duval to stroll through the door."

So they waited. They ate in the galley, ran diagnostic checks on the weapons, and took turns showering in the captain's bathroom. Severyne considered showing open affection to further distract Azad and keep her off balance, but was afraid it would be seen as manipulation; better to carry on as she had been.

Sleeping with Azad had been enjoyable, she had to admit, if only to herself. Severyne didn't have much time for pleasure for pleasure's sake in her usual life, let alone with someone of a different species, but that sense of the forbidden had ultimately made it exciting instead of disgusting. *Maybe I really* have *misjudged myself my whole life*. She thought, briefly, of what would happen if she took Azad up on her offer, but "Come with me" didn't mean "Travel through the stars committing various interesting crimes and having sex" – not really. It meant "Defect, and sit in a Federation of Sol military interview room for one million hours describing Barony security protocols." That was not appealing. It was even less appealing than going home a failure and being executed; at least that would be over relatively quickly, and cause her less shame.

Severyne's comms buzzed with a message from the squad leader on the garbage scow. "We engaged the enemy, assistant director," he said, and his tone was so stiff she couldn't tell whether he'd succeeded or failed. "They disabled our ship and escaped."

"How did they disable your ship?" she demanded. "They were in a long-distance exploration vessel, not a gunship!"

"They utilized a weapon of unknown provenance."

"What? Did they steal some kind experimental weapon while they were on Jol-Nar too?"

"I lack necessary data to draw a conclusion–"

"Never mind. Can you repair the ship?"

"We are attempting repairs, and expect to have partial function restored to the engines within seventy-two hours, which should allow us to return to the scrapyard. Unless you would prefer to rendezvous with us in the *Grim Countence* – if you can bring repair parts, we would not have to fabricate them here, and that would greatly reduce our–"

"You'll have to make your own way. I'm going to be busy succeeding at the mission where you *failed*."

"Yes, assistant director. I will send status updates–"

She cut the connection, squeezing the armrests of the captain's chair tight. "Duval apparently has some kind of super-weapon now."

Azad, standing at the tactical board, shook her head. "I bet they just plugged the ship's shitty little cannons into the power source they stole. That's what I would have done."

Severyne blinked. "That would work?"

"Your basic energy cannon is just a conduit for and focuser of power. How strong the cannons are depends on the energy source. That thing they went to steal is supposed to be like a hundred fusion reactors, only so small you can carry it around in a backpack."

"Then the power source, in itself, has great value," Severyne mused.

"If you brought that back to the Barony, you might not get executed, it's true," Azad said. "Unfortunately, I can't let you have it, since Thales needs it to power his prototype. Sorry about that. Maybe we can get you the schematics or something, and your people can reverse engineer the thing, if you want to give that a shot."

"How very generous."

Azad shrugged but didn't look up from the panel. "I like you, Severyne. I'll help you as much as I can without hurting myself. But that's as far as I can go. Would you respect me if I did anything else?"

"This is a miserable situation," Severyne said. "I am miserable."

"Ah, but there's an upside. Duval is on his way back here. And if your crew played your video like they were supposed to–"

"Of course they did. They follow orders to the letter, without deviation. The Letnev are not as prone to improvisation as humans are." Though Severyne herself had done some improvising lately, hadn't she? Azad was corrupting her.

"Then Duval thinks *we're* floating in a dead ship in the

void," Azad said. "He's going to walk in here with supreme and misplaced confidence. Even more than usual."

"And then I can kill him?" Severyne said.

"And then you can kill him."

"I feel slightly less miserable now."

"Aw, hell," Azad said.

Severyne hurried over to the security station. "What is it?"

"Two people just stepped into the airlock. *Only* two." She pulled up the camera feed and saw Thales carrying a rucksack, and the Hacan security officer, Calred, holding a file box. He was awkwardly juggling the box in an attempt to hold it one-handed while unlocking the ship with his fingertip.

"Where is Duval?" Severyne demanded.

"Maybe he had to take a piss."

"Then where is the Yssaril?"

"Could be lurking invisibly, I guess, though it's bad etiquette to sneak around on Sagasa's station, and they've got no reason to expect an attack, so she's probably with Duval. Yssaril have to piss sometimes too."

"They'll be on board any moment!"

"They'll *try* to get on board any moment. They'll be unconscious a moment after that. Let's get down there and collect them."

Sev grabbed her arm. "We have to wait for Duval."

"Sev, it's Thales, and his stuff. What I need is Thales, and his stuff. I'd like to see Duval dead, too, but that part isn't mission critical."

She tightened her grip, nails digging in. "It is critical for *my* mission. My only mission is revenge."

Your only mission is killing me and taking Thales for yourself, Azad thought. But… Sev really did want to kill Duval, and waiting for him would put off her inevitable betrayal for a while longer. Azad did enjoy having the Letnev woman alive. She calculated risk and came up with an acceptable number. "All right. But only because you're so cute when you're homicidal. Let's secure the owl and the pussycat, and then we'll wait for the others to show up."

They went down to the airlock, weapons ready.

CHAPTER 25

Azad was listening to the feed from the airlock on her comms, so she heard the Hacan swearing about how the inner door wasn't working. She learned a few new Hacan blasphemies in the process. She took up her position in the corridor, facing the airlock doors, and checked that Severyne was in her spot. "Ready?"

"I wish I was about to shoot Duval, but yes."

"Keep it non-lethal," Azad reminded her. "We can't risk a stray shot hitting Thales."

"I know." Severyne's voice was even more grim than usual.

Azad triggered the inner door to open. As soon as the doors slid apart enough to give her a sliver of a sightline on the people on the other side, she aimed at Thales and hit him with a shock-pulse, carefully calibrated to lock up his nervous system without doing any permanent damage.

She was aware of the Hacan, and of Severyne firing at him, but she was focused on her own target, and when she shifted her attention, it was too late.

Calred's right arm hung loose at the shoulder where

Severyne's pulse had hit him, off-center and thus ineffective. Maybe Azad should have taken point on disabling the Hacan, but Thales was the more important target, and she'd made a judgment call. Now a few hundred pounds of enraged humanoid lion came barreling toward them, bellowing. If Calred had stopped to fight them, she could have subdued him, but instead he just straight-armed Severyne out of the way and rushed deeper into the ship.

Azad fired after him, but he was around a corner and gone. Azad heard him shout, "Felix! We have a problem!"

"That could have gone better." Azad put the ship into lockdown, then checked on Severyne, who was leaning against a wall, rubbing her chest where the Hacan had struck her, face stoic. "But it's not a total disaster."

"There is an angry Hacan weapons expert loose on this vessel."

"Sure, but I just locked everything down – he's stuck in a corridor, banging on a door. He's no danger to us. I shielded comms too."

"Not before he warned Duval," Severyne said. "We can't surprise him now."

"That's true. I'm sorry, Severyne. Revenge will have to wait. I promise, we'll get Duval, OK? I want him too. But for now, we've got Thales, and we've got his data, his prototype, the power source–"

A dry laugh crackled from the floor of the airlock. They both turned to look at the scientist, who was still mostly paralyzed, but conscious. "You've got three out of four. Which isn't enough. This is an all-or-nothing situation.

Duval still has the power cell. Idiots. I'm surrounded by idiots."

"That is a complication," Azad said.

"Hello, Duval," Azad said. She was calling him from the *Temerarious*, which made him vibrate with rage.

"Get the fuck off my ship." He paced up and down in the corridor as he spoke, while Tib stood against the wall, seemingly lost in thought. Felix hoped she was figuring out some angle. He was too angry to figure out anything other than a direct attack, personally.

"Your people are pirates, Duval. You know how this works. I'm in control of the ship. That makes it my ship. That's not the only thing of yours I've taken, either. I've got your lion in a cage here."

"If you hurt Calred–"

"Then Calred will be hurt very badly indeed. Stop blustering, Duval. It's unbecoming. I don't want to hurt anyone, oddly enough. I'm a pragmatist, not a sadist. I just have a problem you can help me solve. You have a power source. I need a power source. I have one of your crew. You need one of your crew. That means we can make a deal. Straight trade. The battery for your boy. Oh, and I'm going to need your ship, too. Fortunately, you can pick up another one at the scrapyard."

"You can't be serious."

"It's not only serious, it's a limited-time offer. Think it over. Don't make me wait too long, or I'll start cutting off non-essential parts of your security officer. Then you'll have to pay the same amount to get less and less in return.

It's a brutal negotiating tactic, I know. I learned it from the Disciplinarian. I'll give you a few minutes. I know it takes time for that 'I'm totally fucked' feeling to really sink in."

She clicked off. Felix stared at Tib. "What can we do?"

"Lots of things."

"What can we do that will get Thales back and won't kill Calred in the process?"

"Many fewer things. I can think of… zero things."

"Maybe there's nothing we can do on our own, but…" Felix opened another channel. A bored voice said, "Sagasa Scrap and–"

"Let me talk to Sagasa!"

"Captain Duval. Perhaps I can be of–"

"I don't *want* to talk to you!" Felix bellowed. "Get me Sagasa, now!"

It wasn't "now," but after a long interval, Sagasa rumbled into Felix's comms. "How may I be of further service, captain?"

"You let those assholes get on my ship!"

"Which assholes are those?"

"Severyne and Azad!"

"Ah. Those assholes. I thought they were adrift in a disabled ship many parsecs away?"

"Yeah, well, so did I. But it turns out they sent their crew to harass us while they stayed here, in *your* scrapyard, and broke into my ship. What are you going to do about that?"

"You paid me to dock the ship here, captain." The Hacan's voice was mild and untroubled. "If you wanted me to guard it, you should have said so. I offer very reasonable rates for security services. What's the problem? I won't let them leave with your property – that much is covered by our agreement. Would you like to employ some of my personnel to help you take the ship back?"

"I can't go in hot. They have Calred."

"Ah ha. A hostage situation. I see. What do they want in return for his freedom?"

Felix hesitated. Sagasa was honorable, in very specific ways, but the power cell would be a morality-warping temptation for even a less shady businessperson. "They're demanding a certain item in my possession."

"Then you should decide whether to give it to them, or not. I'm still not clear about why you're calling me. Did you want to secure my services as a negotiator on your behalf?"

"Doesn't breaking into my ship and kidnapping my security officer count as an act of aggression on your station?" Felix said. "Shouldn't you discipline them?"

"Arguably. But such things bother me less when they don't happen right outside my office. If someone starts shooting in the corridors, I will be moved to intervene, but it sounds, at this point, more like an aggressive business negotiation than anything else. I don't meddle in such affairs. Besides, you said you don't want to go in hot. It's not as if I have options for retaking the ship other than the use of force, captain."

Felix was getting desperate. "What if they kill Calred?"

"I would mourn the loss of a brother Hacan. Then I would offer my security forces for hire again, since the impediment against violent intervention would be removed. I might even carry a weapon myself."

"None of this is very helpful, Sagasa."

"Alas, being helpful to Duval's Devils is not one of my duties. I wish you luck." He paused. "I will remind you, though, that if *you* start shooting in my corridors, I'll consider you the aggressor instead, and subject to my discipline."

"Unless I hire you to help."

"Of course. In that situation, *you* wouldn't be the one shooting – I would."

"Right. I guess that's all, then."

"Until next time. Thank you for using Sagasa's Scrap and Salvage. We tear down the past to build a better future." The comms went dead.

Felix slumped against the wall. The clock was counting down, and he didn't doubt that Azad would carry through on her threat. He glanced at his first officer. "You look like you're thinking, Tib. What are you thinking?"

Tib shrugged. "I was just thinking back to the propulsion laboratory. I took the real power cell and switched it with the fake Thales made. I don't know why I bothered. The whole point of swapping it was to make it look like no crime had even occurred, and at that point, there was already a murder victim in the next room. But that was the plan, and I executed the plan. If I hadn't, we'd still have the fake power cell, and we could trade *that* for Calred. Azad and Severyne would still have Thales, but they wouldn't be able to use his device. We'd still have *some* hope of winning."

Felix nodded. "That would have been nice. Elegant. Roguish." He sighed. "But we don't have a fake power cell, and I don't have the skills to build a new one. You?"

"I skipped constructing-fake-technology class at the academy."

"So."

"So."

"I guess we lose."

"It's the second time today we thought we'd lost," Tib said. "Last time, we thought we'd lost, and were about to *die*."

"True. But last time we didn't think anyone else was going to win, either. I am really not happy letting Azad win."

"I'd say there's a good chance that she and the Dampierre woman will end up murdering each other," Tib said. "They have mutually incompatible goals, when it comes down to it."

"That's a comfort," Felix said. "How mad do you think Jhuri will be that we lost Thales?"

"He hasn't invented anything yet," Tib said. "So only roughly the same amount of mad as he will be about you losing the *Temerarious*."

Felix groaned.

There was no way the parties involved were going to trust one another to make the exchange without some attempts at murderous treachery, so they enlisted Sagasa's help after all. He, his Naalu, his N'orr, and two armored guards went with Felix and Tib to their dock. The airlock doors opened, and Azad stood there with Calred, who was clearly sedated and shackled.

"Where's Severyne?" Felix called across the airlock. "Did you kill her already?"

"Nah, she's watching our pet scientist," Azad said. "Hey,

Sagasa. Thanks for stepping in to facilitate matters."

"It is sad when two parties cannot trust one another to deal fairly," the Hacan said. "But such mistrust enriches me, so I cannot bring myself to hate it entirely." He gestured. "Captain Duval? The object in question?"

Felix opened his bag and handed over the sphere. Sagasa could hold it in one huge paw. "This little bauble is the cause of so much strife?"

"Only about a quarter of the cause," Azad said. "But we've got the other three-quarters already."

"Intrigues buzz about me like flies around a carcass," Sagasa said. "It is fortunate that I am fundamentally an incurious man." He strode into the airlock. "Release Calred, please."

Azad gave him a nudge, and Cal stumbled forward. Tib hissed in frustration at Felix's side. "I know," Felix murmured.

Sagasa snapped his fingers, and the Naalu slithered forward, undulating across the deck, and helped Calred out of the airlock. Sagasa handed the power cell to Azad. "Does this conclude your business?"

"Once Captain Duval gives you permission to release the docking clamps and let us go on our way."

Sagasa turned to him. "You'll allow her to take your ship, captain?"

"That's… the deal." Hard to speak, through gritted teeth.

"I assume we'll be discussing the purchase of a new vessel, then? Or another rental?"

"Probably," Felix said.

"Just don't use your new ship to chase after us, OK?" Azad said.

"If you were me, would you give up?" Felix said.

"Of course not. There's no fun in giving up. But I figured I'd give you fair warning. I've got a ship with *big* guns, and a power source that will make them even bigger."

Felix winced. They'd talked to their goons on the other ship, then, and deduced the nature of the secret weapon. "Your advice is noted."

"All right, then. See you in the void."

"Not if I target lock you first."

The airlock slid closed. Calred slumped against the wall, blinking. "Sorry, captain." His voice was slurred. "They sealed me in a corridor and gassed me. I couldn't do anything about it."

"We're just glad you're OK, Cal." Felix turned to Sagasa. "Hey. You sold them that cruiser we disabled."

"I don't comment on my business affairs. Confidentiality is key."

"I already *know* you sold it to them – Severyne said so. What I want to ask is, where's the ship they *came* here in? They didn't swim to your station."

"Why do you ask?"

"Because they took my ship," Felix said. "I'm interested in taking theirs."

"It just so happens that I'm in a position to sell it," Sagasa said.

"The *Grim Countenance*." Sagasa stood in the middle of the Letnev ship's black-metal bridge and spread his arms. "A top-of-the-line Letnev battle cruiser, one of their famed thorn ships, sure to strike terror into the hearts of et cetera.

A fine choice for the unaffiliated privateer, because you can sow terror throughout the stars, and since the ship is so distinctive, the Barony will be blamed – their reputation for dark deeds providing cover for your own."

"Are all the original data banks intact?"

"I haven't even had the vessel cleaned," Sagasa said. "I didn't know I owned this ship until those two flew away without returning the ship they traded this one for. They left the *Grim Countenance* as collateral. I have now collected it. It is new inventory, ready to move."

"Name your price."

Sagasa named one. Calred, who was nearly recovered from his sedation, roared. "That's more than it cost the Barony to build it!"

"Try buying one from the Barony, then," Sagasa said.

Felix sighed. "You two negotiate, and come to an agreement that won't bankrupt us, OK, Cal?"

He went to the command station, considering the unfamiliar controls. The Mentak Coalition studied how to operate all sorts of different vessels – that was the raider's life – and though it had been a while since he'd done his Letnev tutorials, he thought he could muddle along.

Tib joined him. "Apart from the symmetry of taking their ship when they took yours, is there a reason you wanted this boat in particular?"

"It's fast," he said. "It's got guns. It's a match for the *Temerarious* in a fight."

"Except that they have umpty-petawatt-laser cannons, and we don't."

"It's as close as we're going to get to a match for the

Temerarious in a fight, then," Felix said.

"Fair enough, but we don't know where they *went*. They'll shut down the transponder and run dark. They might go back to Jord. They might go to the Barony. Thales said he had various test sites in mind, so maybe they'll go to one of those, but we don't know what those sites are. We're good at hide-and-seek, but we're not *that* good."

"We can find them." Felix figured out how to pull up the ship's personnel roster. The information he wanted was locked, but he had his fob full of Mentak Coalition pirate tools to break that security. He put them to work. "Once we own this system, we can track them down, if we hurry."

"How?" Tib said.

"The Letnev are a paranoid, suspicious, distrustful culture. Their culture heroes are all snitches and informants. They sell out their own grandmothers for promotions."

"The version of the Letnev that appears in sims as villains is all that, absolutely, but it's an exaggeration–"

"They're paranoid enough to track their officers, though." He pulled up Severyne's file, her frozen face on the screen. "Anyone who might defect or sell secrets or who poses a danger to the motherland is fitted with a tracking device, the kind you can't get out without a bomb disposal unit that's also capable of thoracic surgery. If we get moving before that device is out of range, we can track them."

"Calred!" Tib shouted. "Hurry up and close that deal. We're going to cheat at hideand-seek!"

CHAPTER 26

"I can't believe we left the *Grim Countenance* behind." Severyne sat with her head in her hands. "I delivered one of the Barony's finest ships into the hands of a Hacan crime lord."

"It's a shame," Azad said. They were in Felix's cabin, Azad lounging on the bed, Severyne seated at the small desk. "If I'd seen a way to keep both, I would have."

"Loss of a Barony warship is an offense punishable by death."

"You've committed a couple of those. The nice thing about death sentences is, they aren't really cumulative. It's not like the Barony can execute you twice."

"They *can*," Severyne said. "They kill you, then restart your heart, then kill you again. It's fairly common."

"Wow. I stand corrected. So, have you considered my offer?"

Severyne sighed. "My people are taught to choose death before dishonor, Azad."

"But are you really expected to choose *double* death

before dishonor? That's a lot of death." Azad rose and stood behind the desk, where she began to massage Severyne's tense shoulders. Severyne willed herself to relax into the touch. Azad had skillful hands. She should have killed the human by now, but it was nice having her to talk to. Without Azad, Severyne would be stuck here alone with Thales, who had not proven pleasant based on their brief acquaintance. Shelma had been annoying, but Thales was vile.

"Maybe I can make you feel better, or, at least, make you feel *good*," Azad purred.

Then the comms blared. "This is Thales!" the scientist yelled, as if there were anyone else it could be. "We need to talk about my experiment, ladies, right now."

"He does not seem to realize he's a prisoner," Azad said. "He appears to believe he is our boss."

"I have noticed that," Severyne said.

"We'll meet you in half an hour in the galley," Azad replied, shipwide.

"Half an *hour*? I demand we meet–"

Azad turned off the comms. "So. What do we do with half an hour?"

They only got ten minutes, because at that point, Thales started pounding on their door and screaming, which rather ruined the mood.

"You two are disgusting," Thales said. "You aren't even the same species."

"You grew up on Nar." Azad leaned way back in one of the galley chairs, her boots up on the table. "You never kissed a squid? No sense of adventure."

"When I think of you two—" Thales began.

"We aren't here to listen to your fantasies, Doc," Azad interrupted. "You insisted we meet. What's the ruckus?"

Thales composed himself. "I assume you plan to deliver me to your superiors in the Federation of Sol?"

"That's the idea," Azad said. "We sure took the long way around, but the end is in sight."

"You shouldn't take me back there yet."

"Oh? Why not? You have some more errands you need to run? More old rivals to gas or poison?" Azad and Severyne had both read Duval's private log entries, including his speculation about what Thales had done. Azad had checked, and the ship was still running diagnostics on Shelma's corpse. She was curious to see what it turned up.

"It is a long trip back to the heart of Federation space," Thales said. "There is only one nearby wormhole you could plausibly use to get there. We're in a stolen Coalition warship. Their raider fleets will be on alert, looking for this vessel. Don't you think they'll be waiting for you at the gate?"

"Oh, probably," Azad said. "You forget I'm a covert operative by training, Doc. There are ways around that problem."

"Are those ways entirely without risk?"

Azad shrugged. "Taking a *shower* isn't entirely without risk. You could slip and fall. There could be a fault in the heating system, and you could get electrocuted. I guess, if you were particularly stupid, you might even manage to drown."

"I think avoiding Coalition forces is riskier than taking a shower, woman."

"Call me Amina, Doc. We're all pals here."

I don't even call her Amina, Severyne though. *It would feel far too familiar.* Considering some of the things they'd done together, that should have been a ridiculous thought, but it wasn't.

"Damn it, admit I'm right," Thales said.

"Yes, fine, there's danger." Azad yawned in his face. "So what? It's the only path. I was sent to fetch you, and here I am, fetching you. I know you don't want to work with the Federation any more—"

"I don't care who I work with," Thales said. "These idiots, those idiots, you idiots. I only left the Coalition because it seemed wise to put some distance between myself and the ruins of my lab. All I care about now is the work. Duval and his crew acquired the last pieces I needed – the prototype trigger and the power source. I've been working on them in my lab, and the activation engine is ready. We don't *need* to go through a heavily guarded wormhole, risking our lives in the process. We can open our *own* wormhole, and return to the Sol system directly."

Azad whistled. "Really. Your magic button is done?"

"It isn't *magic*."

"Shelma was that close to completion?" Severyne said. "She told us it would be years before she had a device ready for testing!"

"Shelma was toying with you," Thales said. "By the time I got her prototype, it was practically done, except for the power supply – which she didn't even mention to you. She didn't want the Barony to have this power. I don't think she wanted anyone to have it, frankly. She was afraid of harnessing such power. Coward. I would like to note, her design was based entirely on *my* research–"

"You'll get full credit, Doc, don't worry," Azad said. "The dead can't demand a byline. So the thing really works. In that case why shouldn't I just kill you and take it home? We don't actually care about Phillip Thales. Just about what Phillip Thales can build – or, in this case, steal from a Hylar and plug into a battery."

Thales sniffed. "Such threats are so predictable. Only I know how to operate the device, and, moreover, most of my additions to Shelma's design were instituted to make the whole thing tamper-proof. Anyone who tries to open the case to examine the interior, or do a more than purely passive scan, will fuse all the components into melted slag. I will share my designs only when I have proper assurances from the Federation authorities that I'll be compensated to my liking."

Azad nodded. "I thought you'd have something slippery in mind. Your brain is powered by grievance and paranoia."

"How do you know it really works?" Severyne said. "You haven't even turned it on yet."

"When the theory is sound, the practice is mere formality, young lady."

"That is not even a little bit true," Azad said.

"It is easier to sell a finished product than just the plans for one," Thales admitted. "That's the only reason I stooped to doing actual engineering."

Azad said, "I admit, I'm curious to see if it works. It's not like my bosses are expecting me back anytime soon – they probably assume I'm dead, since I've been gone this long.

Being presumed dead offers some operational flexibility. What do you say, Sev? Should we see if this guy's as smart as he thinks he is?"

"It would be advantageous to verify the functionality of the device," Severyne said.

"You are so hot right now," Azad said. "I'd like to verify the functionality of your—"

"Stop!" Thales roared. "You repulse me. I never thought I'd miss Duval and his cretinous crew." He put his hands flat on the tabletop. "We need to travel to an appropriate test site."

"I thought the whole point of your wonder-device was that it can open a wormhole from anywhere to anywhere?" Azad said. "Fire it up right here and now."

"I would rather not. It's possible there could be ripple effects in space-time after I open the wormhole. Or the wormhole might not open precisely where I intend. We're within a few thousand kilometers of an inhabited asteroid belt right now. I don't expect any problems, but I want to open the first wormhole in an uninhabited area, to *another* uninhabited area, until I can verify all the readings fall within expected parameters."

"So we're headed to the big empty. I can see how opening a wormhole in the middle of a civilization would be a big problem."

"Or a huge opportunity," Severyne said.

"What do you mean?" Azad said.

"I mean, if you opened a wormhole directly above, say, Jol or Nar, the resulting warping of space-time would destroy the planets." That was why the Barony really wanted the device – for the remote planet-killing capabilities. The ability to move a fleet from anywhere to anywhere was of secondary importance.

"Now, 'destroy' is an overstatement," Thales said. "But opening a wormhole near a planet would have powerful gravitational effects, and would likely cause mass casualties. There are safeguards in place that won't permit the wormhole to open if–"

"Huh. So could you open a wormhole inside an enemy ship?" Azad said. "Just tear them to bits?"

"Again, there are safeguards against such accidents, but if those safeguards were disabled, then in theory–"

"Theory is just practice that hasn't happened yet, isn't that what you were saying?" Azad interrupted. "Oh, I like this. I like this a lot. You should have led with the whole 'I can destroy planets' thing, Thales – you would have gotten way more funding."

"That is not the purpose of this device. My activation engine is meant to facilitate exploration, and trade, and to help galactic civilization flourish. I don't want my legacy to be that of a war criminal."

"Nobody gets to choose their legacy. One side's war criminal is the other side's war hero, usually, anyway. Besides, the Federation researched you thoroughly, Thales. The purpose of this device is to make you so rich and powerful you never have to do what anybody else tells you to ever again. That's all you really care about."

"I also want respect, Amina." His eyes blazed. "I have been belittled, dismissed, laughed at, for my entire life – that stops. The moment I turn on this device, I will prove my brilliance. Even *you* will be forced to admit that I'm the man who transformed the galaxy."

"Fine by me," Azad said. "Let's find a place to turn it on. Someplace where we *won't* kill a bunch of asteroid miners by accident."

"I have considered the nearest options." Thales called up a star chart on his tablet and showed it to them, zooming in on a marked point in space. There was nothing there, which, Severyne supposed, was part of the point. "I say we go here."

"Does that work for you, Sev?"

Severyne looked at the scientist. "Do you have anything else you'd like to share about your device, Thales?"

"Nothing that people with your lack of education would understand–"

"I worked with Shelma," Severyne said.

"Yes, I'd assumed you were sent to fetch her back. Why else would a Letnev and a human be working together? Do you expect me to express some sympathy for the loss of our mutual colleague? Fine. Her death was a tragedy. She simply couldn't handle the strain of–"

"I don't care about sympathy," Severyne snapped, and was pleased to see his face shut down. "I wasn't friends with Shelma. She was infuriating – though having met you, I must say, I miss her. But she told me about her work, and her worries. She was concerned about that ripple effect through space-time, too, Thales. But she wasn't *just* worried about harming nearby inhabitants. She said there was a chance the ripple effect would propagate. That the wormhole would become unstable, and spread, corroding the fabric of space-time, in all directions… forever."

Thales sniffed. "I obviously don't think that's a serious concern. Shelma was always too cautious. There are legends about the first humans to discover the power of atomic energy. When they built an atom bomb, they were afraid to test it, because some of their scientists theorized that setting off an atomic weapon might create a chain reaction that would ignite the hydrogen and nitrogen in the oceans and the atmosphere and kill everything on the planet in a cataclysm of endless flame."

"I assume that didn't happen," Azad said. "Since there are still a few humans around."

"It did not happen. Shelma's worry is even *less* likely. She didn't want the Barony to have this technology, as I told you, so she over-emphasized the risks."

"And yet, I am not reassured," Severyne said. "You are a megalomaniac with a device that might burn down the galaxy."

"When you put it that way, even I get a little shiver," Azad said. "But, hell, he built the thing already. One thing you should know about humans, Sev, is that once we've built something, we're gonna turn it on."

CHAPTER 27

"We've got them." Calred loomed over the security station on the *Grim Countenance* – or the *Incontinence*, as Felix had taken to calling it. "We're gaining on them, even. They don't seem to be in any particular hurry."

"Are they heading toward the wormhole to Sol, or to Barony space?" Felix asked. "Tib bet me that Azad would kill Severyne and head back to Jord, but my money's on Severyne killing Azad and heading to the Barony – people underestimate her."

"I could go either way," Calred said. "But *they* didn't. Go either way, I mean. They're headed, as far as I can tell, for a big old stretch of nowhere."

"They're going to test the device, then," Felix said. "They must be."

"It's a working hypothesis," Tib said. "What do we do about it? Hang back and see if the activation engine even works? If it doesn't work, we can just slink away and let *them* kill Thales."

"If it does work, though…" Felix shook his head. "If they

open a wormhole, they might go through it, and then they could end up anywhere. I say we take back our ship."

"You want to fight them hand-to-hand in the corridors, huh?" Calred said. "All right. As long as Severyne doesn't have a halberd this time."

"I think it was a glaive guisarme," Tib said.

"Weapons nerds," Felix said. "How long before we intercept?"

"A couple of hours if I push it," Calred said. "Longer if I try to creep up on them, hiding in the sensor-shadows of asteroids along the way. The problem is, they're headed for wide-open nothingness, so if we go in slow, they're definitely going to see us coming at the end, and they have horrible super lasers they can use to blow us up."

"Fortunately, we don't really care if they shoot holes in this ship. And we have our secret weapon."

"Secret weapon nerd," Tib said.

"Set the fastest intercept course you can," Felix said. "We'll– hold on." A priority message lit up in his comms. It had been sent some hours ago, but to the *Temerarious*. Felix had only now gotten close enough for his ship to recognize his personal comm system and forward the message.

Undersecretary Jhuri gazed at him in his heads-up display. "I know I said you should act with autonomy, Felix, but you need to call me, right now, and explain why you just bought a Barony warship from the most notorious criminal in the vicinity of Vega Major."

Connecting a call all the way back to Moll Primus from said Barony warship was tricky, but eventually Felix got through, using the right call signs and passwords to reach the undersecretary's desk, since he lacked the proper encryption protocols on the *Grim Countenance*. The Barony ship's ready room was all black metal and dim light, and Felix worried he'd get tetanus from sitting in the ornamentally spiky captain's chair, but he settled himself as comfortably as he could.

Jhuri appeared, a figure drawn in light above the desk. "I refuse to believe you've defected to the Barony, Felix. They make their alcohol out of fungus."

"I can explain. But only if you *want* me to explain. Explaining will involve telling you things that officially you should not know about."

"I'm good at compartmentalization, Felix."

"This is a secure channel?"

Jhuri barked a laugh. "It's so secure we can barely talk to *each other* through the layers of encryption. You're on a Barony ship, and I'm communicating with you like you're a deep-cover double agent. Tell me your tale of woe."

Felix filled him in on everything: the jailbreak, Shelma's death, their run-in with Severyne and Azad at Sagasa's station, the heist on Jol, the propulsion lab director's death, their *additional* run-in with Severyne and Azad, and their current situation.

Jhuri blinked at him when it was done. "Have you had time to eat or sleep?"

"Not enough, sir."

"Duval's Devils, eh? So. What's your plan?"

"Overtake, board, and recover the *Temerarious*, and bring back Thales–"

"I thought it would be something like that," Jhuri said.

"No. The chance of successfully reclaiming Thales and the device is minimal. Destroy them instead."

Felix leaned back, and one of the spikes on the chair poked him in the side of the neck, so he leaned forward again. "Sir, this isn't a lost cause – we can get Thales and his device back – I know we can. Boarding ships and taking their stuff is what we *do*."

"This whole situation has become very messy, Felix. They don't know you're behind them. You can target them, all weapons hot, and annihilate them. We won't get the wormhole tech, but neither will anybody else. Tipping the balance in our favor would be wonderful, but maintaining the status quo is a decent second option. If you try to board them and fail, and they get away… I don't like to imagine the consequences, especially since Sol *and* the Barony have reasons to be annoyed with us after all this. If either or both of their governments gain the power to open a wormhole over the skies of Moll Primus…"

"If you order me to destroy them, sir, I will. But I'm asking you to have faith in me. What's the motto written on the seal of the Table of Captains?"

Jhuri sighed. "It says, 'Who Dares, Wins.' It's a nice sentiment, Felix, but the truth is: who *wins*, wins."

"If we do it your way, sir, the best outcome is: we don't lose. At least let me *try* to win."

The undersecretary gazed at Felix – or, perhaps, off into space – for a long moment. "I'll offer you a compromise," Jhuri said.

"That's great, sir."

"The terms of the compromise might require you to die."

"That is less great, sir," Felix said, "but I'm still listening."

"I don't get to board the ship and shoot people?" Calred said. "The only thing that's been keeping me going is the thought of boarding the ship and shooting people! Specifically, Severyne. She shot me in the arm. It's still tingly."

Felix shook his head. "Someone has to stay here. It's Jhuri's compromise. Tib and I can try to board, and fight, and recover Thales, and seize control of the ship, but if we fail, you have to blow up the *Temerarious*."

"With you two on board?"

"If we fail, we'll probably be dead anyway," Felix said.

"That is a terrible compromise," Tib said. "Why aren't we going with option one, and just blowing them up? That's also the only plan where Thales dies, so that's a plus."

"Not you, too?" Felix said. "They stole Thales from a colony we were supposed to be protecting. They stole my ship, Tib. They stole Shelma's research. They stole the power cell. They stole all that stuff that we stole in the first place! We're the Coalition. We don't get robbed. We *rob*."

"I am very excited to blow up a spaceship," Calred said. "I am significantly less excited to blow up a spaceship with my friends on board."

"Consider it avenging our deaths," Felix said. "You have your orders, Calred. Come on, Tib. Let's go get in our secret weapon."

Azad woke up with a yawn, looked around, and saw Severyne was gone.

She checked in with the ship while she got dressed. There

was nothing showing on their sensors except some distant asteroids. Nobody had messed around with the life-support functions or security controls. Everything seemed in order. Ostensibly, Azad had given Severyne full control of the ship, but of course, she'd kept her own backdoor access. She scanned through the ship's cameras. Thales was still bustling around in his lab. There were some cleaning and repair drones doing their thing. No sign of Severyne at all.

The ship had a lower deck. That space was usually meant as crew cabins and support spaces, but on this ship it was all just cargo storage for relief supplies. There were, for reasons Azad had been unable to determine, no working security cameras down there. Maybe the Coalition hadn't bothered to install any, figuring nobody would ever go down there anyway, or maybe Felix had disabled the cameras so he could have discreet sex with prostitutes, or he ran an illegal knife-fighting ring back in the colonies. Who knew? That deck was a surveillance dead zone, though. "Sev," she said over the loudspeakers. "Where are you?"

"I'm on the lower deck," she called back promptly. "There's something down here I think you'll want to see."

Here we go, Azad thought. Time to play hide-and-seek.

"I'll be right there," she said, and went to the galley to pick out a knife.

Severyne waited in the darkness. She'd shut off all the lights, even the emergency ones, and she wore a helmet with gas filters and a heads-up display featuring thermal imaging and night-vision overlays. She'd raided the armory and supplied herself with small arms, then disabled the armory door controls, locking the other weaponry inside. Even if Azad was suspicious, she would be relatively defenseless... though someone like Azad was never entirely so.

The lack of cameras down here left her as much in the dark as anyone, but she could monitor the rest of the ship and see Azad coming – until suddenly her feeds went dark. "What?" she said aloud. She tried to reboot, but her system said, "Authorization revoked."

"Oh you're clever," she muttered. Azad had access to the ship's core controls after all. "'You're the one sitting in the big chair' indeed." Her attempts to distract the human had failed, then. Azad knew exactly what was happening here.

"You know, it doesn't have to be this way, Sev." Azad's voice over her personal comms was low and insinuating and right in Severyne's ear, just like it had been earlier, but it was saying much less pleasant things now. "I really do like you. There's zero incentive for me to kill you. Your death gains me nothing. Keeping you alive is good for me, even – my superiors will be excited to have a Barony defector. Let me keep you safe and happy."

Severyne crouched behind a pallet of shrink-wrapped air purifiers. She wasn't going to chat. She wasn't going to roam around. She was going to wait for Azad to creep close, and then shoot her in the back of the head. Severyne wasn't Azad's equal as a hunter, but she could be a very capable spider, lying in wait for prey to stumble into her web.

"You have choices here, Sev. I know they're shitty choices! I get that. But you're betting you can beat me in a fight in the dark, and that's just... Look. You know I think the world of you. You've got talent, and you've got potential.

The dance you did with Duval back on Sagasa's station, that was a thing of beauty, and you've got some real steel in you. I've seen that. I respect it. But, babe. You can't win in a fight against me. Especially not a dirty fight. Come out, drop your weapons, and we'll forget this ever happened. If Thales comes through, my superiors are going to be delighted, and I can negotiate a great deal for you. I'll visit you. Conjugals, even. What do you say?"

Briefly, Severyne considered. She decided to speak. "Azad. If we could go on like this, you and I, traveling and fighting and winning, that would be a temptation. But you offer me a future locked in a secure Federation facility. I used to *run* a facility like that. I would be in the same position Shelma was in: something between a pet and a prisoner. I can't take that. Could you endure such a thing, if our positions were reversed?"

"I guess not," Azad said. "But now you're tempting me. We could do it, huh? Just go our own way. Take this activation engine Thales made and sell it to some third party – the Naalu would love it, and I know people over there. We could get rich, buy a ship, do crimes, make out. Is that your proposal?"

"Amina," Severyne said. "That sounds wonderful." It really did. Severyne didn't have to lie.

"Yeah, it does. It's a shame you'd never actually do it. I'm not saying I would either – I'm fifty-fifty on the idea, I see pluses and minuses – but I know you wouldn't. You're Letnev, Sev. All the way through. Death before dishonor, and being with me, as much as it might turn you on, it's still dishonor."

"Then we do what we must," Severyne said.

"That we do."

There was a sound, a sort of *thump*, and Severyne's heads-up display went dark. She cursed, tried to reboot it, but found the system entirely unresponsive. The faint glow of the charge gauge on her sidearm was dark, too, and that meant –

It had to be an electromagnetic pulse. Azad must have used an EMP grenade, and just having one of those on hand meant she'd planned for this scenario, or something like it.

Severyne no longer had the advantages she'd so carefully created. In fact, she had *disadvantages*, because when it came to fighting with nothing but your bare hands, Azad was much better.

"Hey, Sev!" The voice was not on comms, but echoing through the air. "I'm down here in the dark, and you're down here in the dark. We used to have so much fun together in the dark, huh? I bet you have some guns that don't work any more. I don't have guns either, if that makes you feel better. I do have a knife. I'm guessing you probably don't, though. Just remember, even a gun that won't shoot is a pretty good club. I'm the sharp edge, and you're the blunt object. So, let's see who's going to be dead, and who's just going to be heartbroken."

Carefully, silently, Severyne began to move.

CHAPTER 28

Down in the belly of the *Grim Countenance* rested the *Endless Dark*, burnt-out laser cannons and all. "This is not a boarding craft, Felix," Tib said. "It is barely even a craft at this point."

"Secret weapon," Felix said stubbornly. "It's so small, they might not even notice our approach, and if they do, we'll be harder to hit, because we're small and maneuverable. We're going to creep up on them and cut our way in." Sagasa had loaned them (for, of course, a price) a set of "salvage tools" – which were really the sort of drones raiders used to breach ships that didn't want to open their doors voluntarily. The drones squatted in the *Endless Dark*, filling much of the limited space inside the small craft, their bodies round and matte black, their wicked little manipulator arms and cutting torches all tucked away.

"We are going to die," Tib said.

"You always think that. If we do, Calred will make sure *they* die too."

"That will be no comfort to me, because I will be dead."

"Don't the Yssaril have the concept of an afterlife?" Felix said. "I read about it once. Your heaven is some kind of jungle, full of endless game, prey too slow to run away, and there are miniature versions of the predators that used to eat your people, and instead, you eat *them*–"

"That is what one tribe, out of a very large number of tribes, believes, yes. It's not the tribe my ancestors come from, but that doesn't matter. I'm from the Coalition, Felix. All I believe in is drinking, pillaging, and having a good time before you die."

"Are you telling me we haven't been having a good time?"

"I'd like to have a good time for a *longer* time."

Felix bowed his head. "Tib, if you want, you can stay here with Calred. I know I'm asking a lot of you, that it's dangerous, that–"

"Oh, shut up, you stupid human," Tib said. "I'm not going to let you die by yourself." She clambered into the ship. "Let's go. Time to put all that hide-and-seek training to use."

Felix strapped into the cockpit and called up to Calred. "Ready when you are."

The bay doors opened, and the *Endless Dark* dropped into space and began to accelerate toward the distant *Temerarious*. "Be safe, you two," Calred said.

"I think we'll be dangerous instead," Felix said. "Hang back at the very edge of effective weapons range. You know what to do if we don't call you from the bridge before time's up."

"Boom boom," Calred said. "The most depressing boom boom in the history of all boom booms. I will never forgive you if you ruin boom boom for me, captain."

•••

Felix sat in the pilot's chair, with Tib right beside him. "I like having you in that chair much more than Thales."

"I can't believe we're going to all this trouble to get that asshole back."

"Mostly I want my ship. Thales is a side project."

"They're going to see us coming," Tib said. "I know we're small, I know we're flying manual, but if they bother to look, they'll see us. You know it."

"Maybe Thales is keeping them busy." The *Temerarious* grew in the viewport as they crept closer. "He is very distracting."

"I should have given more thought to my last words," Tib said.

"I heard a story once about Erwin Mentak's last words."

"The glorious founder of our glorious Coalition? What did he say?"

"According to this guy I met in a bar," Felix said, "Erwin Mentak's final words were, 'Don't let it end like this. Tell them I said something.'"

Tib snorted laughter. "Thanks for amusing me as I wait to die."

But they didn't die – at least not yet. The *Endless Dark* reached the *Temerarious*, and sailed beneath its belly. "We're here," Felix said. "They can't hurt us now unless they open up a window and lean out to shoot us with a sidearm. Their sensors can't pick us up, either – we just look like part of the ship. See, Tib? Optimism."

"I can't understand how they didn't notice us," Tib said. "Is nobody monitoring their sensors? What are they *doing* in there?"

"Maybe they all killed each other." Felix spun their ship upside down and activated the magnetic clamps, so the *Endless Dark* could cling, parasitically, to the belly of the *Temerarious*. He unstrapped and went to the back of the ship, activating the boarding drones. They scuttled out of the small airlock, crouched on the hull of the *Temerarious*, and started cutting.

Once the hull was breached, Felix and Tib planned to enter a service tunnel, then slip through an access panel onto the lower deck, where there were no security cameras, because that's where they liked to play hide-and-seek. From down there, unseen, they should be able to sneak up and retake the ship.

Waiting was hard, and Felix checked and re-checked his weapons while the drones did their work. They finally beeped a completion tone to their comms, and Tib and Felix made their way out of the *Endless Dark* into the endless dark.

Felix took a moment, clinging to the skin of his ship, to look around. There was nothing out here. He couldn't even see many stars. Which, he supposed, was the point: Thales wanted a big stretch of empty to punch a hole in, out where no one would see the triumph of the human mind over the physics of the cold and uncaring universe.

"Felix, we have pirating to do," Tib said. "Stop striking a noble and thoughtful pose. There's nobody here to appreciate it."

The drones had deployed a temporary airlock, a sort of rounded tent made of "densely woven polymer" – which was to say, a plastic tarp. Felix unsealed the opening, and Tib slipped in. Felix clambered after and resealed the airlock. The hole the drones had cut in the hull was big enough for his body to fit through, but only just. He followed Tib up – or down – or through – the layers of armor and radiation shielding, on into the ship. The walls vibrated around him as the drones placed a more permanent seal over the hole they'd cut. They wouldn't be getting out the way they got in.

Felix wasn't particularly claustrophobic, but tight spaces *and* darkness *and* a mission to retake a stolen ship *and* the low-level discomfort of wearing an environment suit all combined to make him sweaty and tense. He waited, vibrating himself with tension, while Tib unsealed the access hatch to the service tunnel. They moved on into that objectively cramped but relatively generous space. They were still in the dark, though. Hmm. That wasn't right.

Once the hatch was closed behind them, they took off their helmets and shrugged out of their suits. "Why are the lights off?" Felix said. "There should at least be safety strips on in here. Did those assholes break my ship?"

"There's still air and artificial gravity," Tib said. "Maybe they just wanted mood lighting."

"It is very romantic," Felix said.

"Do you think everyone makes jokes before they walk into possible death, or is that just a Mentak Coalition thing?" Tib said.

"I'm not convinced the L1Z1X or the Nekro do it, being partly or wholly mechanical, but otherwise, I'd guess it's a pretty universal urge."

"I know a Nekro joke," Tib said. "Want to hear it?"

"I might not be alive to hear it later."

"Knock knock."

"Who's there?"

"Zero."

"Zero who?"

"Zero one one zero zero one zero zero zero, zero one one zero one zero zero one, zero one one zero zero one zero one–"

"OK, I get it. We've had the laughter. Let's move on to the tears. Stay quiet on comms until there's something to report. I'll get the bridge, and you secure the armory."

Tib went dim, just a shimmer in the corner of Felix's eye, and the access hatch opened seemingly by itself. Felix crawled out after he was sure she'd had time to get clear.

He was in a corridor, not far from the ladder that led up to the crew quarters, but he only knew that because he'd spent so much time down here playing hide-and-seek with Tib, and could navigate the space blindfolded if need be. The lower deck was totally dark. Had there been some electrical fault?

"Last chance, Sev!" a voice called. Felix went still. Was that Azad? "If I find you down here, I'm going to stab you, and that's way down on the list of things I want to do with you."

Oh, no. Or… oh, yes? Severyne and Azad were trying to kill each other *now*? That explained why they hadn't noticed the approach of the *Endless Dark*. Felix considered. He could just climb up to the next deck, lock the hatches, and leave them trapped down here to kill each other in peace. He opened his comms to suggest that idea to Tib.

Then light glimmered – someone had opened a hatch on the deck above, letting illumination in. "Are you idiots

Twilight Imperium

down there?" Thales bellowed. "There are alarms going off up here, it's *distracting*."

"What alarms?" That was Severyne – and she was very close to Felix, it sounded like, right around the corner.

"Something about a hull breach, though it stopped saying that a minute ago, and now there's a call to repel boarders – not that I've seen any boarders. I think your sensors are malfunctioning. This is not my *job*, ladies. I'm trying to work up here. You'd better not be having sex down there. Duval's bed isn't enough for you?"

"Sev!" Azad called. "Truce? Just while we make sure we aren't being attacked? By someone other than each other, I mean?"

A long, long pause, and then, "Truce," Severyne called. She walked right past Felix and into the shaft of light. Azad joined her. "It's always something, isn't it?" the human said.

Severyne ignored her and clambered up the ladder, bickering with Thales as she vanished from sight.

Azad started up the ladder, then paused and looked around in the dark. "I know you're there," she said. "You may as well come out."

Felix twitched, but didn't move.

Azad waited a moment longer, then snorted. "Worth a try." She climbed up the ladder.

Tib let her get almost all the way to the top before shooting her with a stun charge, so Azad had farther to fall. Tib shimmered into sight next to her supine form, peering up the ladder. Severyne and Thales were gone, and hadn't noticed Azad's tumble.

Felix hurried out of concealment and began binding

Azad's arms and ankles with tape while Tib kept lookout. Azad groaned but didn't wake up. "I got the drop on her twice," Tib whispered. "She only got me once. I win." Tib plucked a kitchen knife from Azad's belt, frisked her, then held up the blade. "This is the only weapon she has on her. What were they *doing* down here?"

"Playing hide-and-seek," Felix said. "Just like we used to. But for somewhat higher stakes."

They dragged Azad to one of the store rooms and propped her between a pallet of chemical toilets and stacks of shelf-stable mayonnaise. "Did Thales say they were having sex?" Tib asked. "In your bed?"

"I haven't even had sex in that bed. Now I have to set the whole thing on fire. I'll be moving into your cabin. You can have Cal's. Cal can sleep in the gym."

Tib looked at Azad's limp form. "I guess it wasn't true love, if they were still trying to kill each other."

"They were trying to kill each other over who got the privilege of keeping Thales," Felix said. "Can you imagine?"

The electrical locks weren't working down here for some reason, so they blocked the cabin door with about fifty bags of mulch, piling them up nearly to the ceiling. It probably wouldn't hold Azad back for long, but for now, it was the best they could do.

"Now we go for Severyne," Felix said.

"Leave me alone, Thales, I'm trying to read this. I thought you had work to do." Severyne stood at the security station in the bridge, though she hated having her back to the door. Where was Azad? Shouldn't she be doing this? Was her "truce" just a trick to make Severyne let her guard down? The ship had detected a hull breach, but now it didn't – which either meant it was a glitch in the system, or someone had breached the hull and covered their tracks. "Shipwide scan," she said. "I want to know everyone who's on board."

"Two sapients onboard," the ship replied.

"Just two?" That didn't make any sense. "Does that include the lower deck?"

"Lower deck systems offline. System rebooting."

So Azad was still down there. But why? Severyne was sure she'd been right behind her –

Something cold struck her back, and then her vision went white, and then dark. Some unknowable moment later she returned to herself, her face pressed into the smooth floor, her arms bound behind her. She wriggled and rolled over – and saw Duval sitting in the captain's chair, his horrible Yssaril second-in-command leading Thales off the bridge. "Ambush," she spat. "A cowardly strike from behind. The Coalition has no *honor*–"

"Probably true," Duval said. "But I still won. You know the old saying, Severyne: Who wins, wins."

"That is not an old saying. You are a very stupid person who is also annoying," Severyne said. "And unattractive. And you need to shave. Your haircut is a disgrace. You–"

"The Letnev," Felix said. "Magnanimous in victory, gracious in defeat."

CHAPTER 29

Severyne and Azad were in the ship's brig, secure behind a set of bars and an energy field. Severyne sat on a bench, dressed in hideous soft pants and a plain gray shirt. Azad was similarly garbed, but she was shackled by wrists, ankles, and waist to the wall, and wore a metal collar with an ominous blinking red light on the front. Severyne was annoyed that she wasn't considered enough of a threat to bother restraining so thoroughly.

"I'm glad I didn't have to kill you," Azad said.

That was the first time either of them had spoken since being locked up here. Severyne considered ignoring her, but what was the point now? "I am glad I did not have to kill you, too. What is your plan to escape and retake the ship?"

"Oh. Babe. I have no such plan."

"You escaped a Coalition dreadnought, did you not?"

"They didn't have me in shackles and a collar that explodes if I leave a ten-meter radius. Sometimes, Sev, you're just beat."

"A Letnev never admits defeat."

"That's a funny thing about defeat. It's still defeat, whether you admit it or not."

Sev considered. "If I can neither escape nor fulfill my mission, I would like to accept your offer to defect to the Federation now."

Azad chuckled. "My ability to follow through on that deal depends on various factors, like us not being Mentak Coalition prisoners forever, but I'll see what I can do."

"I might have bested you, on the lower deck. I found a screwdriver down there. I was not unarmed."

"Lovers turned deadly enemies, armed with screwdriver and knife, fighting for their mutually exclusive futures in the dark. It's kinda romantic, in a way."

"You are a ridiculous person, Amina Azad. If we had not let our personal rivalry distract us, we might have stopped Duval from retaking the ship."

"You're not wrong."

"Perhaps there is a valuable lesson there."

Amina belched. "Probably. Let me know when you figure out what it is."

"You disgust me."

"I love you too, Sev."

Severyne blushed.

"I mean, I guess, since we're already here, we might as well let him do his test." Felix was back in his ready room, because he wasn't ready to face his defiled cabin.

"You've gone this far," Jhuri said. "No reason to stop here. At least if his device malfunctions horribly, no one is likely to get hurt."

"Except us."

"Except you."

"What if the Creuss show up and declare war on all the biological entities in the galaxy when we switch this thing on?"

"What if the kelp fairy appears and wraps you all in ropes of kelp?"

"Is the kelp fairy even a real thing?" Felix said. "Like from Jol-Nar folklore or something?"

"How should I know?" Jhuri said. "I've never been to Jol-Nar. I hate long space voyages. Maybe if you can open a wormhole from my office to Wun-Escha I'll finally take the trip. I'll let you get to work."

"Wait! I wanted to know... What do I do with the prisoners?"

"What prisoners?"

"What do you mean, what prisoners?"

"I mean, I wish the human and the Letnev had died in a dramatic firefight. This whole situation is a potential diplomatic nightmare. A probable Federation operative, and a *definite* Barony security officer, knowing all the things they know about our own covert activities? I don't want a whisper of either one on the official record."

"Then what should I do with them?"

"What should you do with *who*? Let me know how the test goes." Jhuri flickered and vanished.

OK. Severyne and Azad were a problem for later. Other problems came first.

"I'm ready," Thales said simply. Thales, Felix, Tib, and Calred – who'd shuttled over from the *Grim Countenance* –

stood together on the bridge. The huge viewscreen showed the expanse of empty space before them.

Thales had his torpedo-shaped device resting on top of a workstation, attached to the stolen power supply, and wired into the ship's weapons systems – he'd be using some of the focused energy weapons to direct the force he was about to unleash. "We'll open the wormhole, and then launch a probe into it," he said. "I have programmed the other end of the wormhole to open a safe distance from the wasteland world Xanhact – the probe should be able to confirm that location from the configuration of stars, and return to us with data on the journey."

"Oh, good," Calred said. "I was afraid you'd want us to drive into the wormhole to test it."

"I'd love to jettison all of you into space," Thales said. "All this pointless to-ing and fro-ing and fighting and stealing you've dragged me through. I understand I'm valuable, but this inter-faction squabbling has been a grievous distraction." Thales gazed at the empty screen. "Would you transmit an image of this screen to the brig, captain?"

"What? Why?"

"So Dampierre and Azad can witness my triumph."

Felix scratched his chin. "Huh. I'm not opposed to a little gloating, I guess, but why do you care?"

"I want more witnesses, captain," Thales said. "More eyes on the moment I transformed the galaxy. More voices to tell the tale of this achievement."

Felix sighed. "Cal, go ahead and give the brig a screen. I don't need them on comms, though. I've heard enough out of both of them."

Thales cleared his throat. "I've prepared a few words for this occasion–"

"I've heard enough out of *you*, too," Felix said. "Just push the button, Thales."

The scientist glared at him. "This is history happening, right now, you ignorant thug. The occasion must be marked–"

"I promise we'll make sure the official records reflect whatever long speech you wanted to give, Thales. Let's just get this over with."

"We're not getting anything over with. This is a glorious *beginning*–"

"Shut up, or *I'll* push the button," Tib said.

"It's not a button," Thales muttered, but he turned his attention to his terminal. The power cell began to emit a faint hum. They all looked at the screen expectantly.

"Shouldn't beams of coruscating light be shooting from the cannons?" Calred asked.

"The energies involved aren't visible." Thales spoke through gritted teeth. "Don't ruin my enjoyment of this moment."

They watched, and nothing happened... until something started to happen.

At first, Felix thought it was just his eyes inventing things, an optical illusion caused by staring too long at emptiness, but there was a flicker, like a snake slithering through the grass, only the snake was space-time and the grass was more space-time. Thales made more adjustments to his terminal, and a sinuous bright line appeared, gleaming yellow like a thread of gold. "Pretty, isn't it? That's the sort of visual the idiot masses will appreciate when they watch this recording in their classrooms for all time going forward."

"I'm sure they'll appreciate being called idiots, too."

"You already said you're going to manipulate the record. I can say what I please."

"That doesn't look much like a wormhole," Calred pointed out. The golden thread rippled. "I've been through a few wormholes in my time. They're big, bulgy, and round. Not a wavy line, golden or otherwise."

"I'm still adjusting the calibration," Thales complained. "Give me a moment. Altering the fundamental physics of the universe doesn't happen in an instant."

"I always thought going through a wormhole was like passing through a giant water droplet," Tib said. "You know, the way it shimmers a little, and you can faintly see what's on the other side."

"I never understood why they call them 'holes' at all," Felix said. "They're more like… crystal balls."

"Because 'wormballs' sounds disgusting," Tib said.

"Fools," Thales muttered, still adjusting his controls. "If space were two-dimensional, then yes, wormholes would appear as circles punched in the surface of space. Passing through those circles would lead to a *three-dimensional* shape, a cylinder, and you would emerge from another flat circle on the other side. But space isn't two-dimensional, so instead we perceive wormholes as three-dimensional spheres, and they lead to a *four-dimensional* space that your minds can't visualize, until you emerge from another sphere."

"That is not a sphere," Calred said. "It's more like a rip. A tear in a piece of cloth." The gold thread widened, becoming a ribbon of uneven width, and the light became less yellow and more white.

Thales grunted. "I would expect it to start coalescing into a sphere by now."

"Do we need to abort the experiment?" Felix said.

"Of course not," Thales barked. "I think I see the problem. The other end of my wormhole isn't where it should be. Damn it. These readings about the far end of the wormhole are just gibberish. The other side must have opened in the Shaleri Passage – that's the only place I know of where normal physics are twisted, and it's where the Creuss live, so they must be meddling, trying to ruin my triumph!"

"You think the *Ghosts* are doing this?" Felix demanded.

"They must be. There's no other explanation. It's called deductive reasoning, captain."

"So, what, the Creuss are going to come out of that hole?"

"That tear," Calred said.

"I am trying to *determine*–" Thales said.

The light brightened, and suddenly the ribbon became a yawning chasm, a ragged tear big enough to swallow their ship.

Felix scrabbled for the device, but Thales hunched over it, blocking him with his body. "Turn this thing off, Thales!" Felix shouted.

"No, I can get control back, I just need to boost the power." Thales twisted the controls, glaring out the viewport at the shimmer in space. "This is *my* moment – I won't let some aliens who don't even have *bodies* spoil it."

"We're going to get murdered by the Ghosts of Creuss,"

Tib said. "You find such interesting ways for us to die, Felix."

The power source started humming much more loudly, and – was the spherical case *vibrating*? "There!" Thales said. "The connection is stable! It – no, that *still* doesn't make any sense. Why isn't the wormhole opening where I told it to?"

"Why is it a *gash*?" Felix said. "What the hell did you do, Thales?"

The tear in space widened before them, and beyond it, something moved. Colors flickered in there, like aurora, but there were other things, too. Writhing things. Felix thought of maggots in rotting meat. Of baby spiders bursting out of a wound. Of worms wriggling up out of a wet hole.

"Send the probe," Thales said.

"*Why*?" Felix said. "That's not Xanhact through there! It's not even a wormhole!"

"Maybe artificial wormholes present themselves differently!" Thales said. "Send the probe!"

Felix caught Calred's eye, shrugged, and nodded. Calred operated the panel at the security station, and a small gleaming sphere studded with sensors burst out of the ship and sailed toward the rift.

They watched the probe get closer and closer to the chasm – and then tendrils of coruscating darkness lashed out of the rift, grabbed the probe, and pulled it in.

"What," Thales said flatly. "What are you getting from the probe?"

"It's just throwing error codes," Cal said.

"Is that the Shaleri Passage on the other side?" Felix said. "Damn it, Thales, did we just shoot a Coalition probe at the Creuss?"

"I… I don't think…"

"Look," Tib said. "There's something in the crack. A shape, a structure, I can't quite make it out, it's–"

Felix heard a whimper. He realized a second later it had come from his own throat.

There was something inside the crack. Felix had no sense of scale, so he couldn't tell how big the thing was – the size of a starship, the size of a star, bigger. He just knew, whatever size it was, it was impossible.

The thing beyond the crack in space was a burning wheel, facing them side-on, slowly rotating, flickering with a corona of white fire. The spokes of the wheel seemed to be made of yellowed, splintered bone. The rim of the wheel was an immense red serpent, devouring its own tail. The hub of the wheel was an open, bleeding eye.

The eye stared at them. The eye *saw* them. More tendrils began to reach out of the rift, this time, toward the *Temerarious*.

CHAPTER 30

Felix reached for the power source, but Thales hugged the battery and the trigger to his chest. "No! I can fix this!"

Calred tackled him, and the sphere fell from his hand, clattering to the deck, the case cracking loudly on impact. The power cell whined louder, and thin, acrid smoke started to rise from the crack in its side. "Look out!" Felix shouted, diving for Tib and throwing himself on top of her.

The power cell overloaded with a loud *pop* and filled the bridge with a flash of white light and a buzz that made Felix's teeth ache. He staggered upright and looked, through blinking eyes, at the viewscreen. The rift was already shrinking, like a sped-up recording of a wound healing, and the dark tendrils receded into the dark just before it closed. The afterimage of that brightness – and that burning wheel – floated in Felix's vision, though.

Felix leaned against the nearest station, breathing hard. "Tib, Cal, are you OK?"

"I'm a little bruised from you jumping on me," Tib complained.

"I thought it might explode like a grenade," Felix said. "I was being selfless."

"Be selfless on top of someone else next time, captain."

Calred was all right too, but Thales was picking over the remnants of his device, sobbing. The power cell had ruptured into several pieces, and the trigger was cracked too. "You broke it open when you knocked me down!" he shouted. "The interior is fused, it's a melted mess, I'll have to start from scratch–"

Cal stomped down on the device and ground his heel. "That was not a wormhole," Cal said. "That was something else. That was something bad." He was breathing hard, like he'd just run an obstacle course. "Sagasa the Disciplinarian comes from a sect that believes that in the afterlife evildoers are punished forever by demons of blood and fire. I have never believed in that place. But now... now I've seen it, and you, Thales, *you* opened that door. You nearly let that hell into our world."

"It... the device just needs refinement, is all, I'll look at the math–"

Felix grabbed Thales by the back of the neck and dragged him to his feet. "It's over, Thales. Your machine didn't work. That thing, that place, whatever we saw... no one should ever see that again. There are some rocks you shouldn't turn over."

"I- I don't know what went wrong," Thales said.

Felix frowned, remembering. "The Ghost. The one that destroyed your lab. What did it say to you again?"

"What? Why are you talking about that? It's ancient history, and anyway, this wasn't the Creuss, I don't know what it was, but–"

"The Ghost said, 'you must not fracture the void,' right?"

Thales stared at the empty screen. "Something like that."

"The Ghost wasn't trying to scare you off," Felix said. "It was trying to warn you. The Creuss weren't upset because you'd figured out their technology. They were upset because you *hadn't*, not correctly, and they knew if you kept going, you were going to… to do *that*. To open a passage to that place. To the things that live there."

"I… you…" Thales was never slow with a vicious comeback. Until now. "You can't know that. Not really."

"I know enough. Watch Thales for a few minutes, you two. I need to call our boss."

"Then what are you going to do with him?" Calred said.

"Then I'm going to escort him down to the brig," Felix said. "That's where we keep our murderers."

Felix shoved Thales into the cell beside Azad and Severyne. "Hello," he said. "Did you two see the show?"

"That was real?" Severyne said. "It wasn't a trick, to make us think the experiment failed?"

Felix pointed at Thales, who sat on a bench, weeping. "Would he be doing that if he'd succeeded?"

"No, he'd be doing a little dance," Azad said. "Huh. I have seen some messed-up things in my day, captain, but that hole he tore in space was beyond the beyond."

"I devoted years of my life, and ruined my career, for a project that would have failed anyway," Severyne said. "That is disheartening. What will you do with Thales now?"

"Oh, I'm offering this fine specimen of human theoretical

physicist to the highest bidder," Felix said. "What will you give me for him?"

Azad frowned. "Even if I had access to funds, why would I pay for something like that? I'm not saying *nobody* wants a weapon that rips open holes in space and lets nightmare monsters out, but I'm not going to give my superiors the option. Can you imagine, Severyne, if the humans could do *that* on demand?"

"The humans might actually use such a thing," the Letnev said.

"Exactly. So, no, captain. You can keep him."

"What do you think, Severyne?" Felix said. "Would the Barony be interested in Thales?"

"I… Why do you ask? Are you sending me back to the Barony?"

Felix shrugged. "I just assumed that's where you'd head after I let you go."

"Ha," Azad said. "The Coalition doesn't want us, huh? We're a big old can full of way too many worms, and some of those worms might bite."

"I don't understand," Severyne said.

"You don't bring prisoners back from a covert operation," Azad said. "Not prisoners like us, anyhow, from an operation like this. Now, if it was me in the captain's place, I'd shove us out an airlock without suits and let nature take its course. But Felix is sentimental, isn't he?"

"I've killed enough people because of Thales. I don't want to kill any more, if I can avoid it. I never want to see either one of you ever again. Can we arrange that? None of us want to talk about anything that went on here, I bet. As far as I can tell, there's no reason for us to try to shoot or strangle each other any more. No reason beyond personal vengeance, anyway."

"Don't discount the power of personal vengeance," Azad said. "But, nah, I'm good. Live to fight another fight."

"Will you give me back the *Grim Countenance*?" Severyne said.

"The *Incontinence* is yours. I don't have any use for it."

"Ha," Azad said. "*Incontinence*. Nice one."

"My people disabled all the weapons," Felix went on, "just in case you *do* feel a twinge of vengeance. Take your ugly spiky ship and fly far away. But back to Thales. He kidnapped and then murdered a Barony scientist. Don't you want to haul him back to your superiors and put on one of those show trials your people like so much?"

Thales finally seemed to realize what they were talking about. "You can't *sell* me, Duval! You have no right!"

Severyne ignored him. "I seem to recall you were involved in those crimes as well."

"Yeah, but I have a warship, and the key to your cell, and Thales doesn't, so he's easier to apprehend."

Severyne shook her head. "I see no advantage in taking him. Officially, no crime was committed. The research facility was secret, and Shelma's research was, too. As for myself, I am not even sure I can return to the Barony–"

"Sad story, hate to hear it," Felix interrupted. "I'll take that as a no. There's no profit in you at all, is there, Thales?"

"I was thinking, Sev," Azad said. "I can make a report to my superiors that only massages the truth a little, tell them

I recaptured Thales and decided to test his prototype, and it was a disaster. I can cover my own ass—"

"Why would they believe you?"

"Oh, I got footage of the eldritch horror show on my eyeball cams." She tapped her temple with a forefinger.

"Wait. Your eyes are recording devices? Does that mean…"

"I don't record everything. Though if you wanted…"

"Stop!" Severyne shouted.

"Listen. What I'm saying is, *I'm* going to be all right. I don't need to bring in a Barony defector to appease my bosses – I'll just show them Thales was a dead end and no great loss."

"So. You deny me my only chance at survival." Severyne slumped.

Azad rolled her eyes. "Will you listen to me? Try this: go home after all, and give them a gently massaged report too. Tell your superiors Thales murdered Shelma, so you took him instead, tested the device, all hell tried to break loose, and you left him stranded in space. We can stitch together some footage to support that narrative. We can even include you kicking Felix's ass in the scrapyard."

"She did *not* kick my ass," Felix said.

"Only because Sagasa stopped her," Azad said. "But it doesn't matter, because Duval's Devils are covert. There won't be any kind of official report to contradict Severyne's story." She grinned at the Letnev. "We're going to give you a total hero cut, Sev. I mean, I'll have to escape your custody at the end of the story, but I'm Amina Azad. I escape stuff. No one will be too mad."

Severyne frowned thoughtfully. "It could work, especially if I shift blame to the director of the research facility. After all, ultimately, Shelma's kidnapping was *her* responsibility. If you look at events in a certain way, I just went into the field to correct her failure–"

"I have some friends in the Barony who might be able to weigh in on your behalf, too, and support your version of events," Azad said. "I didn't mention that before, because I wanted you to defect."

Severyne's head snapped around. "Friends? In the Barony? Do you mean *assets*? You have spies in my government?"

"I told you, Sev, I make friends wherever I go."

"Speaking of going," Felix said. "Can you two get your story straight *elsewhere*?"

Azad shook her chains.

"Don't try to kill me when I let you loose," Felix said.

"I don't kill people for fun. What kind of sicko do you think I am? I only kill for the mission, and the mission is over."

Felix released Azad from her bonds with the push of a button. Azad tore the collar off, flung it into a corner of the cell, and then went to Severyne, putting an arm around her. "You know, Sev, I could get one of my friends in the Barony to recommend a new career path for you. You're wasted on a space station. You should be out in the field, like me, kicking ass. Just think – we might get to try and kill each other again someday."

Severyne looked at Azad, a speculative glint in her eyes, then stood up straight and fixed her gaze on Felix. "Farewell,

Captain Duval. You were an intermittently capable adversary."

"Thanks?" He opened the cell door and stepped aside.

Azad and Severyne walked past him, still arm in arm. "When we get back to the *Grim Countenance*," Azad said, "we can celebrate our mutual survival. I'll do that thing. The thing you like. With the thing."

Felix watched the play of expressions that flitted across Severyne's face. He could only identify a couple of them – disgust was in there, and lust – but that was enough to get the general idea. Everyone was having more fun in space than he was, even the joyless Letnev.

Well, almost everyone. Thales was still crying.

"Calred will escort you to your ship," Felix said. "I look forward to never seeing either of you ever again."

"Bye, captain. Good luck with Doctor Bullshit there." Azad gave a little finger-fluttering wave and sauntered out of the brig with Severyne.

Thales looked up, his eyes rimmed with red. "What happens now?"

"There's no profit in you," Felix said. "In the absence of profit, I have no choice but to pursue justice."

"You're going to kill me, then."

"It would be an execution, but no. I've been thinking about it, and I want you to live a long time, marinating in your own failure." Felix grinned. "I hope you enjoy our fine Mentak Coalition prison facilities."

"Prison. On what charge? You can't prove any crimes. I was working for your Coalition–"

"The *Temerarious* finally finished the tox screen we ran on

Shelma. It turns out she was killed by a synthetic neurotoxin introduced into her tank. Something pretty unusual, which is why it took so long for the computer to isolate the cause. We have video of you touching her armor, right next to a valve where we found traces of the toxin. We have records of you synthesizing that chemical in your lab the day she died – you deleted the chem-jet printer's local history, but the ship keeps a backup. Not just murder, but premeditated murder, and an attempt to cover it up. That, along with testimony from me and my crew, should be sufficient to put you away."

"This whole operation was covert," Thales said. "You can't have a trial."

"Not a public one, it's true. But my boss, undersecretary Jhuri, says he's happy to lead a secret tribunal. He's Coalition through and through, but he's also Hylar, Thales. He takes you murdering two of his species personally." Felix closed the door and rapped his knuckles against the bars of the cell. "That's about it. Enjoy your ride back to Moll Primus. Get used to confinement."

"At least you won't get *your* promotion," Thales said. "This failure sticks to you too."

"You'd think so, wouldn't you? But it turns out, Jhuri sees potential in my little group, and wants to keep us on in our new capacity. The *Temerarious* is being reassigned, and I'm now special attaché to the undersecretary of special projects." Jhuri had actually said "because I want to keep an eye on you," but Felix decided to gloss over that part. "Don't worry about us, Thales. Duval's Devils will ride again."

EPILOGUE

Phillip Thales – that was as good a name as any, and how he usually thought of himself these days – woke in the cell where he'd spent more time than he cared to remember, and gazed up at the dark.

Mentak Coalition prisons weren't the overcrowded hellholes he'd first expected based on the culture's bloodthirsty reputation – indeed, the Coalition's history, rooted in a horrific penal colony, had led them to create more benign conditions for their inmates. Thales was better off than he would have been if he'd failed the Barony or the Federation. Still, the irony of being imprisoned in a small space – him, the man who was supposed to open up the whole of the galaxy – was not lost on him.

There was sufficient food and water, and if the meals were repetitive and bland, that didn't matter. Food was just fuel, and his body was only a vessel for what truly mattered: his mind. He'd often thought he was born to the wrong species, first as a human in a world full of Hylar, and later, as a creature of matter at all – he should have been Creuss, composed of light and intellect.

The worst thing about being here was the boredom. There was a prison library, but it was limited and contained almost no technical material – certainly none on his level. When he complained about the lack of mental stimulation, one of the warders – in what she considered an act of kindness! – brought him a thousand-piece puzzle depicting some artist's conception of the Lazax imperial palace. Bah. Thales should have *lived* in a palace. Thales still had the puzzle, unopened, under his bunk. Perhaps someday things would get so bad he'd start putting it together.

His powerful mind had nowhere to go but in circles, retracing old grievances and plotting elaborate revenge fantasies – including revenge against the *universe*.

Why was he awake? His wing of the prison was quiet – the inmates who screamed all night were kept together elsewhere so they could only annoy each other. The dark was deep, no glimmer through the small high window, so morning must be a long way off. He didn't have to urinate, which was *usually* what woke him in the night, as he got older. So then…

"Thales. Thales. Thales."

The voice was whispery, like crumpling paper, and Thales moaned. He'd heard that voice before – and its difficulty with, or amusement at, his assumed name.

That voice belonged to the Ghost of Creuss who'd destroyed his lab, so long ago.

Thales started to sit up in bed, then glimpsed the shape of the armored figure sitting on the cell's one uncomfortable chair, and decided he was fine where he was – on his back, looking up at the ceiling, not at the creature. "Why are you here? I'm not meddling in your affairs any more. I'm in a box. Me, the man who was going to–"

"See." The Creuss gestured, and light appeared on the ceiling, a vision in the darkness. Thales saw a star system, and nearby, a wormhole – not the misbegotten thing he'd made, but a real one: a bulging convex bubble in space-time.

"Acheron," the Ghost whispered.

"Eh?" Thales said. "Never heard of it."

The wormhole bulged, and burst out red light, like a popping blister. The planet below was torn apart by a cataclysmic twist in space-time, a piece of pottery smashed with a hammer, shards and fragments flying everywhere.

"Did you do this?" Thales said. "*Your* mistake this time, so much worse than mine?"

"Mahact," the Ghost said.

"This is something that happened in the age of Mahact kings, then? Why are you showing me this? Why–"

"No. Now. This is now. See."

Thales looked back at the – recording? Dramatization? Where the wormhole had been, there was something new, now – a long tear in the fabric of space, a ragged rift, very much like a wound. Beyond the wound there were writhings, and glimmerings, and light in an alien spectrum.

Thales whimpered. "There. Yes. That. It's – what I saw, when I turned on my device. But, no… ours was smaller. That one, with the scale of the planet and the star… that rift is *huge*."

"It grows," the Ghost said.

Thales squinted. Yes, the rift did appear to be growing, both widening and lengthening, like someone pulling at a rip in a piece of cloth. The star began to distort and twist in the strange gravity, and other planets in the system started to crumble as well. "Why are you showing me this?" Thales said.

"See."

The wound in reality began to spill out new forms. They were too small for Thales to make out at first, but the perspective moved closer, until the rift filled his whole field of vision. There were ships emerging from the tear, but not like any he'd seen before – these vessels were broken, twisted, organic things. There were creatures too, crawling and slithering and flying through the void, which should have been impossible – they were creatures with too many eyes or none at all, teeth and mouths in the wrong places, spines and fur and spikes and scales and feathers, sometimes all on one beast. But… were they ships, too? They couldn't be individual creatures, the scale was all wrong, or else his perception was. None of this made sense, in terms of biology or physics or anything else, so – "This is an entertainment? Fiction? Some sort of horror vid–"

"Truth." The Ghost shifted, and when Thales turned his head, the armored creature was kneeling beside his bed. One of its gauntleted hands touched his leg, and the metal was terribly cold. "Truth. Now."

"What is it? What are they?"

"Vuil-raith," the Creuss whispered.

"I don't know what that means."

"From outside."

"Outside *what*?"

"Outside everything. Outside the universe."

"That's nonsense," Thales said. "There's *nothing* outside the universe."

"Monsters are outside."

Monsters. This coming from the Creuss, who *were* monsters, by most accounts. Thales glanced at the helmeted creature, so strange and blank... but the armor was broadly humanoid, wasn't it? The Creuss made an attempt to take on a form that would be comprehensible to other beings in the galaxy, even though as energy creatures, any shape they took was optional. The things pouring through that rift – insofar as they resembled anything known in the galaxy – were the nightmares of a score of different species.

Something tumbled through the rift. A great burning wheel, with spokes of ragged bone. The hub a single bleeding eye. He'd seen that eye before.

"No," Thales said. "My device. I got something wrong, and I didn't open a wormhole at all. I opened a rift, to another place. One teeming with monsters. That's what happened."

"A crack. A glimpse. Yes. See."

"And now you want my *help*." Thales smiled in the dark. The Ghosts had come to him, because, expert as they were in wormhole technology, *Thales* was the first person to open an interdimensional rift – he was a pioneer in a whole new branch of physics. "Absolutely. Just get me out of here, and–"

"Fault." The Creuss pointed at the rift – how was it still pouring out monsters, how could there be so many, and – and were they far away? Please, let that hole in space be far, far away from here.

"Yes? I suppose it is a bit like a fault line."

"No. This is *your* fault."

"How can it be my fault?"

"You opened the way."

Thales shuddered. "Yes, I opened a crack, but not a great horrible gash like this–"

"You looked. The Vuil'raith looked back. They are still looking. They can *see*."

"You're saying those things only noticed us in the first place because of my invention?" His guts turned to ice. "And they've been, what? Waiting, ever since, all these years? Waiting for a chance to come through? A chance they have now, for some reason you haven't bothered to explain?"

"Yes," the Creuss said. "You see now. Your fault."

Thales groaned. "But what do they want?"

The Ghost held up its armored hands about half a meter apart. "They are here." It waved one hand. "We are here." It waved the other. "They want this." The Ghost slowly pushed its hands together, palm to palm, and then interlaced its fingers.

"They want to… bring our worlds together? But from what little I can see, their universe, or whatever it is, it's incompatible with ours, the rules are different... That would destroy everything. That would turn this universe into hell."

"Yes. You see. You were warned. You ignored our warning."

"All right. I made a mistake. I know that. But I don't know what you want me to do *now*."

"You can do nothing. We can do something. We will do this."

The Ghost stood up, turned its back to him, and stepped into the darkness.

"Do what?" Thales shouted. "What are you doing?"

He tried to get out of bed, but he couldn't. He couldn't, he realized, because his legs were gone. He threw the sheet back, and grains of something like sand sprayed across the cell. He watched his thighs come apart, painlessly, swiftly, reduced to individual inert components, just like the contents of his lab, the first time the Creuss warned him, so long ago.

Soon, his body would be nothing but a thin layer of sand, scattered across the bunk and the cell floor.

No, he thought. No no no.

But then, at least he wouldn't be around to see what this universe would become when the Vuil'raith were done with it. What hope did the galaxy have, against a threat like that?

Last words. He only had a moment to make his final statement, to sum up a life of potential greatness, viciously denied. But there was no one to hear what he said, no one to record it, no one to ponder a final wise exhalation, no one to appreciate him, no one had *ever appreciated him*—

"Idiots," Thales said, and then his heart dissolved.

RETURN TO
THE VOID IN...

THE NECROPOLIS EMPIRE

ACKNOWLEDGMENTS

Thanks to Marc Gascoigne, who bought my first attempts at space opera, the Axiom trilogy, when he was at Angry Robot, and kindly thought of me for this gig too. Further thanks to the Aconyte team, especially Lottie Llewelyn-Wells and my editor Paul Simpson. My gratitude to the *Twilight Imperium* creative team, too; they created a wonderful world for me to play in and answered all my weird questions patiently. How about that artwork by Scott Schomburg, huh?

My agent, Ginger Clark, continues to offer invaluable professional support. My wife, Heather Shaw, and son, River, deliver top-notch personal support. River is twelve now, and great at games, though I haven't gotten him into anything as long and involved as *Twilight Imperium* yet; we've done *Fury of Dracula* and *Dead of Winter*, though, so it's only a matter of time.

My near and dear ones are always there for me, so thanks as always to Ais, Amanda, Emily, Katrina, and Sarah. My community of fellow writers is vast, but I'd like to especially thank Daryl Gregory, Jenn Reese and Chris East, Effie Seiberg (look, I dedicated this to you!), and Molly Tanzer for providing support and advice on matters of art and craft.

Finally, thanks to you readers. I hope this book is at least half as fun as the games you play.

DISCOVER EXTRAORDINARY NEW WORLDS

A brave few fight against nightmarish ancient entities lurking at the edge of our reality, whose powers would lay waste to our world... Welcome to ARKHAM HORROR.

Explore a planet of infinite variety – wild science fantasy adventures on an impossible patchwork world of everything known (and unknown) in the universe, in the first explosive and hilarious KEYFORGE *anthology.*

Warring samurai clans fight with swords and magic
for the Emperor's favor while protecting their borders
from the demonic incursions of the Shadowlands, in
LEGEND OF THE FIVE RINGS.

Courageous heroes battling monsters and saving
the realm from being plunged into darkness, in the
vibrant high fantasy realm of DESCENT.